HEAVEN TO BETSY

HEAVEN TO BETSY

by Maud Hart Lovelace

ILLUSTRATED BY VERA NEVILLE

A HARPER TROPHY BOOK

HARPER & ROW, PUBLISHERS

For Tom and Stella

CONTENTS

1	THE FARM	1
2	BUTTERNUT CENTER	11
3	THE SURPRISE	19
4	HIGH STREET	29
5	ANNA	38
6	THE FIRST DAY OF HIGH SCHOOL	46
7	CAB	56
8	THE SIBLEYS' SIDE LAWN	65
9	THE TRIUMVIRATE OF LADY BUGS	73
10	AND THE TRIUMVIRATE OF POTATO BUGS	83
11	SUNDAY NIGHT LUNCH	92
12	THE TALL DARK STRANGER	100
13	THE FRESHMAN PARTY	108
14	THE TRIP TO MURMURING LAKE	120
15	HALLOWEEN	130
16	HIC, HAEC, HOC	139
17	THE BRASS BOWL	148
18	WHAT THE OUIJA BOARD SAID	157
19	THE WINTER PICNIC	167
20	T-R-O-U-B-L-E?	179
21	T-R-O-U-B-L-E!	186
22	NEW YEAR'S EVE	194
23	THE TALK WITH MR. RAY	204
24	AN ADVENTURE ON PUGET SOUND	214
25	CHANGE IN THE AIR	224
26	OF CHURCH AND LIBRARY	233
27	THE ESSAY CONTEST	242
28	RESULTS	251
29	THE HILL	261

All things must change
To something new, to something strange . . .

—HENRY W. LONGFELLOW.

HEAVEN TO BETSY

Chapter One

THE FARM

BETSY was visiting at the Taggarts' farm. It was Wednesday, and soon the kitchen would swim with warm delicious odors. It was ninety-six in the shade outside, and the wood-burning range gave off a fiery heat, but Mrs. Taggart baked on Wednesday just as inflexibly as she washed on Monday and ironed on Tuesday. Heat or no heat, she would bake today . . . cake, cookies, pie, bread, biscuits. It was sad that Betsy who usually liked such mouth-watering items felt she would choke on every morsel.

Betsy smiled brightly.

"I'll walk on down for the mail," she said, "if there's nothing more I can do."

"Not a thing," answered Mrs. Taggart cheerfully, setting out bowls, an egg beater, a flour sifter, pans. She was a short, bright-eyed pouter pigeon of a woman in an apron that crackled with starch. "It isn't time for Mr. Simmons yet, though."

"That's all right. I like sitting down by the road."

"You're sure you're not homesick, Betsy?"

"Oh, no, Mrs. Taggart!"

"Take Shep along for company," Mrs. Taggart said.

Shep plainly expected to go. In the eight days of Betsy's visit, the old collie who had been a pet of the Taggarts' Mattie, now married and gone, had come to look forward to this morning walk. He rose now, brushed against her ankle-length skirts, and barked.

Betsy took a sunbonnet from a row of hooks on the kitchen wall and climbed to the prim, low-ceiled room which had once been Mattie's. She crossed to the bureau and tied on her sunbonnet, looking anxiously into the mirror.

Every time she looked into a mirror Betsy hoped to find that her looks had changed. They had certainly changed enough in the last two years. At twelve she had been short, straight and chunky with perky braids and a freckled smiling face. At fourteen she was tall, very slender, with a tendency to stoop. Her brown hair waved softly by reason of eight kid rollers, four on either side, in which she slept at night. Her one braid was turned up with a large hair ribbon, red today, matching the tie of her dark blue sailor suit. Freckles were fading out of a pink and white skin, the delicacy of which she guarded carefully.

"It's the only pretty thing about me," she often muttered savagely while rubbing in creams at night. "Straight hair! Teeth parted in the middle! Mighty good thing I have a decent complexion!"

As a matter of fact what one noticed first and liked best in Betsy were her eyes, clear hazel, under dark brows and lashes. But her frown, as she tied on the sunbonnet, expressed disapproval of her entire physiognomy. She picked up a pad of paper and a pencil, ran down the stairs and out the kitchen door, saying goodbye to Mrs. Taggart gaily, and calling out to Shep an invitation to race. This, in view of the heat and his age, he sensibly ignored.

Shep was not fooled by Betsy's vivacity. And in spite of laughing denials, Betsy was homesick. She was . . . to put it mildly . . . wretchedly, desperately, nightmarishly homesick, and had been ever since she came to visit the Taggarts.

Mr. Taggart, a friend of her father's, had come into the store to buy shoes. Seeing Betsy and noticing her droopy thinness, he had told her father that the young lady needed some country milk and eggs. How about letting her come out to visit Mrs. Taggart who felt lost since Mattie had married? Betsy had felt important and flattered. She had been delighted to go.

Tacy Kelly, her best friend, who lived across the street, had been thrilled too. When Betsy drove away on the high seat of the farm wagon beside bearded, mild Mr. Taggart, Tacy waved enthusiastically along with Betsy's sisters,

3

Julia and Margaret. Betsy waved back with a shining face but she had not left Deep Valley behind before this sickish misery invaded her being.

It seemed to her that she had to burst out crying and ask Mr. Taggart to turn around and go back. She couldn't do that, of course, and they drove farther and farther away . . . out Front Street and through the wooded river valley, scene of so many family picnics. They climbed Pigeon Hill, and it was worse after that for the country was not even familiar.

The town of Deep Valley was set amidst hills, and Hill Street where Betsy had lived all her life was barricaded by tree-covered slopes. Beyond Pigeon Hill lay prairie, treeless except for planted groves around the widely separated houses. There were only telephone wires for the birds to perch on. Prairie, poles and wires! Prairie, poles and wires! On the seat beside Mr. Taggart Betsy grew quieter and quieter.

"See what I've brought home, mamma." Mr. Taggart had presented her proudly in the dooryard of a small grey house dwarfed by a windmill and a big red barn and the planted windbreak of trees.

In response to Mrs. Taggart's welcoming kindness, Betsy had ground her teeth and smiled.

It was Julia, and not Betsy, who had a talent for the stage, but Betsy had done a wonderful job of acting through eight endless days. She had swallowed food over a lump in her throat and exclaimed over its goodness. She had chatted in a grown-up way borrowed from Julia, listened radiantly to Mrs. Taggart's brisk domestic conversation when she could hardly keep the tears back. Sometimes she knew she could not keep them back and fled to the barn pretending sudden interest in the calf or baby

4

pigs. There in dark solitude she buried her head in her arms while waves of desolation broke against her.

The hardest time of each day came at the end. Every evening her family called her on the telephone.

It was one thing to fool Mr. and Mrs. Taggart. They were strangers, and easily taken in. Fooling her loving, keen-witted mother was quite another matter. But Betsy felt she would rather die than let her family know that she was homesick. Julia went visiting alone, and she was only two years older.

It wasn't necessary for her to stay. The merest hint over the 'phone, and her mother would find a reason for summoning her home. But Betsy wouldn't give it. She had been invited for two weeks, and she would not by her own act cut those two weeks short. Betsy looked these days like a somewhat wilted lily, but going into her teens hadn't changed *one* thing about her. She was still as stubborn as a mule.

A hundred times a day she checked off on her fingers the days that must elapse before she went home. She checked them off now . . . one, two, three, four, five, six . . . as she walked down the long narrow road to the mailbox. This was the happiest hour of her day; not because of the walk . . . that was hot and dusty . . . but because of the blessed anticipation of mail. Tacy wrote faithfully, and sometimes there were letters from Tib, who used to live in Deep Valley but had moved back to her native city of Milwaukee.

Betsy and Tacy had mourned at first when Tib moved away. They had not known then the fun and fascination to be found in correspondence. Now letters flew from Deep Valley to Milwaukee and back like fat, gossipy birds.

"Maybe there'll be a letter from Tib today," thought

5

Betsy as she and Shep plodded along in the burning heat.

The roadsides offered no shade, only thickets of purple spiked leadplant and gaudy butterfly weed. To the right and the left stretched golden fields where rye was in shock. But down at the main road where the Taggart R.F.D. box waited hungrily on a fence post, stood an elderberry bush. Betsy sat down in its patch of shade and Shep gratefully eased himself to the ground. She took off her sunbonnet. Her curls had quite flattened out in the heat, but fortunately she did not know it. She fanned herself and Shep with the generous bonnet.

A short yard away a picket pin gopher appeared, erect on his haunches. From the telephone wire a meadow lark soared into the air, broke the hot stillness with a cool cascade of notes, dropped into the meadow. Betsy groped in her pocket for the pencil and the pad of paper. She scribbled dreamily:

> *"I sit by the side of the road,*
> *Thinking of times gone by,*
> *Thinking of home far away,*
> *'til a tear springs into my eye.*
> *Then a gopher springs up to amuse me,*
> *And a meadow lark sings me a song,*
> *When the world is so full of God's creatures,*
> *To be homesick is certainly wrong."*

She read this over and changed the first "springs" to "wells." She read it over again, and frowned. The word "certainly" didn't seem very poetic. But before she had found an adverb she liked better, she heard a clop clop of hoofs and saw the mail wagon's halo of dust. She jumped to her feet. Mr. Simmons, red faced and genial, handed

6

her a card from Sears Roebuck for Mrs. Taggart, and a letter bearing Tacy's dear angular script.

"But it's thin," Betsy thought as she told Mr. Simmons that Mr. Taggart was haying today, that it *was* hot enough for her, and that she would see him tomorrow.

When he was gone she sat down again. She did not hurry about opening her letter. The moment was too precious to be hurried. She examined the postmark: Deep Valley, Minn. July 25, 1906. Sometimes Tacy enlivened the envelope by putting the stamp on upside down to signify love, or by addressing her with some grandiloquent string of names such as Miss Elizabetha Gwendolyn Madeline Angeline Rosemond Ray, or by adding BC for Best Chum or HHAS for Herbert Humphreys Admiration Society. Herbert Humphreys, large and bright-blond, had been the beau ideal of the girls through grade school.

Today, however, Tacy's envelope was lacking in lively decorations, and when Betsy opened it, there was, as she had feared, only a single page inside. But its message was potent to hold homesickness at bay.

"Dear Betsy. I don't dare to write much for fear I'll give something away. Your mother said I could tell you that they have a surprise for you, but of course I can't tell you what it is. It's nice for you, but not so nice for me, but that's all right. In a way it's nice for me, too. I'd better stop. You see how it is. If I write I'm sure to give it away. Love. Your sincere friend. Tacy."

Betsy jumped up, her eyes sparkling. Shep sprang up, too, and barked, sending echoes over the fields.

"Shep! What is it? What *can* it be?"

Shep barked as though guessing a bone.

7

A Peter Thompson suit? thought Betsy, striding up the road. But that would not be not nice for Tacy. A bike? Her father had suggested buying her a bike, for it was a long walk from Hill Street to the High School which Betsy and Tacy would enter this fall. But Tacy didn't have a bike, and the town, he had said, would fall down with surprise if Betsy and Tacy stopped going to school together. What could it be? Betsy hurried into the house to get Mrs. Taggart's guess.

Mrs. Taggart promptly guessed a baby, and Betsy laughingly told her that once she had gone to visit on a farm and had come home to find a baby sister. But that wouldn't happen now. She was, she explained complacently, old enough to be told. Besides, Tacy liked babies. What could possibly be nice for Betsy that Tacy would not like?

She puzzled while she shelled peas and at dinner Mr. Taggart joined affably in the guessing. But when Betsy started to eat, the misery came back. The surprise seemed suddenly unimportant and it was nightmarish again that she, Betsy, was out here alone among strangers. She started the now familiar business of pushing food around her plate.

"I never knew a growing girl to take so little interest in her victuals," Mrs. Taggart said when Betsy declared that she really didn't have room for fresh peach pie.

Misery kept her company through the dragging afternoon. Then there was supper to be eaten, harder even than dinner. When the dishes were washed Betsy went out to sit on the back fence and watch the sunset. She had always liked sunsets, and tonight the west was turquoise blue, with banked clouds turning from peach color to pink. But shortly the clouds became grey, the sky dark.

The orchard trees moved slowly in an imperceptible breeze, and the crickets began.

The worst thing about farm evenings was the crickets. The cows were bad enough with their dreary lowing, and the birds flying urgently homeward at nightfall when Betsy could not fly home to Hill Street. But those crickets!

"I must, I must get to feeling better before mamma 'phones," Betsy thought, jumping off the fence.

Winking rapidly, she walked toward the house. The lamps were not yet lighted; Mrs. Taggart was sitting in the dooryard for coolness while Mr. Taggart finished his chores. And just as Betsy came up the telephone bell inside the kitchen rang. Two long and three short rings, the Taggarts' call.

"It's sure to be for you, Betsy," Mrs. Taggart said. "Make your mamma tell you what that secret is."

"I'll certainly try," Betsy answered merrily. She put the receiver to her ear.

"Hello. Bettina?" Julia always called her Bettina. "How're you?"

"Dandy," said Betsy. "I'm having a dandy time."

"Not too dandy, I hope," Julia answered, and laughed excitedly. "I mean . . . there's a wonderful surprise here. Papa and mamma want to know if you'd just as soon hurry up your visit."

"Hurry up . . . my visit?"

"And come home ahead of time . . . tomorrow."

Betsy clung to the receiver as though holding fast to Julia's words.

"Why, all right," she said slowly, after a pause. "Of course, I hate like the dickens to leave."

"But this surprise won't keep," said Julia. "That is, you might hear about it. You might read it in the paper."

9

"In the *paper?*"

Julia laughed out loud.

"I'd better ring off, or I'll give it away. Mamma's too busy to talk, if you're coming home tomorrow."

"I'll come," Betsy said. "Wait. I'll find out what time." Holding the receiver, she spoke to Mrs. Taggart.

"Why, Mr. Simmons can take you along to Butternut Center tomorrow," she said. "There's a train at two-three. Tell your mamma we hope you'll come again."

"I'd love to come again," Betsy cried.

When she rang off the kitchen seemed transformed. Mrs. Taggart had lighted the lamps, and the glow was as cozy as home lamplight. Betsy played with Shep, and ate the piece of pie she had spurned at dinner, said goodnight gaily and ran gaily upstairs to the prim little room that had once been Mattie's.

Whistling to herself she undressed and put on her long-sleeved cambric night gown. Smilingly, she washed in the flowered bowl, and brushed her teeth, and rubbed cream into her face, and wound her hair on eight kid rollers. Briskly, she lifted off the pillow shams . . . one said Good Night, and one said Good Morning . . . and folded back the patchwork quilt and blew out the lamp. After she had raced through her prayers, she climbed into bed and lay there peacefully.

The room still held the heat of the day, but the air coming through the screened windows was cool. Outside the crickets were singing.

"Yes, I must come here again sometime," thought Betsy happily, listening to their tune.

Chapter Two

BUTTERNUT CENTER

Betsy's first thought on awakening was that she was going home. She lay in bed and thought about Hill Street with adoration.

It took its name from the fact that it ended in a hill. Her house and Tacy's, across the street, were the last two houses in the town. The rolling, tree-covered slopes seemed but an extension of the lawns surrounding the white rambling Kelly house and the yellow Ray cottage.

This was growing altogether too small. When they kept a hired girl, Julia, Betsy and Margaret had to share one bedroom. The house had almost none of the modern improvements, Betsy had heard her mother remark disparagingly. Never mind, Betsy loved it, from the butternut tree standing like a sentinel in front, to Old Mag's barn behind the garden, not forgetting the lilac bush by the side kitchen door and the back-yard maple.

She thought about Hill Street through breakfast and farewells. But homeward bound beside Mr. Simmons, she began to give a little attention to the surprise. She told him about it, they discussed it pro and con while the wagon rolled from mailbox to mailbox, between swaying cornfields where red-winged blackbirds foraged. By the time they reached Butternut Center Mr. Simmons was quite worked up about the surprise.

"I'll drop you a card to tell you what it is," Betsy promised at the depot.

Tall and slim in her blue sailor suit, with her flat hat and spreading hairbow, she felt very much the young lady. Butternut Center wasn't exactly Paris, but it was adventurous to be there alone. She went into the small red depot and asked the agent whether she might leave her valise; he said, "Sure." She walked along the platform, past wagons full of milk cans, found a shady spot and ate the lunch Mrs. Taggart had put up. It was magnificent; ham sandwiches, dill pickles, hard-boiled eggs, a chunk of layer cake and cookies. She ate looking off at the fields, her back to Butternut Center, feeling that lunch out of doors, out of a box, was slightly undignified. Her lunch eaten, however, and the box disposed of, she set out to see the town.

There wasn't much of it. Except for a white church and burying ground out on the prairie, it lay along a single road. This was dusty now, but its ruts and gulches showed how rich its mud would be at other seasons. It led in one direction to the grain elevator, in the other past a handful of houses to the general store. The store reminded her that in the excitement of her unexpected return, she had forgotten to buy presents. No Ray ever came home from a trip without bringing presents for the rest.

"I'd like to get something for Tacy, too," Betsy thought, hurrying toward the store.

Willard's Emporium, said the sign above the door. It was one of those stores, perfect for her purpose, where everything under the sun was for sale. A single glance revealed kitchen stoves, buggy whips, corset covers and crackers. Betsy browsed happily along the overflowing counters until a boy sitting in a corner, eating an apple and reading a book, threw away the apple and came forward.

She was struck by the way he walked, with a slight challenging swing. He had very light hair brushed back in a pompadour, blue eyes under thick light brows and healthy red lips with the lower one pushed out as though seeming to dare the world to knock the chip off his shoulder. It was a sturdy well-built shoulder, in a faded blue cotton shirt. He hardly looked at her, but keeping his finger in the partly closed book . . . it was, she noticed, *The Three Musketeers* . . . asked what he could do for her in a tone that implied he hoped she would answer, "Nothing. I'm just looking."

"Nothing, thanks. I'm just looking," said Betsy obligingly. Then, realizing that she really had to buy five presents even though it meant delaying D'Artagnon's greatest feat she added, "That is, I can look around a few minutes if you're in an exciting place."

The boy grinned. "Oh, I've read it six times. Swell book! What are you looking for?"

"Presents. Five of them." She explained, talking very fast, that no Ray ever came home from a visit without bringing presents. "It's an old family custom," she said.

"Hallelujah!" he exclaimed, shutting the book. "That'll be fun, picking out five presents. I hope you have a brother. There's a corking jack-knife here."

"Not a sign of a brother," Betsy answered. "Just two sisters. And Margaret's so young she'd cut herself on a jack-knife, and Julia wouldn't care for one. She's sixteen."

"What's Julia interested in?" he asked.

"Oh, music and boys."

Betsy hadn't intended to be funny, and when the boy laughed, she blushed.

"Well," he said. "We've got a mouth organ."

"But she likes classical music. A mouth organ might do for Tacy, though."

"Who's Tacy?"

"My best friend. I want to take her something, too, if I've got money enough."

"How much do you have?" he asked. He put *The Three Musketeers* aside completely and hoisted himself to a counter, smiling. Betsy sat down on a barrel and opened her pocketbook.

"Three dollars."

"A ticket to Deep Valley is only forty cents."

"But I have to take the hack home. That costs a quarter."

"Can't you walk?"

"In our family," said Betsy, "when we come home on the train, we take the hack."

Again he burst into laughter.

"You have a lot of customs in your family. Haven't you?" he asked.

Pleased and pink, she tried to make it clear. "The hack is part of the fun of the trip."

"All right. Forty plus twenty-five, that's sixty-five. So you have two dollars and thirty-five cents to spend for presents."

"But I want to buy some things on the train. Caramels, maybe, and a magazine. It's . . ."

"I know, I know," he interrupted. "It's one of those old family customs. You never travel without caramels."

Betsy's blushes sank to the V of her sailor suit.

"We'll give you a quarter for caramels, then, and get on with the presents. Would your father like a moustache cup?"

"My father," said Betsy, "hasn't a moustache any more, and moustache cups are out of style." She looked around the store. "He likes cheese," she said, nodding toward a row of giant cheeses.

"Fine. Cheese for your father. Sharp or mild?"

"Sharp."

"If you brought home mild cheese, he wouldn't let you in, I'll bet."

"He'd use it for the mousetrap."

They joked like old friends, choosing the presents. For her father he cut a wedge of cheese so sharp that Betsy could smell it even after it was wrapped. For her mother, they found a glass butter dish. Tacy got the mouth organ; Julia, side combs decorated with rhinestones. They hadn't found a present for Margaret when they heard the hooting whistle of the train.

"You don't need to rush," he said. "They take on all the milk cans."

But in spite of this reassurance, Betsy felt hurried. She had to pick up her valise. She decided quickly on doll dishes for Margaret. Her purchases came to a dollar and sixty cents.

"Fifty cents for the pig bank," said the boy. "Well, back to *The Three Musketeers*."

Betsy hesitated, trying to think what to say. She had no brothers, and she hadn't started going around with boys. Julia would have known how to convey to this one that she liked him and appreciated his help. In fact, thought Betsy enviously, Julia would have him taking the next train to Deep Valley to call. But Betsy didn't know how to do it.

Should she tell him that her name was Betsy? He knew it was Ray. Should she ask him to come up to Hill Street when he came to Deep Valley? Perhaps she ought to mention that she was starting high school this fall? That would make him understand that she was old enough to have callers. Before she could decide anything, the train whistled again.

The boy had picked up *The Three Musketeers*. He was acting almost as though he regretted having been so friendly. Betsy blurted out:

"What's your name?"

"Joe Willard."

"Willard's Emporium?"

"I'm just a poor relation."

"Well, thank you," Betsy said. "Thank you a lot."

It wasn't satisfactory, but it was the best she could manage. At least he smiled again.

"Don't eat the cheese before you get home," he said.

The brakeman ushered her into the day coach, and she sat down in a red plush seat. All the passengers seemed to be eating, bananas chiefly, and an endless line of hot, restless children trotted to and from the water fountain.

Betsy bought a box of crackerjack. She bought a box of caramels and a copy of *The Ladies' Home Journal.*

"Like traveling?" asked the train boy.

"Love it," she answered.

"I'd like to travel all over the world," she thought, munching crackerjack. "I think I'd like Paris especially. I think I just belong in Paris."

Paris reminded her of *The Three Musketeers,* and that brought Joe Willard back into her thoughts.

"He's handsomer than Herbert Humphreys," she decided. "Tacy'll never believe it though."

The speed of the train swallowed up the prairie. In no time at all the river came into sight. They passed a waterfall she recognized; then the train descended along the side of a bluff.

The brakeman called, "Deep Valley!" and at once the car was in confusion. Hats were pinned on; small bonnets tied; all traces of banana wiped away. Valises and suit cases were dragged down from the rack. The train slowed to a stop.

Holding her valise in one hand and the package from Willard's Emporium in the other, Betsy found Mr. Thumbler's hack.

"Good afternoon, Mr. Thumbler," she said. "333 Hill Street, please." As though he didn't know where the Ray family lived! The hack rolled up Front Street, past her father's shoe store. It crossed to Broad Street and rolled past Lincoln Park, and began to climb.

Betsy tried to sit back in careless calm, but a smile as bright as her hair ribbon spread across her face. Neighbors

17

darted out to see who was coming in the hack. Children waved, and dogs barked. It was a triumphal return. And not only was she back on her beloved Hill Street . . . the surprise was still ahead.

"Now for the surprise!" thought Betsy, trying not to bounce.

Chapter Three

THE SURPRISE

Betsy didn't know exactly what she had expected, but certainly not to find everything at home going forward just as usual on a summer afternoon. Margaret was playing with her dolls on the front porch. Julia was at the piano, vocalizing.

"Ni-po-tu-la-he-" Her voice floated out the window as the hack stopped in front of the yellow cottage.

Betsy dug twenty-five cents from her pocketbook.

"Thank you, Mr. Thumbler," she said politely, and thanked him again with downright gratitude when he carried her valise up the steps, just as though she were grown up.

Margaret gave a welcoming cry, and Julia rushed out, closely followed by Mrs. Ray in a dressing sacque with her curly red hair falling on her shoulders. She had just been changing into an afternoon dress.

Mrs. Ray was tall and slim; younger and gayer, Betsy was pleasantly aware, than most mothers. She did not seem much older than Julia who was old for sixteen.

None of the Ray girls looked like their mother. They all had their father's dark hair. But Julia's hair was wavy, not straight like Betsy's. It waved in a high pompadour above a truly beautiful face . . . arched brows, violet eyes, classic nose, even teeth and a delicate pink and white skin like the one Betsy cherished.

Much to her chagrin . . . for she planned to be an opera singer, and longed to be tall and queenly . . . Julia was small. She had a tiny waist, dainty hands and feet, and an air of complete poise. Julia, Betsy often heard, had never had an awkward age. Betsy never heard this said about herself and suspected strongly that she was in the midst of one, but she admired Julia without resentment. During the last year all big-sister, little-sister friction had miraculously melted away.

Margaret was eight years old, and not at all the sort of little girl that either of her sisters had been. She did not have Julia's diamond-bright precocity nor Betsy's gregariousness. Betsy at eight had been habitually surrounded by children, cheerfully smudged and disheveled if five minutes away from the wash bowl. Margaret played

20

sedately alone or with one child at a time, and her brown English bob was always glossy, her starched dresses immaculate. She had large black-lashed blue eyes, and a grave expression. She held herself erect just as Mr. Ray did. It was amusing to see the pair, one so big and one so little, but both with squared shoulders, walking hand in hand. And Hill Street saw this often.

"She's my boy," Mr. Ray used to joke. "All the boy I've got."

She came down the steps now with her usual flawless dignity but her small face was covered with smiles. She hugged and kissed Betsy, and so did Julia, and so did Mrs. Ray.

When these greetings were over Betsy waited to hear some word of the surprise, but none was spoken. They all trooped into Mrs. Ray's room so that she could finish dressing while Betsy told the story of her visit.

"I had the dandiest time," she kept repeating.

"And you weren't homesick?" asked Julia. "Bettina, you're wonderful! I die with homesickness when I go away."

"You're temperamental," said Betsy. "You're a temperamental prima donna." To Tacy, and to Tacy alone would she confess how homesick she had been.

Shortly Tacy came running across the street. Politeness had kept her away until she was sure the family reunion was over. Tacy too had grown tall, taller even than Betsy, and she too wore skirts down to her ankles. Her ringlets were gone, and thick auburn braids were bound about her head. She and Betsy hugged tempestuously, rocking back and forth.

They all sat on the porch then, and Julia made lemonade. At intervals Betsy saw her mother and Julia, or Julia and Tacy, or Margaret and her mother, exchange mysterious glances. She wished she had asked about the surprise the minute she stepped out of the hack. Now she didn't know how.

"I must go and unpack," she said. "I brought some presents. Shall I give Tacy hers and put the others on the supper table? We don't want to open them, of course, until papa comes home."

Margaret looked at her mother and then spoke, beaming.

"We aren't eating supper here."

"Not . . . why not?"

"Papa's taking us to a restaurant."

"But why? It isn't Sunday, or a holiday, or anything."

"Oh, he likes to give me a rest once in a while," Mrs. Ray put in breezily, "when we're not keeping a hired girl."

"And there really isn't room for a hired girl in this house," added Julia with an exaggerated sigh.

"What the dickens!" thought Betsy. But she was too stubborn to ask about the surprise since she hadn't done it in the first place.

"I'll give Tacy hers anyway," she said.

Tacy proved to have a talent for the mouth organ. After experimenting only a short time, she said, "This is in Betsy's honor," and began a recognizable, "Home, sweet home."

> *"Be it ever so humble,*
> *There's no place like home . . ."*

Betsy and Julia and Mrs. Ray intoned in close harmony. They all fell to laughing, but Betsy thought secretly how suitable the sentiment was.

"Come on, Tacy," she said. "Let's look around."

They inspected the front lawn and the back lawn, back-yard maple, garden, empty buggy shed and barn. They ran across the street and Betsy said 'hello' to Mrs. Kelly, and to Katie, Tacy's sister, Julia's age, and to Paul, their youngest brother.

"Let's go up on the hill," said Betsy, still holding Tacy's hand. She wouldn't really feel she was at home until she and Tacy had been up on the hill. "Let's go up to our bench and talk."

But to her surprise Tacy refused.

"I don't dare," she replied. "I'm afraid . . ." She broke off, but Betsy knew what she meant. She was afraid that alone on the hill she would give away the secret. "You see," said Tacy hesitantly. "I'm going downtown with you."

"You're what?"

"Going down to the restaurant . . . for supper. Your father invited me. There comes your father now," she cried, sounding relieved.

Sure enough Old Mag was climbing up Hill Street, drawing the surrey.

"But it isn't five o'clock yet!" exclaimed Betsy. "What's papa coming home for?"

"You'll know! You'll see!" Tacy cried.

All the Kellys began to laugh, and when Betsy and Tacy raced across the street, Mr. Ray was smiling, Mrs. Ray and Julia were hugging one another, and Margaret for all her dignity was jumping up and down.

She whispered to her mother; then, ran into the house.

"And a safety pin, Margaret," Mrs. Ray called.

Margaret returned with a table napkin and a safety pin.

"Sit down, Bettina," Julia commanded.

"But why? What for?"

"We're going to blindfold you. No questions, please."

Betsy sat down on the porch steps. She looked around at the laughing faces. She looked up at the loved green hill which seemed to be smiling, too, and down Hill Street. Obediently she closed her eyes and Julia with deft fingers adjusted the blindfold.

"I'll help her."

"No, let me!"

Betsy was surrounded with clamoring voices. She was interested to discover how helpless she felt with her eyes bandaged.

"It's like this to be blind," she thought.

A soft hand took one of hers. That was Julia. Slender, rougher fingers took her other hand. That was Tacy. A whiff of violet perfume rushed by. That was her mother. There were light feet, Margaret's, and her father's firm tread.

"Bring her along. This way. Careful of the stairs."

"Step up, now!" That was the hitching block.

"Again. That's right. Sit down."

She was in the back seat of the surrey. Julia and Tacy squeezed in on either side. Margaret, no doubt, was sitting with papa and mamma up in front.

"Goodbye! Surprise on Betsy!" Katie and Paul were calling from the Kellys' hitching block. The surrey began to move.

"We're on Hill Street, going down," thought Betsy. She resolved to keep track of where they were going. But she couldn't. Right turn, left turn, down hill, up hill. She soon lost her way.

"I give up. Where *are* we? And what's it all about?"

Tacy giggled and squeezed her hand.

"We're on our way to California to see grandma," said her mother.

"We're on our way to Washington to call on the Teddy Roosevelts," said her father.

"We're almost there," said Margaret. "Oh, Betsy! You're going to be so surprised!"

The clop clop of Old Mag's hoofs stopped at last, and the surrey, too, halted. Betsy was helped out by agitated hands. She was led up a flight of stairs and across a level space and up another flight of stairs.

"You're fooling me!" she cried. "We're back home again."

Everyone laughed uproariously.

"You're not far wrong, at that," Mr. Ray remarked.

A door opened. There was a smell of fresh paint, of new wood, of the paste they stick wallpaper on with. Betsy was pushed forward, turned around three times, and her blindfold taken off.

She stood blinking in a small square room, empty of all but sunshine. A golden oak staircase went up at the right. The wallpaper, a design of dark green leaves, was set in gold panels. The floor was oiled and shone with newness.

"It's the music room," Julia cried. "The piano will stand right here, under the stairs."

Turning Betsy to the left they led her through an archway into another, larger room with a big window pushing out at the front. This was papered in lighter green with loops of roses for a border.

"It's the parlor," everyone cried.

Behind that, through another archway, was a room with a plate rail, papered above with pears and grapes. There was a fireplace in one corner, and a glittering gold-fringed lamp was suspended by a gold chain from the ceiling.

"It's the dining room," came the shout.

They pushed through a swinging door into a pantry, into a kitchen, empty and smelling of newness.

Returning by a small door to the music room they climbed the golden oak stairs. There were two bedrooms at the front. Margaret rushed into the right-hand room.

"Papa's and mamma's room!" she cried.

She rushed into the left-hand room which had a window seat.

"Julia's room!" she chanted.

Back in the hall three doors remained unopened. Mrs. Ray opened the one at the head of the stairs.

"This room is yours, Betsy," she said.

"And down the hall is a bathroom," cried Julia. "A bathroom, Bettina! No more baths in a tub in the kitchen."

"And down at the end of the hall is *my* room," said Margaret, standing very straight. "I can arrange the bureau to suit myself."

"There's a room on the third floor for the hired girl when we get one," Mrs. Ray explained. "But now come in and see your room. It's your very own."

"You don't need to put up with me and my untidiness any more," said Julia, putting her arm around Betsy.

Everyone was talking very fast, perhaps because Betsy was saying so little. She had made a few exclamations of surprise, but for Betsy, who was usually such a talker, she was very quiet indeed.

She looked around the generous room which was to be hers alone, with a great pang of loneliness for Julia who had always slept in the same room, in the very same bed, and for Margaret who when they had a hired girl slept in a small bed in the corner. She forced her lips into a smile and walked to one of the windows.

She saw somebody's house, some stranger's dull ordinary house. Across from her window at home was Tacy's house with tall trees behind it and the sunset behind that. She thought of the hill, the dear green hill where she and Tacy had picnicked ever since they were old enough to take their supper plates up to the bench.

"I won't cry! I won't!" she thought, staring out the window. She forced the smile to her face again. It felt as though her lips were stretched tight against her teeth. But she must have managed a pretty fair imitation of a smile for her father who had been looking anxious smiled in return.

"It's ours, Betsy!" he said. "I've bought it. Mamma has her modern improvements at last."

Mrs. Ray danced across the empty room to hug him.

"I'm going to take one bath after another all day long."

"But what about the new gas stove, Mrs. Ray?" asked Tacy. "You have to stop between baths long enough to cook on that."

"Oh, yes! My darling gas stove! No more horrid wood fires to build."

"And no more lamps to clean," said Julia. "This house is lighted all over by gas. See the fixtures, Betsy?"

"And it's heated by a furnace," Mr. Ray said. "No coal stove in the parlor."

Betsy thought her heart would break. Didn't they know how much she loved that coal stove beside which she had read so many books while the tea kettle sang and the little flames leaped behind the isinglass window? Didn't they know how she loved the yellow lamplight over the small cottage rooms? And she thought it was cozy to take baths

27

in the kitchen beside the old wood-burning range! But her father's face was so proud, and her mother's so radiant . . . Julia and Margaret looked so happy . . . she couldn't say a word. She glanced at Tacy. Tacy, she saw, understood. Tacy smiled now and said, "It's just two blocks from the high school, Betsy. I'm going to stop in here before school and after school, every single day."

"Tacy is going to practically live here," said Mrs. Ray. "Oh, my beautiful house! My beautiful new house!" And she hugged Mr. Ray again, and picked up her long skirts and waltzed around the empty room. Julia began to waltz with her, and Mr. Ray began to waltz in his stately way with Margaret, and Tacy caught Betsy. Everybody waltzed singing, "In the Good Old Summertime," until they were laughing too hard either to waltz or to sing.

Betsy laughed harder than anyone, and she and Tacy, hand in hand, raced all over the house. They looked into every nook and corner, and into the closets, and out the windows. And when they had finished they all went down to the restaurant for supper. There everyone talked at once about the new house, and about how the furniture would be arranged, and what new things would have to be bought.

Betsy talked harder and faster than anyone, but inside she felt terrible. She felt as though she had fallen downstairs and had all her breath knocked out. She felt even worse than when she was visiting the Taggarts.

28

Chapter Four

HIGH STREET

IN A breathlessly short space of time the Rays had moved
from Hill Street where Betsy had lived all her life, to
the new house at the windy junction of High Street and
Plum.

High Street, like Hill Street, was on a hill for Deep
Valley was built upon the river bluffs. But where Hill
Street ran up a hill like a finger pointing to the top, High

Street ran lengthwise, one of a layer of streets of which the lowest was Front Street, parallel to the river.

Two blocks from the Ray house, on the same side of the street, stood the red brick, turreted high school. Opposite were other houses with trees and shady lawns. Above them rows of rooftops indicated layers of streets, all the way to the top of High Street's hill, where the sun came up behind a German Catholic College. It was different from the Hill Street hill, with its gifts of flowers and snow.

Betsy's room looked south to Plum Street. Behind Plum Street's houses the road dipped into a ravine. There was a store where Margaret bought candy as Betsy and Tacy had once bought it at Mrs. Chubbock's store. The road forked, at a watering trough, and one branch led off to Cemetery Hill; the other, with several jogs invisible from Betsy's window, found its way to Hill Street.

"At least," Betsy thought with moody satisfaction, "I'm looking in the right direction."

The house sat proudly on a terrace. It was freshly painted, green. It looked at the moment a little bare but that wouldn't last long. Mr. Ray was transplanting vines from the Hill Street house. The new home would be covered with the old familiar pattern by next summer. Mrs. Ray planned to hang baskets filled with daisies, geraniums and long trailing vines around the porch. Bridal wreath and hydrangeas would be set out on the lawn. This house had no garden, no orchard, no grape arbor; not even a buggy shed and barn. Old Mag lived in a barn Mr. Ray had rented down the street. Betsy missed the comfortable litter, the familiar smell of the barnyard. She wondered whether Old Mag wasn't homesick, and she and Margaret secretly made frequent trips to see her, taking sugar.

On moving day Betsy had been caught up into the excitement of the occasion. While men carried the furniture out of the yellow cottage, all the children and dogs of the neighborhood had looked on and rushed about. With scarcely a glance into the startled empty rooms, the family had hurried off in the surrey to reach High Street ahead of the dray.

Tacy had gone along, bearing a cake from her mother, a bowl of potato salad from Mrs. Rivers, and various contributions from the other neighbors. Mr. Ray tucked a coffee pot under the surrey seat. They had picnicked gaily in the midst of the confusion, and the moment the piano was set down in the music room . . . some people would have called this room a hall, but Julia insisted upon music room . . . Julia sat down and began to trill "ni-po-tu-la-he. . . ." There hadn't been time or opportunity to feel lonely for Hill Street.

But when the new house was comparatively settled and serene, the impact of the move struck Betsy with delayed force. Her mother was still blissfully busy with curtains and new purchases. Julia had joined the Girls' Choir of St. John's Episcopal Church which was directed by her singing teacher, Mrs. Poppy. She was busy with choir rehearsals, talking a language of vestments and te deums that Betsy did not even understand. She had also a new boy on the string, a solid, sober, well-dressed boy named Fred.

Betsy turned to Margaret, but Margaret was six years her junior; Betsy with ankle-length skirts and turned-up braid felt foolish playing childish games. She went up to see Tacy often, but the windows of the empty yellow cottage stared like reproachful eyes. She took to writing long letters to Tib, and when she could find solitude adequate enough, she wrote poems, about childhood and

Hill Street and Tacy. But there didn't seem to be a place to write poems in the new house. Her Uncle Keith's trunk was not in the spacious new room.

Keith Warrington, her mother's brother, was an actor. And his trunk, a real trouper's trunk, flat-topped, four-square, had long served Betsy as a desk. It did not seem to belong in the new room, somehow. At Betsy's own suggestion, on moving day, it had been put in the attic.

"Papa and I will buy you a new desk," her mother said absently. Betsy disliked the new desk in advance. Sometimes she climbed to the attic and stuffed smudged, scribbled papers furtively into the trunk, standing forlorn in a dark corner. On such occasions she often cried a little; never much, for it always occurred to her how romantic it was to be crying about her trunk, and then she stopped, and couldn't start again.

"I'll be glad when school begins," she thought one day, sitting on the porch steps, looking across the street at older lawns and gardens where late summer flowers gave the look of fall.

Her mother came out of the house just then, wearing the abstracted beatific look she had worn since moving day. Her red hair was tied up in a towel and she carried a hammer.

She tip-toed out to the muddy lawn and squinted at the big front window.

"I'm putting the new curtains up," she explained. "Just wanted to get the effect. I'm fixing them in a stunning new way, crossed over, sort of. What I need for that window is a big brass bowl, with a palm in it, you know . . ." She stopped, sensing Betsy's disinterest.

Betsy spoke crossly. "I'll be glad when school begins."

Mrs. Ray came out of her trance. She sat down on the steps, looking troubled.

"I'm sure you will. You'll be happier, too, when you get acquainted with some boys and girls. I don't know why you haven't already. You were always such a one for other children."

"There aren't any around here," said Betsy gloomily.

"Why, there's the Edwards boy."

Betsy could not deny it. The Rays' back lawn ended in an alley, and across the alley was the Edwards' barn. Their house looked the other way, fronting on the street below High Street, but it was as close as Tacy's house had been. And there was an Edwards boy just about her age named Caleb. People called him Cab.

"I don't know him; he went to the other school. And he's always busy with boys, playing ball," Betsy said.

"Go out and play with them."

"Mamma! You seem to think I'm no older than Margaret."

Mrs. Ray sighed. She looked at the stooped slender Betsy.

"Sit up straight, Betsy," she said in an irritated tone, but Betsy only stooped the more. Secretly she thought the stoop attractive. She did not consider it a stoop, but a droop, such as Miss Ethel Barrymore had. She had read in the newspapers about the Ethel Barrymore droop, and she hoped that the Betsy Ray droop was equally fascinating.

Mrs. Ray was yearning to get at her windows but she made another attempt.

"Why don't you go down to the Sibleys?" she asked. "They live so near, and Caroline is such a lovely girl."

Mrs. Ray never mentioned Caroline Sibley without adding that she was a lovely girl which always annoyed Betsy.

"Caroline Sibley is a stick," she said.

"Why, Betsy, you hardly know her. I'm sure she isn't a stick. And they have such a big beautiful lawn, and there's always a crowd of young people there. . . ."

"And her father's a banker," Betsy put in rudely.

Mrs. Ray rose.

"Betsy, I really can't let you talk to me like that. You know perfectly well it makes no difference to me that Caroline Sibley's father is a banker. What interests me is that she is a very nice girl with a circle of friends who ought to be your friends, now that you live near. But there's no use in my talking. I see that I can't help you, at least in your present mood. And I'm busy. I wish to goodness I could get some help."

"Hasn't anyone answered your advertisement, mamma?" asked Betsy, trying to sound pleasant because she felt ashamed.

"Not a soul. And I'm willing to pay top wages, two dollars a week."

"Can I help you?"

"Not with the curtains, thanks. I just have to fuss until I get them right." Thoughts of the new lace curtains, and the big shiny front window, brought the gleam back to Mrs. Ray's eyes. "Why don't you go to the Majestic?" she asked.

"Oh, mamma! May I?" Betsy jumped up, smiling. "I haven't a cent," she added.

"Take a nickel out of my brown purse, and another nickel for ice cream," Mrs. Ray answered, and went back to her curtains, swinging the hammer and humming.

Betsy rushed upstairs to wash. The new bathroom *was* nice, she admitted, running hot water into the bowl. She combed her hair freshly, taking care not to comb out the curls, and tied the big taffeta hair ribbon which matched her pink lawn jumper. She scowled at a shiny nose.

"I think I'll run mamma's chamois skin over my face," she said to herself. "Julia does it sometimes. It isn't really powdering."

Having beautified herself, she took ten cents from the brown pocketbook, caught up a pink ruffled parasol and ran downstairs to kiss her mother penitently.

Starting down Plum Street she saw the Edwards boy sawing wood in his back yard. She had seen him first over the back fence the day they moved in, and several times since. He was about her own height, which was tall for a girl but not for a boy. He was thin and wiry with black hair, snapping green eyes and a dark monkeyish face which was not handsome but undeniably attractive, especially when, as now, he grinned.

A year or two before Betsy would have given him a cheerful hello. Today, although she returned his smile, she did not speak or pause. She knew that her pink lawn jumper was becoming, and hoped that her Ethel Barrymore droop was fascinating, as she sauntered past his back yard and his front yard and on down the hill.

Crossing Broad Street she saw the Sibleys' house, and in spite of the indifference she had shown in talking to her mother, she glanced toward it wistfully. It was a large blue-grey frame house with a generous porch. At the side was a large lawn with a trampled comfortable look. Caroline had several brothers, and there was usually a game of some sort going on.

Betsy acknowledged now that she was prejudiced

35

against Caroline Sibley; perhaps because her mother always praised her so highly.

"Probably I'd like her if I knew her better," Betsy conceded, and at that moment caught sight of her, walking arm in arm with a girl whom Betsy did not know at all. She was short, with smooth yellow hair, a round figure, and skirts a shade longer than the other girls wore. Betsy wondered who she was, but although Caroline Sibley called, "Hello!" and Betsy answered, she did not pause to be introduced. As soon as she had left them behind, she was sorry.

"I don't know what ails me," she thought dejectedly, and hurried on, glad to be going to the Majestic.

The Majestic Theatre, now . . . according to the sign . . . a High Class Place of Amusement, with Up-to-date Moving Picture Entertainment, Especially for Ladies and Children . . . had been just a short time before an ordinary Front Street store. Moving Picture Entertainment had been only a rumor emanating from nearby St. Paul and Minneapolis. There, travelers said, pictures moved on a screen. Deep Valley had seen them move only in nickelodeons, small boxes into which one dropped a nickel and peeped at jerky horse races, prize fights or dancing girls. Then talk of a moving picture called "The Great Train Robbery" rolled over the country like a tidal wave. In Deep Valley as in thousands of other towns a store front was painted red and yellow; a screen was put up inside; a projection machine, a piano and rows of chairs were moved in. The first program was "The Great Train Robbery," and Mr. Ray took the family to see it.

Today the picture was a fantasy called "The Astronomer's Dream." That was the kind Betsy liked best. She sat on the hard chair in the dim stuffy show house and watched the flickering scenes in an enchanted silence. After the main picture there was an illustrated song. The girl who played the piano sang, as colored slides were flashed on the screen.

> *"Keep a little cozy corner,*
> *In your heart for me,*
> *Just for me. . . ."*

Betsy knew it well, for Julia played it.

She had an ice cream soda at Heinz's afterwards, but walking home under her pink ruffled parasol, she felt blue again. A game of prisoners' base was in progress now on the Sibleys' lawn. Cab Edwards had disappeared.

"Down at the Sibleys, probably," Betsy thought.

She was returning more despondent than she had been when she left. And that wasn't fair after her mother had spent ten cents to cheer her up. She didn't know what she could do about it, though. Then in a twinkling she didn't feel blue any more. Her spirits perked up like a terrier's ears. For Mr. Thumbler's hack was driving away from her house, and on the steps stood a stout woman wearing an elegant purple silk dress, a large hat trimmed with feathers, and a feather boa which, flung over one shoulder, shimmered down her ample body. She wasn't just a caller, for she carried a valise. A visitor! How thrilling!

Betsy collapsed her parasol, patted her curls. After the visitor had rung the bell and had been admitted and a suitable short interval had elapsed, Betsy put on her Ethel Barrymore droop and sauntered into the house.

Chapter Five

ANNA

HER mother and the visitor were seated in the parlor. The curtains had been hung. Mrs. Ray's hair was no longer concealed by a towel but rose in its usual high red pompadour, and she was wearing a becoming waist and skirt.

She called, "Come in, dear!" and said to the visitor . . . in a somewhat choked voice, Betsy thought . . . "This

38

is my middle daughter, Betsy. Betsy, this is Anna Swenson who has come to work for us."

"I'm pleased to meet you," Betsy murmured.

Under the feathered hat she saw a wide good-natured face.

"Why, lovey!" said Anna Swenson. "How puny you look! Almost as puny as you are, lovey," she added, to Mrs. Ray.

"We're a very puny family," Mrs. Ray answered in the same choked voice.

Anna nodded.

"So were the McCloskeys. They're the folks I used to work for, lovey. My, how they liked my raised biscuits and my meat balls and my chocolate layer cake! And every last one of them was puny. Charley used to say to me, 'Anna, aren't those McCloskeys the puniest folks?' and I'd say, 'Ja, Charley! They're certainly puny.' They were tony, too."

"And who is Charley?" asked Mrs. Ray while Betsy slipped into a chair and stared with fascinated eyes.

"My beau," Anna answered, smiling broadly. "A bartender down at the Corner Café."

"Is he puny, too?"

"Na," answered Anna regretfully, shaking her head. "He's not puny. He's a nice fellow, Charley is, and a good spender. But I'd never call him puny."

"Are you engaged to him?" asked Betsy, hoping that if she was they would not be married soon.

"I'm not much on the marrying," Anna reassured her. "What I like to do is cook. You may think you know how to cook," she said to Mrs. Ray, who certainly *did* think she knew how to cook and started to say so, but Anna waved her down. "You may think you know how to cook,

39

but wait 'til you taste my cinnamon buns. They melt in your mouth. 'Anna,' Mrs. McCloskey used to say to me, 'your cinnamon buns just melt in my mouth.' " She turned to Betsy. "The McCloskey girl," she added, "always said the same."

"Are you really coming to work for us?" cried Betsy.

"Certainly I am," Anna replied, beaming. "I said so to Charley last night. We were out buggy riding. A hired rig, but very tony. He's a good spender, Charley is. I showed him your ad in the paper. Mrs. Robert Ray of High Street wants a hired girl, five in the family, two dollars a week. I said to Charley, 'That's my place, Charley.' 'Well,' he said, 'I hope you'll like them as well as you liked the McCloskeys.' "

"Do you think you will?" Betsy asked eagerly.

Anna looked around the parlor, and Mrs. Ray flashed Betsy a proud confident glance. The new lace curtains were draped with a dazzling effect. Embroidered pillows made a tidy nest at the head of the leather sofa. A gas lamp with a green shade stood on the mission oak table and photographs marched along a mission oak bookcase. Framed pictures dotted the walls.

Anna spoke reflectively.

"The McCloskeys' house was tonier," she said.

For a moment Betsy wasn't sure whether her mother would let Anna work for them or not. She wanted to hiss 'cinnamon buns' warningly across the room. But to her relief her mother's blue eyes began to dance. She jumped up and took Anna's hands.

"Anna," she said. "It's going to be our ambition in life to make you like us as well as you did the McCloskeys."

Julia came in then, swinging her music roll and looking very pretty. Margaret, too, appeared. She had been visiting a neighbor, Mrs. Wheat, on whom she called almost every afternoon. Anna was introduced, and pronounced them both puny. It was dawning upon Betsy that Anna did not give "puny" its usual insignificant meaning, that it was, on the contrary, the most complimentary word in her vocabulary.

Followed by her daughters Mrs. Ray showed Anna the dining room, the pantry, the shining kitchen. Anna surveyed them with pursed thoughtful lips. She did not say how they compared with the McCloskeys', but it was clear they did not quite measure up.

"I'll show her to her room, mamma," Betsy offered, picking up the valise. It was very heavy.

"Thank you, lovey," Anna said, and Betsy led the way to the second floor and the third, across the open attic where Uncle Keith's trunk stood.

Up to this moment she had thought the hired girl's room very nice. It reminded her of her own room on Hill Street, being slant-roofed and small. There were an iron bed, a bureau, a wash stand with bowl and pitcher, a rocking chair beside the single window, a rag rug on the clean pine floor. It was neat as a pin and looked very inviting, but thinking about the McCloskeys Betsy waited anxiously.

Anna looked around and smiled.

"I'll get along fine up here," she said.

"I like it, too," said Betsy, much relieved. "I'll come up and see you sometimes if you want me to."

"I'd like to have you, lovey. You can stay now and watch me unpack."

Betsy sat down in the rocking chair.

Anna took off her feather boa, smoothed it lovingly and hung it in the closet. She removed her big feathered hat and placed it on the closet shelf. Her hair was wound in a big tight knob that made her broad face look even broader than it was. Her forehead was seamed.

She opened her valise and unrolled a flannel night gown in which an alarm clock had been wrapped. She put that on the bureau. She unrolled another night gown and took out a tall, gilt-topped bottle.

"Perfume," she said. "Jasmine. Do you want some, lovey?"

"Why, thank you," Betsy answered. "I love perfume."

Anna sprinkled her liberally and put the bottle on the bureau. She returned to the valise and lifted out a black silk dress.

"This is my best dress," she remarked. "I wear it to weddings and funerals. I'll wear it to your wedding, lovey, but I hope I won't wear it to your funeral."

"I hope so, too," said Betsy, but the idea was not entirely unpleasant. It was quite romantic.

"The dress I have on is second best," Anna continued.

"It's very stylish," Betsy said.

Anna took out a blue cotton dress, a red cotton dress, and a green cotton dress.

"House dresses," she commented. She hung them all on hangers in the closet and added a well worn wrapper. She took out a pile of aprons, and folded suits of underwear and disposed of them neatly in the bureau drawers. She ranged a pair of worn shoes and a pair of slippers in the closet.

Last of all she lifted out a large square box covered with purple plush. She carried this to the bureau and proudly threw back the lid. Gleaming on white satin were a hand mirror, a comb and brush, a button hook, a shoe horn, a finger nail cleaner and a buffer.

"My dresser set. Charley gave it to me for Christmas."

"It's beautiful!"

"It's mother-of-pearl."

"I'd like to brush my hair with such a beautiful brush," Betsy cried.

"Come up and use it any time," said Anna generously. She closed the valise, put it in the closet and sat down on the bed. The clothing, the alarm clock, the bottle of perfume and the plush-encased dresser set seemed to complete the list of her possessions. Bureaus in the Ray bedrooms bore cherished photographs. There wasn't a single picture on Anna's bureau. Not of Charley, not of the McCloskeys, not of her mother or father or sisters or brothers or home.

"Anna," said Betsy suddenly. "Where is your home?"

Anna's broad seamed face broke into a smile of unexpected gentleness.

"Why, lovey!" she answered. "This is my home."

Anna had found a home . . . or had borrowed one as hired girls do . . . and Betsy had found a friend, her first friend on High Street. She walked to the lofty window and looked out, and for the first time saw beauty in the German Catholic College, grey and dour, on the heights.

"The sun comes up behind that college," she remarked. She sat down again to tell Anna about Hill Street, and Tacy.

"Is she puny?" Anna asked.

"The puniest girl I know," Betsy answered, and praised Tacy's curly auburn hair. "I wish I were punier," she confided abruptly.

"You're plenty puny, lovey," Anna answered. "You're almost as puny as the McCloskey girl."

This Betsy knew now, was real praise. And Anna had

43

more than compliments to give. She knew about a cream that took off freckles in a week.

"I'll buy you some on Thursday."

She knew about metal curlers . . . Magic Wavers, they were called . . . that produced a curl so tight and lasting it put kid rollers to shame.

"I'll find you some on Thursday, too," she promised.

They had a beautiful time until Anna looked at her clock and said it was time to change her dress and go down to start supper.

"What would you like me to make, lovey? It's too late for chocolate cake, and cinnamon buns have to raise, but I could stir up a floating island."

"I love floating island!" cried Betsy.

She bounded down the stairs, spreading waves of jasmine perfume.

Betsy liked High Street better after Anna came, and the rest of August slipped by swiftly. Margaret was still busy with her friend, Mrs. Wheat.

"She's a perfect little lady," Mrs. Wheat said.

Julia was busy with the Episcopal Choir, and "ni-po-tu-la-he," and the new beau named Fred. He had a fine voice and liked to sing and Julia played his accompaniments.

"Love me . . . and the world is mine," he bellowed with such feeling that his face grew red.

He brought Margaret a grey and white kitten which she named Washington. He joked with Betsy about how green she would be on her first day at high school. He enlivened life considerably and so, in a different way, did Miss Mix, the dressmaker who . . . toward the last of the month . . . came to the Rays every day for a week.

"I'm certainly lucky to have her . . . best dress-

44

maker in town . . . three girls and myself to get ready for fall . . ."

Mrs. Ray kept repeating this with variations for Miss Mix's semi-annual visits always upset the house. She sewed only in Mrs. Ray's bedroom, but bright scraps of cloth and snarls of thread, like the hum of her machine, permeated everywhere.

Mr. Ray could find no peaceful spot in which to read his paper. He was irritable. Mrs. Ray was nervous and abstracted, and even Anna was jumpy. Every meal was a challenge; company food, and the best silver and dishes. Miss Mix, wherever she went, expected and received the best.

Miss Mix was a favored character. She went to the twin cities often, bringing back the latest styles, the newest coiffures, not only in fashion books but on her person. Moreover she wore rouge. Women in Deep Valley did not use rouge; not even Julia's singing teacher, Mrs. Poppy, whose husband owned the opera house and the hotel and who used to be an actress. Mrs. Ray sometimes surreptitiously darkened her eyebrows with a burned match, but she never even considered using rouge. Miss Mix used it unreproved . . . on her grave lips, her unsmiling middle-aged cheeks. Unlike most dressmakers she was not talkative. She worked silently, swiftly, intent upon materials, trimmings, patterns, seeming to take little interest in the wearers of the beautiful clothes she produced.

So the sewing machine hummed in a littered bedroom, and Anna baked, and the ends of the maples in lawns along High Street turned yellow.

Chapter Six

THE FIRST DAY OF HIGH SCHOOL

SCHOOL opened on the day after Labor Day. Betsy was
awake at six o'clock. She hadn't slept well, for the Magic
Wavers weren't as comfortable as the familiar kid rollers.
They made a firm curl, though, and a dazzling entrance
into high school was worth any discomfort.

She was glad to be up early in order to have plenty of
time in the bathroom. She could get in before her father

started shaving and ahead of Julia, Margaret and her mother. She had taken a warm bath the night before but this morning she took the quick cold one which . . . she understood from novels, chiefly English . . . brought a glow to the cheek and a shine to the eye. Looking into the mirror afterwards she was not at all sure it had had this effect; she looked a trifle blue and chilly. But it gave her a good feeling, and she didn't worry about her color knowing that her cheeks always flushed obligingly on exciting occasions.

They were gratifyingly pink when, giddy with curls, wearing a large and jaunty pale blue hair ribbon and a pale blue and white sailor suit, closely belted to make her waist look even smaller than it was, Betsy descended the stairs. The family wasn't down yet so she went out to the kitchen.

"Do I look puny, Anna?"

"Lovey, you do!" cried Anna admiringly. "I was saying to Charley last night that you get punier all the time."

"What smells so good?"

"Muffins. They're on account of it's the first day of school. At the McCloskeys I always made muffins for the first day of school."

"The McCloskeys had the nicest customs," said Betsy with a sigh. "Where did they live, Anna? What's become of them?"

She had asked these questions before, but Anna was always evasive.

"They've moved away," she answered vaguely. "They lived in a big tony house. Take the coffee in for me, will you, lovey? And strike the gong? I hear your father coming down."

Betsy took in the coffee and beat a tattoo on the gong.

47

She also ran upstairs to prod Julia. It was Julia's practise to tumble out of bed, not when she was called but after the breakfast gong sounded. Betsy hurried her along now with a tantalizing reference to muffins and rushed back to the dining room where her father, mother and Margaret were assembled. The checked taffeta hair ribbon atop Margaret's English bob was as stiff with newness as her checked gingham dress. Her small face was sober for she, too, was starting at a new school and unlike Betsy was not sure that she was going to like it.

"Where is Julia?" asked Mr. Ray as usual.

"We won't wait for her," said Mrs. Ray quickly, and they sat down at the table. Mr. Ray asked the blessing while Betsy peeked into the sideboard mirror pleased to note the pinkness of her cheeks and the pronounced curl of her hair.

"When I was a boy," said Mr. Ray as soon as the blessing was over, "every child in the family was on time for every meal. There were ten of us, too."

Mr. Ray was a great one to joke, but he wasn't joking now. He had been raised on a farm and believed in early rising, that habit so repugnant to Julia.

Mrs. Ray hurried his coffee across the table and Betsy, as usual, tried to create a diversion.

"I'm starting high school today, papa. How do you like the new sailor suit Miss Mix made for me?"

"Margaret has a new dress, too," said Mrs. Ray.

"I'm glad you have something to show for all that fuss," said Mr. Ray, serving the bacon and eggs. He forgot Julia for a moment, but when Anna brought in the muffins he looked around.

"My dear," he said to Mrs. Ray. "It's too bad for Julia not to get down while these muffins are hot."

"I told her about the muffins, papa. She's hurrying,"

Betsy said and tried to think of another diversion. A sharp ring at the doorbell provided one. Betsy ran to the door and came back with Tacy whose arrival put Mr. Ray into such good humor that Julia slipped into her chair without a reprimand.

"Well, well!" said Mr. Ray. "Betsy and Tacy starting high school together! How many years have you gone off together on the first day of school?"

"This is the tenth," Tacy said. "It's too bad Tib isn't here to go along."

"Sit down and have a muffin and a cup of cocoa with Betsy," Mrs. Ray urged and Tacy slipped into a chair. Betsy's pink cheeks looked pale beside Tacy's which were sheets of scarlet. Under a round hat even her ears were red; and her eyes were shining.

"I'm almost too scared to eat," she said. "Not quite, though. These muffins look so good."

"Well, don't cry and try to go home like you did in Kindergarten," Betsy responded.

"And remember, both of you, all Katie and I have told you," Julia said mischievously. "Don't put Mr. or Miss in front of a teacher's name. Except when you're speaking to one, of course. You always say Bangeter, Clarke, O'Rourke, and so on. Not *Miss* Bangeter, *Miss* Clarke, *Miss* O'Rourke."

"Yes, ma'am," replied Tacy meekly. "What else, ma'am?"

"Did you ever hear of a Social Room?" asked Julia. "Do you know what a vacant period is?"

"Certainly," said Tacy. "I know what it means to flunk, too, and I only hope I won't do it."

"Well, don't act like freshies. Be a credit to Katie and me."

"Don't worry," said Betsy. "We'll act as though we

49

owned the school. We'll saunter in with bored expressions. Won't we, Tacy?"

"Absolutely," said Tacy. "And we'd better stop eating muffins if we're going to saunter in early enough to get those seats."

"What seats?" asked Mr. Ray.

"The back corner seats in the freshman row. They're the seats everyone tries to get."

"I forbid you to choose those seats," Mr. Ray said. "Front seats for both of you. You need to be where Miss Bangeter can keep her eyes on you."

But his hazel eyes were twinkling now.

"It isn't eight o'clock yet," said Mrs. Ray. "School doesn't begin until nine."

"We want to be there when the doors open. All the kids are after those back corner seats."

"Winona Root is after one. And you know we have to hump to get ahead of Winona."

"Goodbye, mamma. Goodbye, papa." Betsy kissed them hurriedly.

"The muffins were grand, Anna. Hope you get a nice teacher, Margaret."

"I'll see you in school," Julia cried.

Betsy put on her hat before the music room mirror, picked up a new tablet and a freshly sharpened pencil. Tacy carried a spanking new tablet and pencil, too. Joining hands, they ran.

Outside there was sunshine. The air smelled and tasted like September, like the first day of school. The flood of schoolbound children was not yet loosed. Betsy and Tacy had High Street to themselves.

At the high school, the grizzled janitor was opening the big front doors. Betsy and Tacy rushed in. They rushed up the broad stairs which turned at a landing where a statue of Mercury was placed, through the spacious upper hall and the girls' cloakroom into the big assembly room, empty and silent.

Freshmen, they knew, were always assigned to the last half dozen rows on the far side of the room. They ran at once to these, and followed the last two rows back to the end. The back seats in these rows had advantages other than the obvious one of being so far from the presiding teacher's desk. They were next to a bulging many-windowed alcove which served as the school library and could also . . . so they had heard from Julia and Katie . . . provide a sociable retreat. The alcove held not only a dictionary on an easel, an encyclopedia and other reference books, but offered a view over descending rooftops all the way to Front Street and the river. Betsy and Tacy paused to look at their own Deep Valley spread out before them on this momentous day.

They sat down breathless, smiling at each other. They examined the inkwells, the grooves for pens and pencils where each one placed her pencil now, the empty interiors of the desks.

"Let's leave our tablets out on top," said Betsy. "They'll stake our claim to the seats while we look around."

So leaving the tablets as evidence of ownership, they drifted down the aisle. They investigated the assembly room. Betsy even went up on the platform where stood a piano, two armchairs and a high reading desk.

"Betsy! Come down! You shouldn't!" hissed Tacy as Betsy sat down in one of the armchairs and tried to imitate tall, erect, queenly Miss Bangeter.

Betsy ran down the steps at the other side of the platform and into the girls' cloakroom again.

Here they were delighted to find Winona Root hanging up a red hat. Winona was tall, thin, angular, yet jauntily graceful. She had heavy black hair worn in Grecian braids like Tacy's but given a different effect by a red hair ribbon at the back. She had gleaming black eyes, gleaming white teeth and an habitual teasing smile. It vanished now when she saw Betsy and Tacy. For Winona too was carrying a tablet and pencil, and she too was breathless, obviously headed for one of the prized back seats.

"Don't bother to go in," Betsy sang out. "We've got them."

"Got what?"

"Got you know what."

"Got what you're after yourself."

"Phooey!" cried Winona, and made a dash for the assembly room, Betsy and Tacy following.

At the back of the room a scuffle ensued, but accepting defeat Winona placed her tablet and pencil on the back seat next to Tacy's and they all raced to the front again. Winona ran up on the platform as Betsy had done, but her imitation of Miss Bangeter was much more daring. She stood up at the reading desk, threw out her chest and said, "Students of the Deep Valley High School . . ." with the strong Boston accent which characterized Miss Bangeter's speech. Boys and girls were flooding in from the cloakrooms now.

"Winona!" Betsy and Tacy pleaded. "Come down!"

And Winona, flashing her white teeth, jumped down from the platform, ignoring the steps. She and Betsy and Tacy ran through the girls' cloakroom, out into the hall, inspected, one after another, the empty classrooms that made a half circle around it, peeped into the Social Room where upper classmen were gathered, and looked at the trophy cups displayed behind glass in a case in the big hall.

"Know which society you're going to join?" Betsy asked Winona. The students were divided between Philomathians and Zetamathians, societies which competed in athletics, in debate and in essay writing as the three cups testified. "Tacy and I are going to be Zets," she added.

"Then I'll be a Philomathian," said Winona sticking out her tongue.

"Just because we got the best seats!" jibed Tacy.

"No. To make things interesting. Besides, the cutest boys are Philos." Winona tossed her head and smiled. She looked around abruptly. "Who's *that* cute boy?" she asked.

Betsy and Tacy followed her penetrating gaze, and Betsy saw a yellow pompadour, an out-thrust lower lip. She looked almost directly into blue eyes which were puzzlingly familiar. While she hesitated the boy passed on. Then she remembered.

"That's Joe Willard . . . Tacy, you know . . . the boy from Butternut Center." She started to run after him, but at that moment a gong clanged. There was a rush for the assembly room, and Joe Willard disappeared.

"Do you know him?" Winona asked eagerly. "Gosh, introduce me! Have you heard that Tom Slade's gone to Cox Military? Weep, weep! Herbert Humphreys is back, though. Don't run like freshies. That's only the first gong." And Winona led the way nonchalantly to the girls' cloakroom. They took turns at the mirror, Betsy and Tacy striving to act as nonchalant as Winona. They delayed so successfully that when Betsy and Tacy were halfway up the aisle the second gong sounded and quiet descended upon the big assembly room.

"A good thing we've got our seats," Betsy thought, trying not to hurry. Tacy was frankly hurrying and her ears, Betsy saw, were as red as fire. Betsy felt all eyes upon them and remembered to assume her Ethel Barrymore droop. Three-quarters of the way up the aisle, however, she stood upright. For lounging comfortably in the choice back corner seats were two boys. Herbert Humphreys and Cab Edwards!

Tacy stopped stock still. If anything was going to be done, Betsy realized, she would have to do it. Forcing a smile she approached them.

"Pardon me," she said politely, in an undertone, "but these are our seats."

"They're ours now," said Herbert Humphreys, grinning.

"We put our tablets on to hold them," Betsy said.

"Looking for these?" asked Cab, pulling two tablets and two pencils out of his desk. He too grinned at them impudently.

Everyone else in the room was seated now. Miss Bangeter was rapping for order. There were several vacant seats in the freshman rows . . . far front, not together, most undesirable. Tacy nudged Betsy and pointed to them. She was agonized with embarrassment.

But Betsy was stubborn.

"We came early to get those seats," she said in a loud whisper. The boys looked at each other and grinned. Betsy forgot herself. She blushed furiously, but not from shyness. "They belong to us. You get out!" she said.

To her amazement the boys, with one accord, slipped out of the seats.

"Take it easy! Take it easy!" Herbert Humphreys said.

"And she looks so sweet and gentle, walking past my house," Cab whispered.

54

Covering their retreat with muttered witticisms, they hurried down the aisle.

Betsy and Tacy sat down, breathing hard. All about them necks were craned. A wave of giggling swept through the room. Miss Bangeter rapped for order again.

Then to Betsy's horror, Miss Bangeter turned and descended the platform. She walked rapidly up the last aisle. Heads were turned to follow her progress. Betsy saw Julia's anxious face, Katie's.

Miss Bangeter drew nearer. No feeble imitation of Betsy's or Winona's had conveyed her height, her sternness, her black-haired majesty. Betsy stole a glance at Tacy who had turned pale, and seemed frozen to her seat.

Miss Bangeter drew nearer the two culprits, nearer, nearer . . .

She passed them by, and going into the alcove, efficiently opened a window.

Chapter Seven

CAB

EXCEPT for the Adventure of the Two Back Seats, the first day at high school did not amount to much. There were the usual opening exercises. The school joined lustily in singing a hymn, and for the first time Betsy and Tacy heard Miss Bangeter, with stern sincerity and an impressive Boston accent, read a psalm and lead in the Lord's Prayer. Long before noon school was dismissed for the day.

In the afternoon Betsy, Tacy and Winona went down to Cook's Book Store to buy school supplies. They went to Heinz's Restaurant for banana splits and back to the Ray house where . . . joined by Julia, Katie and Mrs. Ray . . . they discussed the morning. The banana splits proving insufficient, they made fudge. And Julia played, and all of them sang.

Julia preferred operatic music. Some time before she had written to a music store in Minneapolis, grandly opened an account, asked for a list of their opera scores and ordered . . . because it was cheapest . . . the opera of Pagliacci. When alone, she played and sang Pagliacci by the hour. Not just the soprano part of Nedda, but all the parts . . . tenors, baritones, even the villagers. She told Betsy the story of the clown's betrayal and Betsy almost wept at first when Julia sang, "Laugh, Pagliaccio," with a sob in her voice. But the Rays had grown callous to the sorrows of the strolling players.

When contemporaries were around, as now, Julia played popular songs and with such contagious zest that everyone gathered arm in arm around the piano and sang.

After supper, Betsy telephoned Tacy and Winona for prolonged conversations, then went upstairs to wind her hair on Magic Wavers, take a warm bath with some of Julia's bath salts in it, and rub the new freckle cream into her face. Wrapped in a kimono she sat down to manicure her nails.

She still felt a little strange in the new bedroom. It was always so neat. . . . Julia had kept the old room cozily untidy. And she missed Uncle Keith's trunk, gathering dust in the attic. She had to admit that the room was pretty, though; Mrs. Ray joyfully called it a typical girl's room.

It was papered in a pattern of large blue and white

flowers clambering up vines. There were blue ruffled curtains at the windows, blue matting on the floor, a blue, white-tufted bedspread on the white iron bed. The furniture was Mrs. Ray's old Hill Street bedroom set, freshly painted white.

"You'll have a set of bird's eye maple some day," her mother promised. But Betsy rather liked the low old-fashioned bureau with a tier of shelves at the side, and the chest and rocking chair in their shining new white coats. The walls were liberally sprinkled with photographs and Gibson Girls.

"I'm going to get me a Deep Valley High School pennant," Betsy planned, buffing luxuriously.

Julia and Fred were downstairs. Betsy could hear their voices in the parlor, and that brought to her mind a question dormant since morning. Winona had created it with her talk about boys. Tacy didn't care about boys, and with Tacy Betsy almost forgot how important they were.

But she was in high school now. Would boys start coming to see her, as they came to see Julia?

Tom Slade had come of course, since he was a little boy, but that was because his mother and Mrs. Ray were friends. And Tom had gone away to the military school that Julia's friend Jerry had once attended. She knew Herbert Humphreys pretty well; his parents too were friends of her parents, and at intervals he and his older brother joined the Rays at a family party. But she couldn't imagine Herbert coming to the house independent of his parents.

She giggled to herself remembering the morning's encounter with him and Cab.

"No more H.H.A.S.," Tacy had leaned out to whisper after Miss Bangeter returned to the platform. And Betsy agreed although admitting to herself that Herbert, in vacation tan, blonder, bigger and brawnier than ever, was outstandingly good looking. Cab Edwards was cute, too.

"I wish I were prettier," she thought, depression, like a sudden fog, invading the room. She put away her manicure set, took off her kimono, turned out the gas, said her prayers and slipped into bed.

"I wish I had golden hair," she continued in the darkness. "Wavy golden hair, a yard long. And big blue eyes, and pink cheeks, and teeth close together like Julia's. Or maybe it would be nicer to have heavy black ringlets, and big black eyes with curly lashes, and a white satiny skin."

Before she could decide which she preferred, she fell asleep.

The next day was the first day of real school, and the prospect was almost as exciting as it had been the day before. There weren't muffins for breakfast, but there were pancakes with sausage and maple syrup. While the Rays were at the table, the doorbell rang.

"Tacy, probably," Betsy said, as Margaret went to answer it, and Julia slipped into her chair, late, as usual.

Margaret came back, looking surprised.

"It's a boy," she said. "He asked for Betsy."

"For *me?*" Betsy was sure Margaret had misunderstood.

"Ask him to come in," said Mrs. Ray, and Margaret went back. She returned with the dark monkeyish face of Cab Edwards grinning behind her.

"Good morning, Cab," said Mr. Ray who had sold him his shoes for many years.

"Good morning," said Mrs. Ray.

"Hello," said Julia.

"Hello," said Betsy blushing. Anna who had come to the doorway rolled her eyes at Betsy.

"Won't you sit down?" asked Mrs. Ray. "Maybe you'd like a pancake?"

"Gosh, I should say I would!" said Cab. He drew up a chair beside Betsy's, and Betsy jumping up to get him a plate and knife and fork and spoon managed a hasty glance at her curls in the sideboard mirror. They were still Magically Waved, thank goodness!

"Have you heard how your daughter treated me yesterday, Mr. Ray?" asked Cab.

"Isn't she behaving?"

"Well, did you bring her up to steal? Cold bloodedly steal?"

"She's stolen my pencils for years," said Mr. Ray.

"And my perfume," said Julia.

"And my handkerchiefs," said Mrs. Ray.

"We did not steal those seats. You go jump in the lake," said Betsy. She was enormously pleased. Cab had dropped in to walk to school with her. There was no doubt of it.

To be sure, he wasn't gazing at her soulfully as Julia's beaux gazed. He was devouring pancakes and syrup, and Anna was plying him with more. But he must like her, or he wouldn't have come.

The doorbell rang again, and this time it was Tacy. She looked surprised and confused when she saw Cab. Then the significance of his presence dawned and she flashed Betsy a congratulatory glance. On invitation, she too sat down for a pancake.

"Tacy," said Cab, "was as bad as Betsy."

"Worse, probably," Mr. Ray returned. "These redheads! I know all about them. I've been married to one for twenty years. She's terrific to live with; isn't she, Anna?"

Anna was not yet accustomed to Mr. Ray's teasing. Moreover she thought that Mrs. Ray's beautiful red hair was a curse which it was indelicate to mention.

"Lovey," she said to Mrs. Ray, "I don't think your hair is really red. Just last night, Charley said to me, 'I think Mrs. Ray's hair is more brown than red.'"

"No, Anna," said Mr. Ray. "You can't get around it. She's a carrot top. But I've stood it for twenty years, and I can stand it for twenty more if you'll only bring me another plate of pancakes."

"Betsy, can I walk to school with you every day forever? I like your groceries," said Cab.

"Don't they feed you at home?" asked Betsy. "If you're coming with Tacy and me, you'll have to hurry."

She tried to conceal her gratification at having a masculine escort as she and Tacy joined the river of schoolbound boys and girls.

"Who is that girl with Caroline Sibley?" she asked as Caroline passed, arm in arm with the yellow-haired girl she had noticed before.

"Don't you know?" Cab replied. "Bonnie Andrews. Her father's the new minister at the Presbyterian Church. She's the reason all the boys have started going to Christian Endeavor."

"Where did she come from?"

"Gosh, don't you know anything? From Paris."

"Paris! Not Paris, France?"

"What other Paris is there? There isn't any Paris, Minnesota, that I've ever heard of."

Betsy was thrilled.

"But what's the connection between being a Presbyterian minister and living in Paris?"

"Let's go down to the Sibleys' some day and ask," Cab

replied. "We'd find her there," he added. "Everyone gangs up on the Sibleys' lawn."

It was just what her mother had said. Betsy felt ashamed of the remote bad-tempered Betsy of the days before high school began. "Let's," she replied.

There were real lessons today. Betsy and Tacy had enrolled for Latin, algebra, ancient history and composition. In most classes they sat together, and they needed companionship for high school subjects seemed very strange.

Latin! A language, so Mr. Morse said, that nobody living spoke familiarly now. It was mystifying that one should have to study it. And algebra baffled Betsy from the first, but she liked the algebra teacher. Miss O'Rourke had curly hair and smiling eyes and looked trimly lovely in a white shirtwaist and collar.

Miss Clarke, the ancient-history teacher, was nice, too. She wore glasses, but she was pretty, with dark wings of hair and soft white skin. She was gentle; she trusted everyone. Ancient history, therefore, was supposed to be a snap. Mr. Gaston who taught composition had a reputation for stiffness, but that didn't worry Betsy.

"You're sure to be the best in the class," Tacy remarked, voicing Betsy's own thought.

Joe Willard was in the composition class. Remembering *The Three Musketeers,* Betsy had an idea that he too might be good; and she soon found out that he was. Several times during the first week she tried to catch his eye, but she never succeeded. He must, she thought regretfully, have thought she was snubbing him on the first day of school. He sat in the back row and always slipped out promptly, so she never found a chance to make things right.

62

Returning to school after dinner one day, Betsy and Tacy went into the Social Room. Freshmen were unwelcome there usually, but not today; today they were fawned on by seniors, juniors and sophomores; for this afternoon they would choose their societies, and rivalry between Philomathians and Zetamathians was keen. Betsy and Tacy were sure to be Zetamathians, because Julia and Katie were, so no upperclassmen wasted time on them. But they basked in the short-lived popularity of freshmen and inspected the Social Room.

It was only a classroom, furnished with desks and black boards, but it was particularly pleasant, located in one of the turrets as the library alcove was; and it was given over to social intercourse during all school intermissions.

Julia and Katie, busily wooing Cab, waved at them. Fred hailed them, and so did Leo who went with Katie, and another friend of their sisters', dark-eyed Dorothy Drew. Caroline Sibley was there with Bonnie Andrews and the Humphreys boys.

"This Social Room makes school as good as a party," Tacy observed. "Only no refreshments."

After the afternoon classes there was a big assembly. Miss Bangeter explained about the two societies, about the cups . . . for athletics, debating and essay writing . . . for which they annually competed. The presidents of the societies spoke, and there was rooting:

"Zet! Zet! Zetamathian!"

"Philo! Philo! Philomathian!"

Then lists were passed and Betsy and Tacy became Zetamathians. They were given turquoise blue bows.

"Zet! Zet! Zetamathian!" they chanted in the cloakroom.

"Philo! Philo! Philomathian!" Winona, wearing an

63

orange bow, threw her red hat in the air. "The cute new boy's a Philo. Did you know?"

She meant Joe Willard. Betsy saw him on the steps and he was wearing an orange bow.

Cab, wearing a turquoise blue bow, joined Betsy and Tacy on High Street. They all dropped into the Ray house for cookies and some singing. Then Cab proposed, "How about going down to the Sibleys'? Find out who went what?"

"I can't," said Tacy. "I have to go home."

"I'll go. Love to," said Betsy. She avoided her mother's eyes as she fluffed up her curls in the mirror.

Tacy walked with Cab and Betsy down the Plum Street hill to Broad Street, and left them at the Sibleys' lawn.

"You'll like Carney; she's lots of fun," said Cab as he and Betsy strolled toward a group of boys and girls.

"Is Carney, Caroline?"

"Sure."

"I hope Bonnie Andrews is here," Betsy remarked.

It was exciting to be going to the Sibleys; and gratifying to have a boy by her side. But most thrilling of all was the thought of meeting someone who came from Paris, France.

Chapter Eight

THE SIBLEYS' SIDE LAWN

IT WAS to develop later that the younger high school crowd had the most indoor fun at the Ray house and the most outdoor fun at the Sibleys . . . on the wide, trampled side lawn, and the porch running across the front and around the side of the house. The porch was unscreened and shaded by vines, now turning red. It was broad enough to hold a hammock and some chairs and a table, but nothing too good, nothing rain would hurt.

The porch was deserted today. A bonfire smouldered in the driveway; rakes lay beside it, and a crowd composed of Caroline Sibley's brothers, Herbert Humphreys and his older brother Lawrence, Caroline and Bonnie, were seated on the leaf-strewn lawn. Cab and Betsy dropped down beside them and no one seemed to think it strange that Betsy had come. Caroline said, "Hello," showing a surprising solitary dimple, and introduced Bonnie.

Caroline Sibley was the only girl Betsy had ever seen who had only one dimple. She was also the only girl Betsy had ever seen who looked prettier in glasses than she could possibly have looked without them. They were eye glasses and suited her demure, piquant face. She had slightly irregular teeth which folded over in front, twinkling eyes, and a skin like apple blossoms. Her straight brown hair was parted and combed smoothly back to an always crisp hair ribbon. Her shirt waist was unbelievably white, the slender waistband neat. Caroline's people came from New England, and she had a prim New Englandish air that contrasted with the dimple in a fascinating way.

Bonnie's blonde hair was as smooth as Caroline's and her shirt waist as snowy and fresh. Betsy's hair was forever coming loose, and her waists had a way of pulling out from her skirts just as soon as she forgot them and began to have a good time. She immediately admired Caroline's and Bonnie's trimness.

"Of course they're sophomores," she told herself consolingly. "Probably by the time I'm a sophomore I can keep my waist tucked in, too."

Bonnie had calm blue eyes. She was short, but her figure was more mature than Caroline's and her skirts were sedately long. She had small, plump, very soft hands, and a soft, chuckling laugh that flowed continuously

66

through the conversation. In spite of the laugh, however, she seemed womanly and serious, as befitted a minister's daughter.

Lawrence Humphreys was as dark as Herbert was light, as big or bigger, and equally handsome. But he was quiet. He lacked Herbert's wild high spirits. Not that these were apparent, today. Herbert seemed glum, subdued, and most of the time gazed moodily at Bonnie.

"He has a crush on Bonnie," Betsy thought, proud of her acumen.

Lawrence, whom they all called Larry, played football on the first team. After Saturday, he said, he'd be in training and he had told the girls to spoil him while they could.

Caroline was making a wreath of red ivy leaves from the porch. She was going to crown him, she explained, as the Romans crowned guests at their banquets. She and Bonnie and Larry were all studying Caesar or Cicero and were full of Latin quotations.

"O di immortales!" was Caroline's favorite exclamation. It made Betsy's Latin come considerably alive.

While waiting for his crown, Lawrence was being fed peanuts by Bonnie to the accompaniment of her soft giggle.

"Heck! I'm going out for football, too. What about me?" Herbert protested.

"And what about me?" asked Cab, flexing his muscles. "Boy, what football material!"

Caroline's brothers, all still in grade school, laughed appreciatively.

The Humphreys were Philos, Betsy discovered, and Caroline and Bonnie were Zets.

"What do Philomathian and Zetamathian mean, I wonder?" asked Betsy.

67

Bonnie knew. Philomathian meant Lover of Learning and Zetamathian, Investigator.

"My father told me," she explained, tossing off her knowledge.

Betsy liked her. She liked Carney, too. Already she was calling Caroline Carney, Lawrence Larry, and exclaiming *O di immortales!* with the rest of the crowd. At last Carney's brothers went back to their raking which reminded Larry and Herbert that they too had a lawn.

"And, gosh, I've got a paper route!" Cab said. "But if you'll go home now, Betsy, I'll escort you. Always the perfect gentleman, by gum!"

"I can find my way," said Betsy. "Me and my trained bloodhound!"

"Betsy isn't going to hurry," said Carney. She smiled up at Larry. "I think you're mean to go. You haven't worn your wreath."

"You wear it. You'll look nice in it."

"All right. And I'll make one for Bonnie and one for Betsy!"

"Hey! You'll be a Triumvirate!" What, Betsy wondered, was a Triumvirate?

"Girls! We're a Triumvirate!" cried Carney, flashing her dimple. "I want to be Caesar. He's so cute in the pictures. You can be Crassus, Bonnie, and Betsy, you can be Pompey."

"A Triumvirate of Lady Bugs!" jeered Larry.

"There are three of you boys, too," cried Bonnie, soft giggles bubbling. "You're a Triumvirate your own selves. What's the name of yours? Make one up, somebody."

"They're a Triumvirate of Potato Bugs," said Betsy.

This was a triumph. The boys, departing, yelped, and Carney and Bonnie doubled up with appreciative mirth.

Their laughter continued while they robbed the porch of ivy leaves and Carney made wreaths. Carney and Bonnie laughed at everything Betsy said.

"Betsy, you're so *funny!*" Bonnie kept gasping. And Betsy, delighted, laughed so hard at her own wit that she could hardly keep on being witty.

When the wreaths were finished she put hers on askew, over the left eye. Carney put hers on over the right eye. Bonnie hung hers on one ear. They leered drunkenly, imitating Romans. Exhausted, at last, they rolled in the grass.

Carney sat up suddenly and said, "I hereby invite the Triumvirate to go riding tomorrow after school."

"Will we wear crowns?" asked Betsy.

"We ought to wrap up in bedsheets like those old Romans."

"*O di immortales!*" cried Carney, rocking back and forth. "We'd scare Dandy."

"Who's Dandy?"

"He's our horse. All our horses are named Dandy."

"All our horses are named Old Mag," said Betsy "whether they're girls or boys."

This struck Carney and Bonnie as so supremely comical that they were obliged to fall shrieking into the grass again. But the Big Mill whistle, blowing for six o'clock, brought them all to their feet.

"Gee, I didn't know it was that late," Betsy said.

"I ought to be in helping my mother," cried Carney.

"Walk home with me, Bonnie," Betsy urged. "I hate to think of that long walk all alone."

"But I'd have to walk back all alone."

"No you wouldn't. I'd walk halfway back with you. That would make everything fair."

69

So Bonnie walked home with Betsy, and having gained the new green house on High Street, they turned around and Betsy walked halfway back with Bonnie. From the time they said goodbye to Carney until they said goodbye to each other, they didn't laugh at all. In a sudden shift of mood, Betsy asked Bonnie about Paris, and Bonnie told her a little about it, but she failed to create any picture of Paris in Betsy's mind.

"There are lots of hacks," she said. "They drive like mad. And there was a merry-go-round—carousels, they call them—in the park where I played after school."

"Do you speak French?"

"Of course. Father was in the pastorate there for four years."

"Say some for me," said Betsy.

Bonnie looked embarrassed but obediently murmured something.

"What does that mean?"

"It means I like Deep Valley better than Paris."

Betsy remembered that many years ago Tib had said she liked Deep Valley better than Milwaukee. Deep Valley, Betsy thought, looking up at the hills and down at the town, must be a pretty nice place.

She told Bonnie about Tib . . . how pretty she was, small and dainty with yellow curls. She told her that Tib was going to be a dancer.

"She and Tacy are my two best friends," Betsy explained.

"Carney's my best friend," said Bonnie. "It's wonderful having a chum. We're having our Sunday dresses made just alike."

"Exactly alike?"

70

"Exactly. Miss Mix is making them."

"How marvelous!" cried Betsy. She wished that she and Tacy had thought of doing that.

"Carney's going with Lawrence. Did you know it?"

"I guessed it," said Betsy.

"Do you go with anyone?" asked Bonnie.

With a feeling of unutterable thankfulness Betsy answered carelessly, "Only Cab. He's just a neighbor, of course."

"I'll tell you something, Betsy," said Bonnie. "Promise not to tell a soul. Herbert has a crush on me."

"I noticed it," said Betsy. "I think it's thrilling. Herbert was just the idol of all the girls in grade school. We trembled when we saw him, practically."

"But he's such a *child*," cried Bonnie. "He's such an *infant*. Why, he's only a freshman, and I'm a sophomore. I wish I could hand him over to you."

"And I wish I could find a nice sophomore boy for you," said Betsy. "Not that you need anybody found for you," she added, and repeated what Cab had said about Bonnie having greatly increased attendance at Christian Endeavor.

"How silly!" said Bonnie. "I try not to think about boys at Christian Endeavor." She looked so sincerely devout that Betsy was impressed.

They parted at a point on Plum Street which was exactly half way between High Street and Broad.

Betsy instead of Julia was late for supper that night. Her father gave her a reproving glance when she entered the dining room, but he relented quickly; she looked so radiantly happy. She was full of talk all through supper. Anna, clearing the plates, paused to listen.

71

"But who *is* this Bonnie?" Mr. Ray asked.

"Bonnie Andrews. Her father is the new Presbyterian minister."

"And Carney?"

"Caroline Sibley. Don't be surprised, though, if I call her Julius Caesar. We've formed a Triumvirate."

"What is a Triumvirate?" asked Margaret, looking up from her plate.

"She doesn't even know what a Triumvirate is! *O di immortales!*" Betsy cried.

Chapter Nine

THE TRIUMVIRATE OF LADY BUGS

CAB appeared as usual the next day to walk to school with them, and Betsy and Tacy had small chance for private conversation. During the morning, however, Betsy was able to give some idea of the fun she had had at the Sibleys. And at noon they walked around and around the school block for a really confidential talk.

Betsy told her about Carney and Bonnie.

"They're oceans of fun. You'll be crazy about them."
She told her about the two Triumvirates.

Tacy was not the kind of best friend who felt jealous of a Triumvirate of Lady Bugs which left her out. Of course she and Betsy both knew that any group which included Betsy would shortly expand to take in Tacy too. Betsy said as much and Tacy agreed, but with a reservation.

"You know, Betsy, I'm not interested in boys. When those Triumvirates do things together, I'd just as soon not be there."

"But what do you have against boys?" asked Betsy. "You like Cab, don't you?"

"Yes. Cab's nice."

"You always liked Tom Slade."

"Yes, but he's gone away. And anyway, Betsy, it's not that I don't like boys all right. I don't know how to act when they're around like you and Julia do."

Betsy was flattered to be classed with Julia.

"You're just bashful, Tacy. But, listen! I've got a plan. Herbert Humphreys has a crush on Bonnie, and Bonnie doesn't want him because he's a freshman. So she said she'd hand him over to me, but I don't really need him because I've got Cab, sort of. So I could hand Herbert over to you."

Tacy burst out laughing.

"You can't hand boys around as though they were pieces of cake," she said. "Don't worry about getting a boy for me, Betsy. Boys just don't seem important to me. They don't seem any more important to me than they ever did."

"Tacy!" said Betsy. "You're beyond me!"

"Well!" said Tacy. "That's the way I am."

So after school she went off contentedly with Alice, who

was a friend from the Hill Street neighborhood, a tall blonde girl with glasses, and Betsy dropped her books at home, preparatory to going down to the Sibleys'. She took Carney and Bonnie in to meet her mother. They liked her, as all the girls did, and chattered easily while Betsy foraged. She came back from the kitchen flourishing a box of crackers.

"Nourishment for the ride!"

"I'll get some olives at home," Carney said.

"Those old Romans didn't eat crackers and olives," objected Bonnie with her bubbling laugh.

"They drank wine," said Carney. "But don't forget you're a minister's daughter, miss."

At the Sibleys', they went in to speak to Mrs. Sibley, a slender dark-haired woman with twinkling eyes who looked much as Carney would look at her age. Carney got the olives, and the three girls hitched the bay horse to the surrey.

"I like horses better than automobiles. Don't you?" asked Betsy.

"Yes. Papa's threatening to get an automobile, though."

"Are you allowed to take Dandy out often?"

"Quite often. Papa walks to the bank."

"Papa lets Julia and me drive Old Mag too. I love to go riding," Betsy said.

It was a perfect day for a ride. The sky was greenish blue and misty over Deep Valley's hills. The air was warm, and smelled of bonfires.

They left Broad Street at the Episcopal Church and took the road leading to Cemetery Hill. They passed the watering trough and the little store where Margaret had bought candy, and the road began to climb.

Carney knew this hill as Betsy and Tacy knew the Hill Street Hill. She coasted down it every winter.

"Larry steers. He's wonderful," she said. "How he misses the watering trough is just beyond me!"

The dry gulch beside the road became a brook in the spring, she said. She and her brothers used to float boats there.

Today it was full of yellow leaves and bordered by flaming sumac. On the right, at the crest of the hill, rose the solemn white arch of the cemetery gate.

"Shall we go in?" asked Betsy. "I love to look at gravestones."

"Not today," said Carney. "I'm not in the mood for it."

"Neither am I," said Bonnie. "I feel perfectly wild."

"Let's scream then," said Betsy, and she screamed, and they all screamed. Dandy didn't turn his head, but a flock of blackbirds rose in alarm.

"I think I'll ride Dandy. Would he mind?" Betsy asked.

"Not a bit. He's used to it."

"I could climb on from that fencepost. Pompey always rode horseback." Betsy scrambled down.

"He didn't either," shouted Bonnie. "He rode in a chariot!"

"They raced," yelled Carney. "Whoopee! Remember Ben Hur?"

But Betsy thought Dandy's back was better than any chariot. She sat astride, pretending to be a cowboy, while Carney and Bonnie rolled in the seat with laughter. Her hair came down, and lost its curl in the breeze. Her waist pulled out of her skirt. She didn't mind.

"Look what I see!" she cried suddenly.

"What?"

"Grapes!" She pointed to an old elm, laden with clustering vines.

"Pompey has discovered wine!" shrieked Bonnie.

"He's the noblest Roman of them all," cried Carney. She and Bonnie tumbled out of the surrey while Betsy, with some difficulty, got down from Dandy's back. The grapes were ripe and they picked handfuls.

"There's a good place to eat," said Carney pointing to a field that was empty except for golden-rod, asters and thistles and a jeweled apple tree.

"Swell! We can steal apples."

"Listen to the minister's daughter!"

"I'll get some. My father is only an elder." Carney ran to the tree, returned with six apples and tossed two to each of the girls.

"*Gallia est omnis divisa in partes tres.*"

"*Amo, amas, amat,*" shouted Betsy, not to be outdone.

"Freshie!" the others yelled.

Carney loosened Dandy's checkrein, and he stood without hitching during the Roman feast.

While they ate they talked about boys. Betsy repeated Tacy's remark about passing boys around like pieces of cake. Carney and Bonnie thought it was killing. Bonnie said she was going to entertain the two Triumvirates Friday night. She bewailed Herbert's youth, and Betsy said she was going to ask Julia to look out for a junior boy for Bonnie.

"A junior! Betsy, you angel!"

"Do you like them?"

"I adore them!"

"Larry is nicer than any old junior," said Carney, munching her stolen fruit.

"He is not."

"He is so."

"Herbie's nice too."

"That baby!"

They had a wonderful time, and after eating they made themselves as tidy as they could. Bonnie and Carney weren't very mussed, but they tucked in Betsy's waist and tied her hair up with a ribbon.

"Heavens, I hope we won't meet any boys going home!" Betsy said. "If we do, make Dandy gallop; will you, Carney?"

"He forgot how years ago."

"Besides, if we galloped the boys would think they had to rescue us," said Bonnie.

"Let 'em try," said Betsy. "They couldn't catch up. And we'd yell, 'Help! Help! Help!' like this. 'Help! Help! Help!' "

They raced across the field crying, "Help! Help! Help!" Fortunately nobody heard them but Dandy who ignored them. Laughter drifted behind them like smoke all the way down Cemetery Hill.

Betsy parted from Carney and Bonnie at the watering trough. She raced home through the early twilight and had just time to wash before supper. She could use, she found, a good bit of washing.

After supper she was supposed to do homework but first she telephoned Tacy to tell her about the ride. And Bonnie telephoned to giggle over how funny Betsy had looked on Dandy. And Betsy telephoned Carney to bring her up to date on the other two conversations.

Julia was out at choir practice, and when she returned Betsy went into her room to drum up a junior boy for Bonnie.

Betsy always liked to go into Julia's room. It smelled like her, of a sweet cologne she used. It was often in disorder for Julia was untidy, but she was untidy in a dainty way. The pile of clothes that Betsy now moved from the window seat, in order to sit down, was fresh, lacy and sweet-smelling.

Betsy loved this window seat, which looked up at the Catholic College. She settled into it cozily now while Julia in a white nightgown sat down at the dressing table to take pins out of her hair. Julia didn't wear a hair ribbon any more. She wore her hair in a pompadour all around her head with a knot on top.

Julia was not one of a crowd of girls as Betsy was. She never had been. Katie and Dorothy were her friends, but she didn't feel that she must telephone them every night, nor see them every day. She wasn't inclined either toward a crowd of boys. She preferred one completely devoted swain, but she always tired of him and went on to another, indifferent to the sufferings of the discarded one.

"He'll get over it," was her callous answer to tender Betsy's protests.

She had liked Jerry best, but he had gone away to West Point, and none of them could compete in her interest with music. Her mind was upon music now, while Betsy talked.

"Of course I'll introduce Bonnie to some junior boys," she said. "But Bettina, listen! The choir needs altos badly and Mrs. Poppy wants you to come and try out."

"I'd love to!" cried Betsy. She thought rapturously of wearing vestments and of marching through candlelight. "But, Julia, I'm sure I can't sing well enough. Mrs. Poppy just thinks I can because I'm your sister."

"No, Bettina, you could do it. I wouldn't say so if I

79

didn't believe it. You're really musical. Perhaps because we've always had so much music at home." She laughed as she shook out her hair. "You know, mamma raised us on the Gilbert and Sullivan operas. She sang them to us while we were nursing. And I've been banging a piano in your ears for centuries now. You could carry the alto part without coming up to the soprano all the time the way so many girls do."

"The way I used to do when Tacy and I sang the Cat Duet," said Betsy.

"You've learned since then," said Julia, "shouting around the piano."

"Do you suppose papa and mamma would mind?" asked Betsy after a thoughtful moment. "They don't mind *your* doing it because you have such a talent for music, and they know it's good training. But they might not like to have me going all the time to the Episcopal Church."

"They'd still have Margaret to go to the Baptist Church with them," said Julia. She turned from the mirror to look solemnly into Betsy's face.

"Bettina," she said. "I love the Episcopal Church. I want to be an Episcopalian."

"Julia!" cried Betsy, hardly believing her ears.

"I don't think I was ever cut out to be a Baptist," Julia said.

Betsy was genuinely shocked. It had not occurred to her that one could change one's church any more than one could change one's skin. She was silent, and Julia went on:

"Just because papa and mamma are Baptists is no reason I should be a Baptist. People are different. I'm myself."

"But Julia!" Betsy protested. "You've been baptized."

She well remembered Julia's baptism several years before. At the front of the Baptist Church, behind the pulpit, hung a painted landscape of the River Jordan. Where the canvas river ended there was a deep recess which could be made into an actual pool. On the days when people were baptized, the minister stood there in a rubber coat; each devotee in turn walked down the steps and was dipped beneath the water.

Julia had seemed like an angel coming down. The other girls had looked self-conscious or frightened, but Julia had looked rapt and grave. The people were singing, "Shall we gather at the river?" and Julia had looked as though she were listening to heavenly choirs. The other girls had come up from their immersion sputtering and gasping, but Julia, although her long hair hung like sea weed, had kept a grave, rapt profile.

Betsy had not yet been baptized. And she knew that she could not hope to emulate Julia. She was religious. But she was religious only when she prayed, and when she wrote poetry, and when she talked with Tacy about God and Heaven. Her religion had nothing whatever to do with the Baptist Church. It came to her now that perhaps she, like Julia, was not cut out to be a Baptist.

"But you can't hurt papa's and mamma's feelings," she said, coming back to Julia's problem which was suddenly unmistakably her own.

"I'd die first," said Julia.

"What are you going to do about it?"

"I don't know. You'll have to help me, Bettina."

Julia had a way of leaning on Betsy, of coming to her for advice, which was wine to Betsy's soul. Julia was looking at her now out of tragic, dark-blue eyes, her classic face strained.

"Betsy, I *have* to be an Episcopalian!"

"Girls!" came Mrs. Ray's voice. "It's ten o'clock."

"I'm going to bed, mamma," Betsy called. She whispered to Julia, "I'll think up something."

"Thank you, darling. Turn out the light, will you?" Julia asked, jumping into bed.

Before she turned out the gas Betsy looked at the vivid face framed in a cloud of dark hair on the pillow. Julia had no need to put her hair up on curlers. She hadn't put cream on her face or rubbed her hands with lemon or done a single thing to make herself look pretty on the morrow. But Betsy knew how pretty she would look.

Betsy turned out the gas and went to the bathroom to begin her nightly ritual. She loved Julia dearly, and could not be jealous of her. Yet as her thoughts returned to the two Triumvirates, to Bonnie's party, boys, she felt a little bitter. She wound her hair on Magic Wavers, and scrubbed her face and rubbed in the freckle cream; it was supposed to remove freckles practically overnight, but Betsy had been using it for two weeks now, and the soft brown sprinkle on her nose was as plain as ever.

Chapter Ten

AND THE TRIUMVIRATE OF POTATO
BUGS

As Bonnie's evening party for the two Triumvirates drew
near, Betsy began to worry. It was not the first time she
had gone to a party boys attended, but it was the first time
since boys had emerged from the pest and nuisance class
She wished ardently that one of them would ask to be her
escort.

Thursday night, after winding her hair on the Wavers with special care, she even included in her prayers a request that a boy invite her to the party. It seemed a little frivolous, but she felt sure God wouldn't mind.

Cab walked to school with her Friday morning, and she thought he would surely mention Bonnie's party, but he didn't; he talked about the scrub football team. Betsy listened with what she hoped seemed radiant attention.

"Did I act interested in that football business?" she asked Tacy in the cloakroom.

"You certainly did," Tacy replied. "You acted as though your life depended on whether he made the team or not."

"That's the way you have to be with boys," said Betsy. "Beam about their old football when you're dying to know whether they're going to take you to a party."

Tacy knew all about Betsy's worry.

"Of course, he'll ask you," she said. "Hasn't he called for you almost every morning since school began? I think you're foolish to want to go with boys, but I must say you're not having any trouble doing it."

Betsy glowed at this. She had a secret suspicion that the easy hospitality of her home attracted Cab at least as much as she did, but it was gratifying to hear Tacy's opinion.

"Well, if he's going to call for me, why doesn't he ask me?" she groaned.

"Oh, boys just like to be annoying."

Betsy waited hopefully for Cab to drop in that afternoon. He didn't. But of course, she consoled herself, the scrubs might be practising late. As supper time approached she waited for the telephone to ring. It didn't.

During supper, her mother said casually, "Betsy's going out tonight, a party at Bonnie Andrews'."

84

"What time shall I call for you?" her father asked.

Betsy was grateful to them for assuming that she would be called for as usual when she went out in the evening.

"I'll telephone you," she said.

"Not to come," added Julia in a whisper. This was cheering, for it meant that though Julia had noticed no boy was taking her, she felt sure one would ask to walk home with her. Betsy's spirits began to rise. She excused herself while the rest were still eating dessert and went upstairs to dress.

She wished she could take a bath in the tub but she didn't dare; the steam would uncurl her hair. She sponged carefully, however, put on her prettiest underwear, and pinned starched ruffles across her chest to give her figure an Anna Held curve.

This wasn't a real dress-up party to which she could wear the blue silk mull trimmed with insertion medallions which Miss Mix had made. She felt sure that Bonnie and Carney would wear waists and skirts. So she wore a white openwork waist over a pale blue cambric underwaist, a white duck skirt which Anna had carefully pressed, and a large pale blue hair ribbon.

Julia did her hair . . . she had a gift with Betsy's hair . . . and tied the hair ribbon. Mrs. Ray came in with her best perfume which she sprayed over Betsy's waist. Margaret sat with Washington on her lap and watched with awed eyes. Only Mr. Ray remained in the parlor reading his newspaper.

Betsy's cheeks had flushed a vivid pink. The reflection she saw in the mirror was pleasant. She was excited and happy, but not so happy as she would have been if a boy were calling for her.

Her mother and Julia kept tactfully away from the subject of boys calling for girls.

"Just telephone papa when . . ." Mrs. Ray was saying when a bell rang sharply below.

"Oh, let it be the telephone!" Betsy prayed. But it wasn't. It was the doorbell.

Anna answered it. She always hurried to answer the doorbell in the evening even though she was washing dishes. She took a great interest in Julia's beaux.

"Tell him I'll be down in a minute," Julia called without even waiting for Anna to tell her who was there. She was intent on Betsy's ribbon.

Anna did not reply, but her feet mounted the stairs. She came into Betsy's room, still wiping her hands on her apron.

"Stars in the sky!" she said. "It's for Betsy."

"I had an idea Cab might drop in to walk down with you," Mrs. Ray said carelessly.

"It ain't Cab," said Anna. "It's the puniest young fellow I ever laid eyes on."

Everyone turned toward her.

"What's his name?"

"He didn't say. He just said he'd come to call for Betsy, and he went into the parlor and shook hands with your pa."

Betsy felt a surge of joy.

"It must be Herbert," she said. "He's extremely puny."

"There's a piece of pie left from dinner," Anna said. "Do you suppose he'd like a piece of pie?"

"Anna," said Mrs. Ray, "did you ever know a boy who didn't like a piece of pie?"

Everybody laughed, and Betsy was very glad to laugh

for she felt shaky with joy. An evening party, and a boy had called for her, and Herbert Humphreys at that!

Anna hurried down, and Betsy twirled before the mirror, to make sure that her waist was tucked in neatly, and that no petticoats showed. She was glad she had a slender waist, and pretty ankles when the petticoats whirled; the starched ruffles gave her bust the proper curve.

"Keep him waiting. It's always a good plan," said Julia.

"Especially when he's eating a piece of Anna's pie," said Mrs. Ray, and they all laughed again.

While they were still laughing the bell rang again. Again Anna raced to the door.

"Right down, Anna," Julia called, fastening her best new bracelet on Betsy's wrist.

Again Anna's heavy steps were heard on the stairs, and she burst into the room, her eyes gleaming.

"But 't'ain't for you, Julia. It's Cab, and he said he came to call for Betsy, and then he saw that Herbert sitting in the parlor, looking so puny, and eating the pie. And he said, 'Anna, what's he doing with my pie? There'd better be a piece of pie for me too,' he said. (But there ain't.) He said to Herbert, 'Why don't you get yourself a girl of your own?' "

"Aren't they silly?" asked Betsy blissfully, going to the closet for her jacket.

"I hope you can find Cab at least a cookie," said Mrs. Ray, laughing.

"Bettina," said Julia. "I'm going to keep my beaux away from you. Sisters' beaux are sacred. Do you hear?"

It was glorious. Drooping in her most Barrymorish manner, she floated down the stairs. Margaret and Washington, Mrs. Ray and Anna came behind. Julia stayed upstairs to primp for Fred, but she peeked down to watch Betsy's departure.

Curled and flushed, treading on air, a boy on either side, Betsy went out into the crisp September night.

On the way down to Bonnie's house, the boys continued to wrangle. Bonnie not being present, Herbert was his usual hilarious self, and he and Cab joked and tussled, with Betsy an appreciative audience.

"Ever been to the Andrewses before?" Herbert asked Betsy as they approached the parsonage. It was opposite the Sibleys', a sprawling old house, set back from the road.

"No, it looks romantic."

"It's something, all right."

And Betsy knew what he meant as soon as she entered the hall. The house had a foreign flavor. Bonnie now seemed almost like other Deep Valley girls but her home spoke of far away places.

At the end of the hall a door stood open. Betsy saw books in rich abundance, not in cases behind glass, but on open shelves, up to the ceiling.

"That's Dr. Andrews' library," said Carney, who was taking Betsy's jacket.

"Think of having that many books right at home!" Betsy exclaimed.

"It's a fascinating room. It's full of things the Andrewses have brought from Europe and the Holy Land. The pictures are prints of paintings from European galleries. Bonnie has seen the originals. Just think!"

Betsy was enthralled.

They did not go into the library, although Betsy longed to, but turned into the parlor. This too was remarkable, but in a different way. It was richly carpeted, with curtains

88

of cream-colored lace, paintings in gold frames, damask-covered sofas, small polished tables with statuettes and little boxes on them. A huge, light tan grand piano filled one wall.

"This isn't a parlor, it's a drawing room," thought Betsy. "I'm in a drawing room for the first time in my life."

She stayed there only a moment, for the elegance of the room was unsuited to the occasion, and the two Triumvirates instinctively moved on to the cozy crowded back parlor.

Dr. Andrews, impressive in a beard, came in to welcome them. He left, but Mrs. Andrews stayed on for a time and seemed, indeed, to hate to go. She obviously liked young people and greeted their sallies with a duplicate of Bonnie's flowing laugh.

Her hair was dark and crisply curly. She wore garnet ear rings, and beautiful rings, and a watch pinned to her shirt waist. Her speech had a slight odd twist which charmed Betsy.

"Is she French?" Betsy whispered to Carney who shook her head.

"English. But he met her in Paris."

How romantic! Betsy thought.

After Mrs. Andrews left, the two Triumvirates played Consequences and Fortunes. Later they trooped to the kitchen and made cocoa and drank it with cookies and cake.

For a while Betsy remembered her Ethel Barrymore droop; and she tried to imitate Julia's manner with boys. But before the end of the evening she had forgotten the droop, and Julia's manner just didn't work. Boys worshiped Julia, but they teased Betsy. They teased her about her blushing; they teased her about her curls which they had discovered were manufactured; they teased her about using perfume and about her writing. She had had a poem published long ago in the *Deep Valley Sun,* and Herbert remembered it. He and Larry started calling her The Little Poetess, and Cab took it up.

"Betsy, The Little Poetess!" they mocked, and Betsy pretended to be angry.

Cab and Herbert both walked home with her. Before they reached High Street they were joined by Larry; Carney's mother did not permit a lingering goodnight. Betsy's mother did not permit it either, as Betsy well knew from injunctions she had heard given to Julia. But she paused a moment on the porch steps enjoying the tangy autumn chill, the brilliance of the stars, and the satisfying presence of three boys pushing one another about and making jokes for her amusement.

"Why don't you come to Christian Endeavor Sunday night?" Herbert asked.

"I'm a Baptist."

"Well, Larry and I are Episcopalians but we turn Presbyterian on Sunday night."

"I'm Welsh Calvinistic Methodist," said Cab, "but I turn Presbyterian for Christian Endeavor. I'll call for you if you'll go."

"Not this Sunday night," Betsy said. Tacy was coming for Sunday night lunch. "Some time I'll go."

She ran into the house and up to Julia's room where a light was burning. She had barely bounced to the foot of her sister's bed when her mother came in, in a bathrobe. She too curled up on the bed and Betsy told them all about the evening . . . about the grandeur of the Andrews' house, how nice Mrs. Andrews was, how Carney was undoubtedly going with Larry, and more about Herbert's crush on Bonnie.

The next day she told the whole story to Tacy on the telephone, and she told it again in even more detail on Sunday night when Tacy came to lunch.

Chapter Eleven

SUNDAY NIGHT LUNCH

SUNDAY night lunch was an institution at the Ray house.
They never called it supper; and they scorned folks who
called it tea. The drink of the evening was coffee, which
Mrs. Ray loved, and although Betsy and Margaret still
took cocoa, their loyalty was to coffee for her sake.

The meal was prepared by Mr. Ray. This was a custom
of many years' standing. No one else was allowed in the

kitchen except in the role of admiring audience. He didn't object when Anna or Mrs. Ray made a cake earlier in the day; he didn't mind the girls putting a cloth on the dining room table. But in the kitchen on Sunday evenings he was supreme.

First he put the coffee on. He made it with egg, crushing shell and all into the pot, mixing it with plenty of coffee and filling the pot with cold water. He put this to simmer and while it came to a boil, slowly filling the kitchen with delicious coffee fragrance, he made the sandwiches.

He got out a wooden breadboard, and a sharp knife which he always proceeded to sharpen further. He sliced the bread in sensibly thick slices and he never cut off the crusts. Mr. Ray's opinion of sandwiches without crusts matched Mrs. Ray's opinion of tea on Sunday nights. The butter had been put to soften, and now around the bread-board he ranged everything he could find in the icebox. Sometimes there was cold roast beef, sometimes chicken, sometimes cheese. If nothing else was available he made his sandwiches of onions. He used slices of mild Bermuda onions, sprinkled with vinegar and dusted with pepper and salt. About the use of pepper and salt Mr. Ray had very positive ideas. He used his condiments with the care and precision of a gourmet. Not too much! Not too little! And spread so evenly that each bite had the heavenly seasoning of the one before.

"I'm not," he used to say with sedate pride, "the sort of sandwich maker who puts salt and pepper all in one place with a shovel. No, siree!" And then he would add, for emphasis, "No siree, BOB!"

The onion sandwiches were most popular of all with the boys who flocked to the Ray house.

Mr. Ray didn't mind company for Sunday night lunch;

in fact, he liked it. The larger his audience, the more skill and ingenuity he displayed in his sandwich combinations. Tall, black haired, big-nosed, benevolent, an apron tied around his widening middle, he perched on a stool in the pantry with assorted guests all around.

The guests were of all ages. Friends of Mrs. Ray and himself . . . the High Fly Whist Club crowd . . . friends of Julia, Betsy and Margaret were equally welcome. Old and young gathered in the dining room around the table beneath the hanging lamp. The big platter of sandwiches was placed in the center. A cake sat on one side, a dish of pickles on the other. There was the pot of steaming coffee, of course; but the sandwiches were king of the meal.

After the Rays moved to High Street, there was always a fire in the dining room grate for Sunday night lunch. Often the crowd spilled over to pillows ranged around the fire. Almost everyone ended there, with a second cup of coffee and his cake. Talk flourished, until Julia went to the piano. Mr. Ray always made her play, "Everybody Works but Father."

Tacy came often for Sunday night lunch. And often she stayed all night. She stayed all night on the Sunday after Bonnie's party. Betsy had 'phoned her, of course, to report that not one boy but two had taken her to the party. And in the course of the sandwich making, the sandwich eating, the general talk and singing, she gave her a few more high points. But not until she and Tacy went up to her room did Betsy do the party justice.

Betsy talked on and on, and Tacy listened eagerly, undressing beneath a ballooning nightgown, after the modest custom of Deep Valley girls.

"It's like a novel," said Tacy at last, "by Robert W. Chambers. Imagine a house with a library, and a drawing room!"

"You'll be going there soon, Tacy. Carney and Bonnie both are anxious to get better acquainted."

"I'd love to go. It sounds marvelous. And Betsy you're marvelous, too. Other girls think they're doing well to get one boy for a party, and you had three."

"Not really," Betsy objected, although pleased by the remark. "Larry only wanted to walk home with Herbert, and Herbert, of course, has a case on Bonnie." Honesty compelled a further admission. "Cab likes me, but just as a friend. Mostly he likes coming to our house."

"Who doesn't?" Tacy asked.

"But I mean . . . it isn't very romantic. Cab doesn't feel the least bit romantic about me."

She had finished undressing and now she sat down in the middle of the bed, drawing her knees into her arms.

"To tell the truth, Tacy," she said, "I don't feel romantic about any of these boys. I've known Herbert all my life, almost, and Cab's a neighbor. When I feel romantic about a boy," she added, "he'll be somebody dark and mysterious, a stranger."

Tacy began to laugh.

"A Tall, Dark Stranger."

"That's right. Like in Rena's novels." Rena had been the Rays' hired girl on Hill Street and Betsy and Tacy had read her paper-backed novels. Betsy joined in Tacy's laughter, but after a moment she grew serious again. "I'm just practising on these boys," she said, "so I'll know how to act when my Tall Dark Stranger comes along."

"How *does* a girl act with boys, exactly?" Tacy asked.

"Oh," said Betsy airily, "you just curl your hair and use a lot of perfume and act plagued when they tease you."

September rolled on its slowly goldening way. The stairs and halls, the cloakrooms and classrooms of the high school became familiar ground. Betsy started singing in the Episcopalian choir. Her father and mother didn't object at all. Julia had a birthday, her seventeenth, and Anna made a birthday cake and Fred was invited to supper.

Chauncey Olcott came to Deep Valley in his play, Aileen Asthore. Mr. Ray took the family to hear him. Usually Betsy saw her rare plays at matinees with Winona who had passes because her father was editor of the Deep Valley Sun. But once a year when Chauncey Olcott came, she went to the Opera House in the evening with her parents.

The Irish tenor was growing old and stout, but his swagger was as gallant as ever, his voice as honey sweet. Always in the course of the evening the audience made him sing a hit song of earlier years called, "My Wild Irish Rose." At the end of the second act when he came out to take his curtain calls, someone in the audience would shout, "My Wild Irish Rose," and others would take up the cry. Chauncey Olcott would laugh, shake his head, make gestures of protest, but the cries would continue, and at last the curtain would go up again, he would hoist himself a trifle heavily to a table or bench, and the orchestra would begin the much-loved song.

Mr. Ray would take Mrs. Ray's hand then. Julia, Betsy and Margaret . . . whose eyes were blazing like stars in the excitement of going to the Opera House . . . would settle back to enjoy each honied note.

"Of course," Julia said to Betsy afterwards, "that isn't great music."

"Why, the idea!" cried Betsy. "If that isn't great music, I'd like to know what is."

"Grand Opera," answered Julia.

"Like that Pagliacci you sing?"

"Of course. But Chauncey Olcott is a sweet old thing."

A sweet old thing! Betsy was indignant. She and Tacy agreed that Chauncey Olcott was the finest singer in the world.

September brought the first football game . . . the game with Red Feather. Carney, Bonnie, Betsy, Tacy, Winona and Alice drove in Sibleys' surrey to the football field at the far end of town. The school colors were pinned to their coats, bows of maroon and gold, with yard-long streamers.

Larry was halfback on the team which made Carney very important. Once Larry was knocked out for a few seconds and Carney turned white, and Bonnie held her hand. Cab and Herbert sat with the scrub team praying for an accident which would give them a chance to play.

Betsy didn't understand the game very well but she tried to shout and groan at the proper places. Bonnie didn't understand it either, and she was earnest about trying to learn. Carney and Tacy and Alice, having brothers, knew all the fine points and watched the game with interest. Winona excelled at cheering. They all chanted together:

> "One, two, three, four, five, six, seven,
>   All good children, go to heaven,
>   When we get there, we will shout,
>   'Red Feather High School, you get out!'"

But Red Feather High School didn't get out. It played to a triumphant score of forty to nothing.

"Larry will feel bad," Carney said soberly as they crowded back into the surrey. They returned to the Sibleys' for cocoa, and Cab and Herbert came shortly, but not Larry.

"He's got the blues," Herbert explained.

"He shouldn't have. He played well," said Carney. "I'd send him some cakes except that he's in training."

"Those Red Feather players weigh two hundred pounds apiece," said Cab.

"Everybody knows," said Herbert scornfully, "that they're practically grown men. They only stay in school for the football season."

Everyone was indignant, and the cocoa tasted very good.

In September also, Betsy entertained the two Triumvirates. It was the last time the Triumvirates were to meet. The group was bursting out in all directions, outgrowing its fixed mould of three boys and three girls. For one thing Betsy did not like leaving Tacy out, and Carney and Bonnie had grown fond of her too; and Tacy wasn't bashful with Cab or Herbert or Larry although she still refused to consider them important. Then, Bonnie had a new junior boy to whom Julia had introduced her, a tall, thin, freckled boy nicknamed Pin, who had gone around with Katie but didn't any more because Katie was busy with Leo.

The two Triumvirates merged into what was called simply, The Crowd.

"When are you going with The Crowd to Christian Endeavor?" Cab asked Betsy.

"I'll go next Sunday night," Betsy replied.

"Good!" put in Herbert. "I'll call for you at a quarter to seven."

"*You'll* call for her, you big stiff!" said Cab.

"And both of you come back here for Sunday night lunch afterwards," said Betsy.

No boy ever objected to that.

Chapter Twelve

THE TALL DARK STRANGER

THE Presbyterian Church stood on a corner of Broad
Street. It was built of white stone with a pointed steeple
and a round stained glass window on one side. But no
colored light flowed from this window in the early Sunday
evening when Cab, Herbert and Betsy approached to at-
tend Christian Endeavor.

"Christian Endeavor's held in the Sunday School room," Cab explained, heading for the side door.

"What's it like, anyway?" Betsy asked. She paused in the doorway to settle her hat.

"Religious exercises first," said Cab. "But a social hour afterwards."

"Refreshments?"

"Only cocoa on Sunday nights. Once a month they have a Friday meeting with games and real grub. The Presbyterians give you a good time; and then of course there's Bonnie."

"Bonnie's president," said Herbert. His tone was gloomy. Bonnie now walked to Christian Endeavor with Pin.

In the spacious Sunday School room, rows of folding chairs were ranged in one corner, and Carney and Larry were sitting there in devout silence with Pin. Cab, Herbert and Betsy tiptoed to seats beside them. They too sat in devout silence while at a table in front Bonnie conferred with another girl in whispers. She did not even glance their way.

The chairs were filling up, and Betsy saw that the boys had been telling the truth when they said that almost all denominations came to Christian Endeavor. She saw fellow Baptists, and boys and girls she knew were Methodists, Congregationalists, Camelites, Lutherans. The Humphreys represented the Episcopal Church, and Cab, of course, was a Welsh Calvinistic Methodist.

Bonnie looked sweet enough to have drawn them all. She gazed over the group with calm blue eyes. Then, grave and efficient, she called the meeting to order. She announced a hymn and they all stood up and sang: "Let a Little Sunshine In."

Cab, Herbert and Betsy looked on one book. Betsy took the alto part, and they sang loudly and with spirit.

Bonnie prayed. It was amazing to Betsy that a 'teen-age girl could pray just like a minister. She didn't use a prayer book, either, as they did in the Episcopal Church. She made it all up out of her head. At the end she led the others in saying the Lord's Prayer. Then she turned the meeting over to her companion. It was the practise, she explained, for a different member to take charge each week.

The new presiding officer read haltingly from the Scriptures. Bonnie paid conscientious attention but the boys began to grow restive. Cab found a pencil and scribbled:

"Gosh, I feel religious. How about you?"

"Me, too," scribbled Betsy, and passed the note to Carney who wrote, "Me, too," and passed it on to Larry who wrote, "Maybe our Little Poetess will write an appropriate poem," and passed it to Betsy who wrote "Brute!" and passed it back.

Herbert, the usually irrepressible, would take no part in these doings. He could not remove his adoring eyes from Bonnie. Herbert would stop being crazy about Bonnie, and then he would see her presiding at Christian Endeavor and it would all come back on him. So he had told Betsy one day in a confidential moment.

The meeting ended and the social hour began. It wasn't a full hour; it merely spanned the interval between Christian Endeavor and the Sunday evening service. Members of the hospitality committee had slipped out to the kitchen during the final hymn and now came in with trays full of steaming cups. Bonnie in her friendly way was calling everybody to come and get cocoa when the door opened and two boys entered.

One of them was familiar to Betsy; he was a sophomore

boy named Pete. The other she had never seen before.

"They've got their nerve," muttered Cab. "If you drink the Presbyterians' cocoa, you ought to come for their prayers. Don't you think so, Betsy?"

But Betsy only nodded absently. The second boy was Tall, Dark, and a Stranger. He might almost have walked out of her conversation with Tacy. She stared with fascinated eyes.

He walked with a slouch that was inexplicably attractive. His hair, parted at the left side, stood up on the right side in a black curly bush. He had heavy eyebrows and large sleepy dark eyes and full lips. He looked about with an almost scornful expression which melted as Bonnie, mindful of her duties as president, crossed the room and held out her hand.

"I am Bonnie Andrews," she said.

"My name's Tony Markham," Betsy heard him reply in a voice deeper than the voices of most of the other boys.

Bonnie shook hands with Pete, too.

"We're having some cocoa," she said. "Won't you join us? Just introduce yourself," she added to Tony. "We're very informal around here."

Tony smiled out of his sleepy eyes, and sauntered toward the table.

Tony Markham! Tony Markham! Betsy said his name over and over to herself. Cab brought her some cocoa, and she drank it, thankful for the banter between Herbert and Cab which made it unnecessary for her to talk very much. She looked between people's heads and over their shoulders at Tony.

"You're certainly taking a look at Christian Endeavor," Cab remarked.

"Well," she answered, "that's what I'm here for."

"Do you feel yourself turning just slightly Presbyterian?"

"Um . . . what did you say?"

When the meeting broke up Bonnie sought out Tony again. Betsy, Carney, Larry, Cab and Herbert were all within earshot.

"Christian Endeavor begins at seven," she said. "I hope you will come next week for the first part of the meeting." She smiled but the rebuke was apparent.

"Maybe I will," Tony replied. His joking tone robbed the answer of rudeness. But Bonnie would not flirt at Christian Endeavor.

"I'm sure you'll remember," she said with a cool smile.

"Oh, you are, are you?" asked Tony. But he could not get a response in kind. Bonnie smiled again, reprovingly, and hurried away.

"What kind of a girl is that anyway?" asked Tony, turning to The Crowd.

"She's president of Christian Endeavor," said Carney. "She's a wonderful girl."

"She'd make a good school teacher," said Tony.

Herbert stiffened.

"Nobody's asking you to come here," he said. "Why don't you try staying away?"

"Aw, come off!" said Tony with his lazy smile. "I was only fooling. Some school teachers are fine and dandy."

Carney remembered her duties as a bona fide Presbyterian.

"Don't mind Herbert," she said. "We all hope you'll come regularly to Christian Endeavor. And *on time.*" She stressed the last two words but she showed her mischievous solitary dimple.

Tony turned to Pete.

"I didn't think," he said, "that Christian Endeavor was much in my line, but I'm getting to like it better all the time."

Everyone laughed. They moved out into the darkness, and Tony and Pete walked away.

Betsy's heart was pounding. The Tall Dark Stranger, the Tall Dark Stranger, she said under her breath.

Climbing the Plum Street hill Herbert and Cab wrangled and brawled as usual, but Betsy was very quiet. In her mind she was reconstructing Tony's image, recalling his curly bush of hair and the laughter in his eyes. She was startled out of her reverie by hearing Herbert say to Cab, "Who is this Markham guy, anyway?"

"He must be new in town," answered Cab. "I never saw him before. Fresh, isn't he?"

"So fresh he'll get his nose punched if he doesn't look out," Herbert replied.

Betsy shuddered; Herbert was extremely brawny.

"Aw, he didn't mean any harm," Cab said soothingly. "Bonnie isn't sacred, you know. She isn't a plaster saint, with a ring around her head."

Herbert kicked sulkily at the curb. But he cheered as they opened the door of the Ray house with its firelight, and piano music, and the festive smell of coffee. Herbert and Cab ignored the piano and the clamor of Julia's crowd, to charge into the dining room where they pounced upon Mr. Ray's sandwiches and Anna's chocolate cake. Betsy put off her coat and hat and pushed into the kitchen to the niche beside the cellar door where the telephone was placed. She gave the Kellys' number and when Mr. Kelly answered, she called breathlessly for Tacy.

"Tacy, this is Betsy."

"Hello. You sound excited."

"I am. Can you hear me? The piano is making such a racket."

"I can hear you. Heavens, what is it?"

"I have to be careful for the boys might come in. Herbert and Cab are here. Tacy, I've seen the T.D.S."

"The what?"

"The T.D.S. You remember our conversation . . ."

There was a bewildered silence.

"Think hard," said Betsy. "The T.D.S. What I could be romantic about."

"Oh-h-h-h-h-h-h!" Tacy's voice swelled with illumination. "Where?"

"At Christian Endeavor. I'll tell you all about it in the morning."

"I'll call for you early."

"Oh, do! I don't expect to sleep a wink tonight. . . ."

The swinging door from the dining room opened, and her father came in followed by Herbert and Cab. He was going to make more sandwiches, and they wanted to watch him, of course.

"Yes, the algebra lesson is on page ninety-six," said Betsy changing her tone. "Ten problems. They're hard as the dickens, too."

"I hope you've done them," said her father sharpening the knife as Betsy hung up the receiver.

"Julia helped me."

"Mr. Ray," said Cab. "In algebra, your daughter is not quite bright."

"Just leave off the 'in algebra,' " Herbert put in, and Betsy made a face, and thought for the first time to go to the mirror to see whether her hair was still in curl.

Beside the fire she munched an onion sandwich dreamily. And after the boys had gone, clearing the dining room table with her mother and Julia she was still silent and dreamy.

Julia came into her room to undress. She was full of talk to which Betsy gave but abstracted attention.

"Bettina," said Julia. "Do you have something on your mind?"

"Not a thing," said Betsy.

"You didn't meet anybody new at Christian Endeavor, did you?"

"Not a soul."

"I didn't meet him; I only saw him," she whispered after Julia was gone.

She turned out the gas and went to the window and looked out into the night.

"The Tall Dark Stranger, The Tall Dark Stranger," she murmured dreamily, liking the sound of the words.

Bonnie   Carney

Mrs. Ray

Julia   Betsy   Tacy

Chapter Thirteen

THE FRESHMAN PARTY

TACY came so early the next morning that Betsy was not
yet downstairs. Red-cheeked from her long walk, bright-
eyed with curiosity, Tacy burst into the bedroom and
found Betsy, fully dressed, standing before the mirror staring into her own hazel eyes.

"Oh, Tacy!" she said in a lowered voice. "I wish I was
prettier."

"Why, Betsy, you're plenty pretty enough. You're better than pretty."

"I don't want to be better than pretty. I'm tired of being better than pretty. Sweet looking! Interesting looking! Pooh for that! I want to be plain pretty like you are."

"Look at my freckles," said Tacy.

"But look at your beautiful auburn curly hair and big blue eyes. And you have the reddest lips, and not a quarter as many freckles as you used to have."

"Neither have you," said Tacy. "Your skin is peaches and cream."

"It's the only decent thing about me."

"It isn't either. You have the smallest waist of any girl in The Crowd and the prettiest hands and ankles."

"My ankles aren't half as pretty as Carney's, and she has a dimple besides."

"Betsy, don't wish to change the way you look," said Tacy indignantly. And putting down her school books, she gave Betsy a hug to which Betsy responded by snuggling her head for a long comforting moment on Tacy's shoulder.

"But he's so unutterably marvelous, Tacy."

"So are you."

"Betsy!" came Mr. Ray's stern voice from below. "Your breakfast is getting cold. And will you see whether your sister Julia is ready to come down?"

When Mr. Ray said, "your sister Julia," he was really annoyed. Straightening up, Betsy called, "Coming, papa!" She ran into Julia's room, pulled the covers off the bed and threw them on the floor.

"Papa's mad," she hissed. Then she rushed downstairs, followed by Tacy.

She ate hurriedly so that they could get away before Cab arrived. For once they did not want a boy's company. They went to the high school and sat down on the lawn, littered with colored leaves. The maples were all yellow now, or coral pink, or crimson. It was a beautiful place to sit and talk about a Tall Dark Stranger.

"But who is he?" asked Tacy after Betsy had finished her description of the upstanding curly black hair, the black eyes, the lazy saunter.

"His name's Tony Markham. That's all I know."

"His family must have just moved here. But why hasn't he come to school?"

"He will. Oh, Tacy, I hope he doesn't show up in any of my classes! I couldn't recite! I'd drop through the floor!"

"You'd do no such thing," replied Tacy. "You'd put on your Ethel Barrymore droop and fascinate him like you do Cab and Herbert."

Betsy knew that she didn't really fascinate Cab and Herbert, but it was good of Tacy to say so.

"Look at you!" Tacy continued. "Only in high school a month, and two boys on the string. You'll have this Tony too. See if you don't!"

Silently Betsy squeezed Tacy's hand.

"I hear the first gong," she said after a moment.

Tony did not appear at school that day, or the next, or the next. There wasn't a sign of him anywhere, although Betsy and Tacy looked both in school and out of it. They had agreed that if she saw him Betsy was to say, "T.D.S." But the week passed without a sign of the Tall Dark Stranger.

By the end of the week they were almost talked out on the subject. Betsy could not even remember just exactly how he looked, nor just why she had been so crazy about him. She began to take some interest in the Freshman Party, scheduled for Friday night.

A get-together, it was called. Ten cents admission. Cab had not invited Betsy to go, and she suspected that the ten cents was standing in the way. Cab earned his pocket money by delivering papers; his family thought this was good for him; and it undoubtedly was, for when he had money he spent it lavishly. There weren't many spare dimes clinking in his pocket.

"If no boy asks you, come with Alice and me," said Tacy. "But I'm sure some boy will, worse luck!"

Betsy didn't particularly care whether one did or not, unless it were the Tall Dark Stranger, but on Friday morning she received a note from Herbert.

"Dear, dear Betsy,
It makes no difference to me which way you take the following. Will you accompany me to the High School this evening? My mother is going to serve punch, and I'm glad because then you can't flirt with me. Of course, you'll have to pay your own way. If you answer this, and if affirmative, tell me when to call. I remain
                              Yours very truly
                              Herbert W. Humphreys."

Betsy passed the note to Tacy and both of them rocked with mirth, to the great satisfaction of Herbert, who had turned around in his seat to watch the reception of this masterpiece of wit.

After much pencil-chewing Betsy produced an answer Tacy approved, and they passed it furtively down the aisle.

"Dear Herbert,

I'm surprised that you don't want me to pay your way too. Are you sure you wouldn't like me to rob a bank for you? I am glad your mother is going to be there for she won't let you monopolize the punch bowl. I saw you in action at Christian Endeavor, remember. I'll be ready at half past seven with a rose in my hair.

Your obedient servant,
Betsy Warrington Ray."

Betsy almost forgot about the Tall Dark Stranger in the fun of getting ready for the party. Here was an occasion suitable for her pale blue silk mull. Worn with a large hair ribbon and with stockings of the same soft blue, it was very becoming, and as usual on important occasions Julia dressed her hair.

Herbert called for her early, thinking perhaps that there might be an extra piece of pie, and when Betsy appeared he was eating it. He looked very big and handsome in his best blue serge suit. Anna was stealing admiring glances around the swinging door. Among all the boys who came to the Ray house, Herbert was Anna's favorite.

When he saw Betsy he actually was startled into a compliment.

"Golly, you look nice!"

"For a change," said Betsy pertly.

"I'm going to pay for you. Darned if I'm not!"

"Triumph of triumphs!" said Betsy.

She kissed her father and mother, Julia and Margaret . . . the Rays were great ones for kissing one another . . . and started off in a glow. She did look pretty, and she knew it.

At the corner they found Cab waiting.

112

"Well of all the bums!" said Herbert. "Can't raise a dime to take a girl himself, so he horns in on me and my girl."

"I thought you needed a chaperone," Cab grinned. "Betsy's getting to be a terrible flirt."

"These poetesses!" said Herbert. "When they get started they're worse than any girls."

"You two behave yourselves!" said Betsy blissfully.

She floated into the high school between them. And in the cloakroom she encountered Tacy who remarked at once upon how pretty she looked.

"If only I could wear blue silk mull all the time!" Betsy sighed, fluffing out her curls.

Everyone looked festive, the girls in their prettiest dresses, the boys in their Sunday suits. The women teachers looked curiously unnatural wearing trailing silk dresses instead of shirtwaist suits. And the upper hall looked unnatural, decorated with potted palms, and with rugs and cushions brought from people's houses by the decorating committee. An unnatural air of propriety hung over it.

But presently a program of games was begun. Ruth and Jacob, Going to Jerusalem, Bird, Beast or Fish, Jenkins Says Thumbs Up. The air of propriety gave way to increasing noise and confusion. Betsy, having a very good time, forgot about her curls and the becomingness of blue silk mull.

In the game of Pass the Ring she found herself next to Joe Willard. This surprised her for he was not much in evidence outside of classes. He worked after school, Cab had told her. He worked at the creamery; couldn't even go out for football. He didn't have much to do with girls. Winona had tried in vain to fascinate him.

Knowing that she looked pretty now, feeling successful and gay, Betsy smiled.

"How do you like high school?" she asked.

"I like it. Do you?"

"I think it's just Heaven."

"Heaven to Betsy!" he said.

She paid this sally the tribute of a laugh so hearty that
he laughed himself. The hunter found the ring just then,
and there was a scramble while a new hunter took his place
in the center, then Joe Willard asked: "How did your
family like the presents?"

"Crazy about them. My mother adored the butter dish."
She had a daring impulse. "Wouldn't you like to come to
see how it looks on our dining room table?"

"Maybe I could walk home with you tonight and find
out where you live?" he answered. He said it stiffly as
though it were an effort for him to make the request.

"Oh, I'm sorry!" said Betsy. "But I came with a
boy . . . two boys, that is." She didn't mean to sound
braggy, but she realized at once that he might think she
had. She felt confused, and all the more so when he said,
"Request withdrawn," not as though he had thought she
was bragging but as though he thought she had rebuffed
him which she certainly, Betsy thought indignantly, had
not.

Unfortunately at that moment the ring was found
again, and when the circle broke he streaked away so
rapidly that she did not have a chance to say one conciliat-
ing word. She was put out. She had liked him so much at
Butternut Center, and since high school opened she had
not been able to get a word from him, and now their first
conversation had ended badly.

"Refreshments will be served in the Domestic Science

Room," Miss Bangeter called. "Form for the Grand March."

Betsy found Tacy.

"Let's fix our hair," she said, and along with most of the other girls they crowded into the cloakroom and strove for a glance at the mirror.

They were returning to the hall, properly beautified, when Betsy clutched Tacy's arm.

"Betsy! What's the matter?"

"The T.D.S.," Betsy whispered urgently.

"Where? Where?" Tacy looked in all directions.

"Over there by the piano. See him? He *would* come just in time for refreshments!"

Tacy stared eagerly. The curly black hair, the laughing eyes, the slouching pose were just as Betsy had described them. Tacy did not feel the magic Betsy felt, but she was sympathetically enthusiastic.

"He's very nice looking. He seems older than us."

A teacher at the piano plunged into a rousing march. Herbert and Betsy, Cab and Tacy joined the line which wound around the hall and down the stairs, past Mercury, to the Domestic Science Room.

Betsy loved to march. She always went lightly on the tips of her toes, and tonight she was almost dancing. The Tall Dark Stranger had come; he was here; and she looked so pretty, wearing blue silk mull. When they reached the Domestic Science Room she looked around. He was there, and he was still alone. As at Christian Endeavor, he was surveying the scene with a superior gaze.

Betsy and Tacy, Cab and Herbert filled their plates with sandwiches, pickles, olives and Athena wafers. They received punch from Herbert's pretty mother, and perched on a table in the corner of the room. Betsy still had that glorious feeling of being successful, attractive. She waved to Alice and Winona who, with two boys, were on an adjacent table. She hardly glanced at Tony Markham and yet she knew that he was watching her. He had surveyed the whole room and his eyes had come to rest on her.

Now he helped himself generously to sandwiches and sauntered up to the table where they were perched. Betsy didn't feel frightened. She had known that he would come. He shifted the plate to his left hand and saluted with his right.

"Christian Endeavor!" he said, addressing Herbert. "Who's your girl?"

"Christian Endeavor, my eye!" said Herbert angrily. "You go way back and sit down."

"Come, come!" said Tony. "I'm a stranger here."

At that Tacy poked Betsy, her eyes brimming with fun, and Betsy laughed.

"What's so funny?" asked Tony. "What's so funny about me being a stranger?"

"It's a secret," Betsy answered, "and you might as well not ask us what it is, for we wouldn't tell you in a thousand years."

"The room is large. Vamoose! Skiddoo!" said Herbert.

But Tony leaned against the wall, his eyes on Betsy.

"Do you want the scrub team to go into action?" Cab asked Herbert, flexing his arms.

"I can handle him with one arm tied behind me," Herbert said.

"Maybe," said Betsy, "we ought to let him stay. For hospitality's sake. The honor of Deep Valley High School."

"Do you go to high school?" asked Herbert relenting. "Or are you just horning in, like you did at Christian Endeavor?"

"I'm starting next week," said Tony. "Can't get out of it any longer. And because I've changed schools, I'm put into your pee wee freshman class."

As before, at Christian Endeavor, his smile made his rude words acceptable. Herbert grinned.

"I'll bet you flunked whatever school you went to."

"They couldn't catch me long enough to make me take the exams. So I have to start the weary grind all over."

"I give in. I'm Herbert Humphreys."

"Caleb Edwards."

"Tacy Kelly."

"Betsy Ray."

"Little Ray of Sunshine, eh?" asked Tony. Betsy blushed.

"Going out for football?" Herbert asked.

"Scrub team any good?"

"Any good? It's got Humphreys and Edwards. Need I say more?"

"Nary a word. Nary a word."

Herbert and Cab, Betsy was glad to see, were beginning to like Tony. He was a master at their form of banter. He started presently on Tacy's red hair and as soon as the boys apprised him of the fact that Betsy had manufactured curls, he teased her harder than they did. When the party broke up he joined them on the homeward walk.

Tacy had gone off with Alice. Herbert walked on one side of Betsy and Cab on the other, and Tony walked on the outside quite as though he belonged in their group, looking at her with laughing eyes.

"Aren't we asked in?" he inquired at the Ray steps.

"Not as late as this," said Betsy. "It's eleven o'clock."

"After Christian Endeavor you're asked in," said Herbert.

"And boy!" said Cab. "How her sister bangs the ivories!"

"Well! I may drop in," said Tony, quite as though he had been invited.

"I may drop in!" Betsy whispered as she went into the darkened house. She was glad that Julia was out at a dance, and for once she almost regretted her mother's sociable habit of coming into her room after parties. She wanted to think about this one instead of talking about it.

She told her mother . . . she hoped casually . . . that there was a new boy in school named Tony Markham. But she didn't say that he might drop in for Sunday night lunch. There was always room for one more, and it might be bad luck to make special preparations.

On Sunday she refused Christian Endeavor. She told Cab and Herbert they could come up afterwards if they liked. Evening approached, but she did not even change her dress. And she must have cajoled destiny properly, for when the doorbell rang Cab and Herbert were not alone on the porch. Tony was with them.

"Waiting for us here," Herbert said. "Didn't have the nerve to come in alone."

Tony laughed lazily.

"I told you before . . . I'm a stranger."

Tall and dark he certainly was, but he did not long remain a stranger. From the first step across the threshold he felt at home in the Ray house. He fell in love with the family, and they with him.

His appreciation of onion sandwiches won Mr. Ray;

Mrs. Ray enjoyed his cheerful impertinence; Margaret liked him because he liked Washington, and Washington crawled up to his shoulder and licked his ear.

His rich baritone voice delighted Julia, and he was a real asset to the group around the piano. He knew all the songs The Crowd sang: "Shy Ann," "Crocodile Isle," "Cause I'm Lonesome," "My Wild Irish Rose."

Julia had a new song that evening, a waltz:

> *"Dreaming, dreaming,*
> *Of you sweetheart, I am dreaming . . ."*

Tony threw back his head and his resonant voice rolled about the room. Fred was annoyed, but he had no need to be, for Julia's manner toward Tony was markedly sisterly. Betsy had discovered him; he was Betsy's property.

When the time came to say goodnight, Tony looked around the glowing music room.

"Say!" he drawled. "I'm going to just about live at this house."

"You big stiff!" said Cab. "*I* live here."

Humphreys slapped his chest.

"Where Humphreys is," he said, "there's no room for Markham. Begone now, and don't come back."

"See you tomorrow," said Tony looking at Betsy with a special look from his laughing black eyes.

"T.D.S., T.D.S.," Betsy whispered to herself.

"That Tony Markham is nice, isn't he?" said Julia as Betsy wound her hair on Magic Wavers.

"Yes, he's a cute kid," said Betsy carelessly.

After that Tony came to the Ray house almost every day. He came as faithfully as Cab and Herbert did.

Chapter Fourteen

THE TRIP TO MURMURING LAKE

On a Sunday in mid-October, Mr. and Mrs. Ray and Margaret attended the Episcopal Church. Julia was singing a solo, and the event fell fortuitously upon the Rays' twentieth wedding anniversary. It seemed intended that they should worship that day in the church to which Julia and Betsy now gave so much of their time.

"All that kneeling down and getting up, kneeling down

and getting up! But I can stand it if you can," Mr. Ray grumbled to his wife.

"I think our church is more *sensible*," said Margaret. "Don't you, Betsy?" But Betsy did not answer.

Like Julia she now loved the new church. And it was not just a matter of wearing a black robe and a black four-cornered hat, of marching down the aisle in candlelight and singing. She loved the kneeling down to pray and the standing up to praise.

"*O All ye Works of the Lord, bless ye the Lord . . .*" That was her favorite canticle. As she sang breathlessly, calling upon Angels, Heavens, Waters that be above the firmament, Sun and Moon, Showers and Dew, Ice and Snow, Light and Darkness, Lightnings and Clouds, Mountains and Hills, Green Things upon the Earth, Wells, Seas and Floods, Whales, Fowls of the Air, Beasts and Cattle, and the Children of Men to "praise him and magnify him forever," the panorama of the earth and the seasons seemed to wheel majestically before her eyes.

They sang this today, and glancing down she saw her father, looking patient and Margaret looking polite.

"Julia's right. People just are different about the kind of churches they like," Betsy thought.

Mr. Ray perked up when Julia sang her solo at the offertory. He and Mrs. Ray tried to hide their pride, but it was difficult, for Julia's voice soared and she looked rapt and saintly.

Larry and Herbert were in church with their father and mother. Betsy pretended not to notice them, emulating Bonnie at Christian Endeavor.

When she and Julia, having changed from vestments into fall coats and tams, came out of the church, the Humphreys were standing beside the Ray surrey. Ordinarily the Rays walked to church but today they were bound for Murmuring Lake. This had been Mrs. Ray's home as a girl; she had been married there; and the trip was in honor of the wedding anniversary.

"Going to be gone all day?" Mr. Humphreys asked.

"Yep. Anna has the day off, and the front door key's in my pocket."

"Which is funny," said Mrs. Ray, "for we never lock the back door."

"Having dinner at the Inn?"

"That's the plan. Then we're going across the lake to Jule's old home. We'll drive back late and rustle up some supper. We do it every year."

"It's a sweet idea," Mrs. Humphreys said.

"It's a bum idea," said Herbert in an undertone to Betsy. "Cab and Tony and I don't like it a little bit."

Betsy gave him a gratified smile.

Rolling down Broad Street Betsy relaxed in the back seat of the surrey between Julia and Margaret. It was delicious to hear that Tony would mind her absence. She treated him just as she treated the other boys, and not even her mother and Julia did more than suspect that she had a special feeling for him. But she had a very special feeling.

Tacy knew it, of course. To Tacy Betsy poured out all her sensations. When they did homework together, eulogies of Tony came between algebra problems. Tacy stayed all night, and they talked about Tony until long past midnight. If Tacy grew bored she never showed it. She listened with inexhaustible sympathy, always pointing out in the most heart-warming way how quickly and successfully Betsy had added Tony to her train.

It was true that Tony showed some liking for her; his

teasing was affectionate. But there was something big brotherish in his attitude that Betsy did not like. She kept hoping this would change, and give place to an attitude more like Fred's to Julia, Larry's to Carney.

She did not mind being away from him today. Just thinking about him was almost more satisfactory. Besides she loved this trip to Murmuring Lake. They took it at all seasons; the Inn was a favorite vacation ground. But the October anniversary trip was the nicest.

The countryside seemed to be on fire. The maples had the red and gold of flames. Orange colored pumpkins glimmered among shocks of corn and Mr. Ray stopped and bought one for Margaret's Halloween.

Murmuring Lake was encircled by two golden rings as the trees on the shore looked down at their mates in the water.

"Just the thing for a wedding," Mr. Ray pointed out.

The Inn with its flock of cottages looked like a hen surrounded by chicks, and there was an excellent dinner in which a real hen was served with dumplings. For dessert there were two kinds of pie, ice cream and cake. You could have all four if you wished; and after they had eaten to contentment and beyond, and Mr. Ray had smoked a cigar and Old Mag had had a chance to eat and rest, they drove around the lake to Mrs. Ray's old home.

Betsy thought her mother's girlhood home extremely romantic. Its shady acres were enclosed . . . except on the lake side . . . by a white picket fence with an arched gate bearing the sign, "Pleasant Park." A twin line of evergreens led to the house, the barns and the kitchen garden. There was a rose garden, too, and a little summer house covered with vines.

"But I didn't have half the fun here that you girls have

on High Street," Mrs. Ray said. "One reason I'm so easy with you is that my stepfather was so strict with us."

By "us" she meant herself and Uncle Keith. It was a family legend that Step-grandfather Newton's severity had caused Uncle Keith to run away and go on the stage. He was a boy then, and for years Mrs. Ray had not even known where he was. But they had corresponded since a joyful reunion when he came to Deep Valley playing in Rip Van Winkle.

With the passing of years Step-grandfather Newton had become much less prickly. Betsy was quite fond of him, in fact. But she saw him only rarely now; he and her grandmother lived in California. "Pleasant Park" had long since been sold to a farmer. The farmer's wife was hospitable and seemed to enjoy the annual October visit from the Rays.

"This is the bay window where we stood when we were married," Mrs. Ray said as usual. "There never was a happier marriage made."

"This is the oak tree she hooked me under," Mr. Ray said, leading the way across the lawn, ankle deep in leaves, to an oak with leaves the color of Mrs. Ray's hair.

"I was camping down by the lake shore," he went on, "with a bunch of young fellows. We needed salt and knowing Jule Warrington I came up to her house after supper to borrow a cupful. That was my finish, that cup of salt. I didn't get back to the tent until midnight, and then I was hooked."

As usual Mrs. Ray put her arms around him.

"You've never regretted it, have you, darling?"

"Not for a second," Mr. Ray answered, and kissed her.

Julia, Betsy and Margaret knew all this by heart. They

looked on benevolently. Strolling back to the house, Julia said to Betsy, "It's wonderful how much in love papa and mamma are."

"Why, of course, they're in love. They're married, aren't they?" asked Betsy.

"It isn't the same thing, you know," smiled Julia. But Betsy thought she was just being cynical as she had been about Chauncey Olcott.

"Married for twenty years! I should think they *would* be in love," Betsy muttered indignantly.

When they started home the sun was getting low, and in withdrawing it seemed to take with it all the brightness of the landscape. The girls were grateful for the warmth of their fall coats and snuggled together under the buggy robes.

Now it was Mr. Ray's turn to talk about his youth.

His father and mother had come to Iowa from Canada, he said, going as far as Chicago by train and the rest of the way behind oxen in a covered wagon. His mother had had eleven children out there on the prairies. She had been poor, and had died in her early forties. Yet she had left her mark on every child, of the ten who had lived.

She had been a school teacher in Canada, and there were always books in the little farmhouse. She had talked to her children as she washed and ironed, baked and scrubbed, about the value of an education. She had implanted in every one of them a yearning for an education, and they had not been satisfied with the little country school house. There was an academy in the town nearby and to this she and her husband had managed to send the older children in turn.

"After she died we older children tried to help the younger ones to get an education," Mr. Ray said.

There was no Protestant church out there on the prairie, although the Catholics had one.

"The Catholics have set us a good example," Grandma Ray had said. She asked her boy Bob to drive her around the neighborhood so that she might raise a fund for a church. Mr. Ray could still remember, he said, the arguments she advanced.

"You want a church here when your children marry, don't you?" "You want a funeral sermon when you die."

"You don't want your children to grow up like Indians, do you?" she'd ask the atheists. Some of the farmers really were atheists, Mr. Ray said.

Grandpa Ray had headed the list of donations with one hundred dollars. It was a great deal for him to give, Mr. Ray went on, a poor man with eleven children. Some men gave fifty, some twenty-five, some ten, five, some just a dollar.

"One man, I remember," Mr. Ray said chuckling, "said he couldn't spare even a dollar. He was one of the atheists. Mother looked at his litter of pigs.

" 'How about one of those pigs, Henry Hogan,' she asked, 'so that your children can grow up in a civilized community?'

"She looked so little and spunky sitting there on the wagon seat. He gave her the pig," Mr. Ray ended.

"Do any of us look like her, papa?" Julia asked.

"Margaret does, a little. She was small and dark—she was Welsh, you know—and she had big eyes like Margaret's."

Margaret sat straighter than ever with pride.

"Did she get the church, papa?" asked Betsy. She knew the answer. They all knew the story, but they liked to hear it through.

"She did," said Mr. Ray. "It was the first Protestant church in that part of Iowa. It had a steeple, it was painted white, it stood under two pines out on the prairie. It's standing there still, and my mother is buried in the churchyard. We'll all go down to see it some day."

After a moment Julia asked hesitantly, "Was it a Baptist Church, papa?"

"All the Protestant denominations worshiped there," he answered.

"Episcopalians, too?"

"They would have if there had been any around, I suppose. But there weren't any high falutin' Episcopalians out there on the prairie. My mother was a Baptist, and that's why I'm a Baptist."

Betsy swallowed hard and spoke. "Is that a good reason for being a Baptist?" she asked.

"Why, come to think of it, I don't know that it is," Mr. Ray replied. "And I don't even know that I made a true statement. Probably I'm a Baptist because I like to be a Baptist. I certainly wouldn't like to be getting up and down all the time the way the Episcopalians do."

"Neither would I," said Margaret. She volunteered, "Mrs. Wheat is a Baptist. Her husband is a deacon. I watched her wash the communion cups one day."

Julia and Betsy said nothing.

The conversation had brought them to the top of the hill overlooking Deep Valley. The valley was full of mist through which the lights of the town were shining.

"Home already," said Mr. Ray.

"The ride went quickly."

"There's nothing like a story for passing the time."

"I'm starving, I'm famished," said Mrs. Ray. "And *how* I want a good cup of coffee!"

The girls cried out that they were hungry too.

"I'll rustle up some sandwiches in a jiffy," Mr. Ray said.

"Let's build a fire in the fireplace," said Mrs. Ray. "And get the lights turned on. The house always looks so dark and cheerless when everyone's away. But perhaps Anna will have come in ahead of us."

They drove down High Street, and as the house came into sight Mr. Ray exclaimed, "By George, Anna *did* get in ahead of us! I thought her Charley kept her out late on Sunday nights."

"She's in all right," said Mrs. Ray. "Look at the lights!" Lights were blazing all over the house.

"Doesn't she ever think of the gas bill?" grumbled Mr. Ray.

They stopped in front of the house, and instead of taking Old Mag to her barn, Mr. Ray went in with the others to see what was up.

At the front door the smell of coffee greeted them, savory and strong. The music room was empty. A fire was crackling in the dining room grate. And as the surprised Rays moved toward the dining room, a trio of voices broke into song. They were masculine voices, one deeper than the rest.

"Here comes the bride, here comes the bride . . ."

"For Heavens' sake!" cried Mrs. Ray, rushing ahead.

The table was set, not too elegantly. Tony, Cab and Herbert were dressed out in Anna's kitchen aprons. Tony was waving a knife.

"Fried egg sandwiches coming up," he said. "Do you like your eggs flopped or unflopped? Speak quick."

"Flopped," said Mr. Ray. "Two of them."

"Flopped." "Flopped." "Unflopped." "Unflopped."

Julia, without stopping to take off her tam and coat, went to the piano. Everyone sang together, "Here comes the bride."

Chapter Fifteen

HALLOWEEN

At one of the late October football games Larry sprained his ankle. He was laid up for several days, and the girls went to his house after school with fudge and candy kisses.

Carney had been planning a Halloween party for The Crowd, but when she found that Larry couldn't come she decided to invite only girls. Betsy, Tacy, Bonnie, Winona and Alice! It was to be a sheet-and-pillowcase party.

After supper on Halloween Mr. Ray and Anna brought into the kitchen the ash cans and everything movable from outside the house. Windows and doors were locked. Deep Valley boys weren't well behaved on Halloween.

Julia was going to a dance, but before she put on her own party dress she helped Betsy into the sheet and pillow case. Shouting "boo" at Margaret, Betsy started off for Carney's.

For a week the weather had been stormy. Wind and rain had stripped the trees and made sodden masses of the leaves. But tonight a white merry moon sailed in a freshly washed sky and caused the damp sidewalks to shine.

Groups of children were already roaming the streets. Feeling safe in her disguise, Betsy booed at them and waved her sheeted arms. She didn't see Cab, or anyone she knew. The boys, she had heard, were indignant at their exclusion from the party, but Betsy thought a hen party was the best kind on Halloween. Undoubtedly they would try in magic ways to peer into the future. Betsy shivered and hoped that the omens for her would point to Tony.

Not that she was anxious to get married. Far from it! She had been almost appalled, when she started going around with Carney and Bonnie, to discover how fixed and definite their ideas of marriage were. They both had cedar hope chests and took pleasure in embroidering their initials on towels to lay away. Each one had picked out a silver pattern and they were planning to give each other spoons in these patterns for Christmases and birthdays. When Betsy and Tacy and Tib talked about their future they planned to be writers, dancers, circus acrobats. Betsy certainly had no wish at all to settle down, but just the same she hoped she would see Tony's face if she walked down the cellar steps backward holding a mirror tonight.

Two sheeted figures approached the Sibley house just as she did, and at the door each one secretly showed her face to Mrs. Sibley. She was too wise to admit masked figures indiscriminately. For some time after entering, the ghosts talked in sepulchral voices, trying to conceal their true identities, but at last with uproarious laughter they threw back their pillow cases.

At the end of the Sibleys' hall were dining room and kitchen. At the right in a row were front parlor, back parlor, and a library. The rooms could be closed off with folding doors, but they were all open tonight. There was no light except from grinning jack-o'-lanterns in the corners and a fireplace blazing in the library.

The shades in all the rooms were closely drawn. When tappings on the windows began the girls raised one shade a trifle and saw a jack-o'-lantern peering in, but later there was almost continuous tapping and they pulled the shade down.

"Probably the boys," said Bonnie.

"They're furious that they're not invited," Carney agreed. "Herbert came down before supper and teased like a baby to be allowed to come."

"He only wanted to gaze on his Bonnie," Betsy said. "He knew she would make an elegant ghost."

While they were bobbing for apples in the kitchen the front doorbell rang violently. Mrs. Sibley answered it and came back laughing.

"Three ghosts," she said, "tried to make me believe they had been invited. But they couldn't fool me. I have boys of my own."

They drenched themselves bobbing for apples; then there was an hilarious struggle to take a bite from an apple suspended in a doorway. After such routine Halloween amusements, Mrs. Sibley withdrew.

"You know where the refreshments are, Caroline. Have a good time," she said, and went upstairs to join Mr. Sibley.

"We have a freezer full of ice cream in the woodshed, so don't eat too much popcorn," Carney warned. Waving the popcorn shaker, she led the way to the library.

Betsy loved the Sibleys' library, even more than the Andrews' library although it didn't have so many books. It had the fireplace, and a window seat full of cushions and Mr. Sibley's armchair. This was a tremendous black leather-covered armchair, deep and soft with pillowy arms. It swung on a patent rocker so that it could be luxuriously tilted, and there was a footstool in front.

The girls made a rush for it, and Winona got it, and Tacy piled on top of Winona, and Betsy on top of Tacy, and Alice on top of Betsy, and Bonnie on top of Alice. But Bonnie scrambled off to help Carney with the corn.

Tapping began now on the library windows but the girls wouldn't raise the shades.

"Those ghosts had better go home," said Carney. She didn't take much interest in the prowling boys, since Larry was not among them.

When the corn was popped and buttered, more apples were brought out, and the girls started peeling them and throwing the peelings around. The peelings were supposed to make letters, and the letters were supposed to represent the initials of future husbands. Future husbands were very important that night. Betsy flung her peeling but it didn't look like a T. It was hard to get a straight letter like T out of a crooked peeling. They began the time-honored game of snapping apples.

One girl snapped another's apple while saying the name of a possible future husband. The owner ate the apple and then counted the seeds to the accompaniment of the magic rhyme:

> *One I love*
> *Two I love,*
> *Three I love I say;*
> *Four I love with all my heart,*
> *Five I cast away.*
> *Six he loves,*
> *Seven she loves,*
> *Eight they both love,*
> *Nine he comes,*
> *Ten he tarries,*
> *Eleven he courts and*
> *Twelve he marries.*

If there were more than twelve seeds, you started over again with "One I love."

Bonnie snapped Carney's apple . . . for Larry, of course. Betsy snapped Winona's Teddy Roosevelt, which brought roars of laughter. One apple was snapped for Hank Weed, senior captain of the football team. Another was snapped John Drew, the actor.

Tacy snapped Betsy's.

"Um, let's see!" Trust Tacy not to betray Betsy's feelings. "Oh . . . Tony," she said in an offhand way.

Betsy gobbled the apple, counted the seeds feverishly, chanting:

> *"One I love,*
> *Two I love . . ."*

There were sixteen seeds, so it came out, "Four I love with all my heart."

"Hi, girls! Betsy loves Tony with all her heart."

It was the usual cry, but Winona happened to be looking at Betsy. And Betsy blushed such a rosy red that it could be discerned even by firelight.

"Betsy's blushing!" Winona shouted. "Betsy loves Tony . . ."

Betsy leaned over to pommel her, and it caused an uproar that ended the apple snapping.

"Come on now," said Carney. "We're going to walk down the cellar steps backward and *settle* this matter of our future husbands."

They took turns, and each girl returned to the kitchen shrieking. When Betsy's turn came she discovered why. Carney had placed a particularly hideous jack-o'-lantern just where it would grimace into the mirror on the lowest step. This was fun but Betsy felt disappointed.

Refreshments came next. Mrs. Sibley had left the dining room table all ready, the girls discovered peeking in. It was decorated with fruit and colored leaves and in the center was a Halloween cake, frosted with orange.

"It has favors in it," Bonnie said. "A penny, a thimble, a button, a boat, a key and a ring."

"Betsy'll get the ring, I'll bet," teased Winona, dancing about.

"Don't be silly."

"Betsy loves Tony!"

"Come along and help me bring in the ice cream,"

Carney said. "Mamma made it herself, and I turned the freezer for absolutely hours. It's yummy."

"I hope the woodshed was locked up tight," remarked Alice.

"Don't worry. We locked and double locked it." Carney lighted a candle and led the way.

But when they opened the woodshed door, even the flickering light of the candle revealed disaster. The outside door stood open. The wind blew the candle out, but Carney was already screaming, "The ice cream's gone! The ice cream's gone!" She ran outdoors, her long white draperies fluttering behind her.

The other five followed. Like six ungainly white birds they flapped about the Sibley lawn. Soon there were nine white birds.

"I've caught Herbert," shouted Winona clutching the tallest. The rest of the girls bore down upon him. Star of the scrub football team Herbert might be, but they forced him to the ground.

"Tell us where our ice cream is! Tell us where our ice cream is!" Six girls sat on him to enforce the demand.

"Cab! Tony!" moaned Herbert.

Two sheeted figures tried to pull six sheeted figures from Herbert's struggling body. A magnificent free-for-all fight was impeded by sheets which sent more than one tangled warrior to the ground.

"We won't tell you where the ice cream is unless we can have some!" roared Cab.

"All right," said Carney, yielding suddenly. "Come on in." And the boys dragged the ice cream freezer out from under a denuded lilac bush.

"How did you get in anyway?" Carney was asking. "I locked that door myself."

"The spirits let us in," said Tony in his deep voice.

"The strong right arm of Humphreys," Herbert said.

"And his little friend Edwards," added Cab.

They all trooped through the woodshed to the kitchen where the boys dished out ice cream while the girls put their hair to rights. Then they gathered around the dining room table where the candles had now been lighted.

Everyone was still breathless. The boys told how they had found a crack beneath one of the shades around the window seat, and by standing on a barrel had managed to look in.

"We saw you snapping apples," Tony said.

"Betsy loves you with all her heart, Tony," Winona called down the table.

Tony turned his head and looked at Betsy.

"Can I help it if someone snaps my apple for you instead of John Drew?" asked Betsy. She spoke with commendable lightness but she felt a hot wave creeping into her face.

"Betsy's blushing!" cried Herbert. "Look at her blush!"

"Why, Betsy, I thought you loved me!" said Cab.

Tony said nothing but the expression in his eyes made Betsy tingle. She was glad when Carney distracted his attention by finding the thimble in her cake.

"You're going to be an old maid," everyone shouted.

"I am not!"

"Wait 'til Larry hears this!"

The excitement had barely died down when Bonnie created more.

"Girls! Here's a mystery. There are nine of us at the table, and nine places set, but Carney only expected to serve six."

"*O di immortales!*" cried Carney.

"Ghosts did it," said Herbert, grinning.

"I sneaked in and did it while you were snapping apples," said Cab.

"But you couldn't have!" cried Carney. "It's set so artistically. No one could have done it but mother. When you called at the front door she told you to come around to the back door later. She unlocked that woodshed door for you.

"Mother!" Carney called, jumping up and running out into the hall.

Mr. and Mrs. Sibley leaned over the banisters, laughing.

"Leave enough ice cream for your brothers," Mrs. Sibley said.

Chapter Sixteen

HIC, HAEC, HOC

By the time November was under way, homework reared
its ugly head. At first Betsy had managed very well with
study periods but the habit, now flourishing, of writing
notes to Herbert had interfered considerably. A forty-six
in an algebra test brought her up short.

And not only was her algebra teacher depressingly un-
complimentary. Her Latin teacher was plainly not im-

pressed. Betsy and Tacy were delighted when they were introduced to "*Hic, haec, hoc.*" They took the declension for a slogan, and when Betsy called Tacy on the telephone she said "*Hic, haec, hoc,*" and Tacy answered, "*Hujus, hujus, hujus,*" and they shouted in unison, "*Huic, huic, huic.*" This was undeniably very bright, but its good effects were not apparent in the classroom.

Even her English teacher did not appreciate Betsy.

"He picks on me about commas," she complained.

Joe Willard carried off first honors easily, and Betsy was a breathless second.

In Miss Clarke's Ancient History class alone did she find smooth sailing, but almost everyone sailed smoothly in gentle Miss Clarke's class. From the beginning of the year to the end, Miss Clarke did not shuffle her cards.

The names of her pupils were written on cards stacked alphabetically. Miss Clarke sat down each morning with the neat pile before her, lifted a card, peered at it mildly through her eye-glasses, and asked the pupil named there-on a question. When the answer had been given, the card went to the bottom of the pile. The Ancient History text-book was so arranged that each paragraph formed a convenient subject for a question. Knowing exactly when his card would come up, a student had no difficulty in figuring out beforehand just which paragraph it was advisable to study. It was not considered sporting to study anything else.

One day in November Miss Clarke dropped her cards. They scattered widely in all directions and the consternation created in her class was quite out of proportion to the labor involved in picking them up.

"I won't take time to sort them now," said Miss Clarke, lifting the first one at hand. There were frantic mutterings among the seekers after knowledge. Books were furtively opened, pages ruffled. Almost everyone recited badly that day. Even star pupils like Betsy seemed completely in a fog.

"That little accident with my cards upset you children more than it did me," said Miss Clarke sympathetically.

Betsy saw a good deal of Miss Clarke for she was the Zetamathian faculty advisor, and Betsy was from the first an active Zetamathian. This was more or less an accident.

The two societies alternated in presenting monthly programs; Rhetoricals, they were called. Julia, who loved to perform, had long been Miss Clarke's mainstay. Seldom were there Zetamathian Rhetoricals at which Julia did not sing, recite or play the piano. Miss Clarke assumed that Betsy, being Julia's sister, was equally talented, and asked her to take part in the first program.

"Now, what would you like to do?" she asked with flattering confidence after Betsy had accepted.

"Well," said Betsy hesitantly, "Tacy and I might sing our Cat Duet."

They had sung this first in the Fourth Grade, and in every grade thereafter. The costumes had been outgrown long since, but the duet had never been abandoned. It consisted mostly of cat yowls and howls and was popular with grade school audiences. A high school audience received it hilariously at the first Zetamathian Rhetoricals.

The weather was growing wintry. Early in November Betsy looked out her window one morning to find a thin layer of white over the world. The snow was wet, and melted promptly, but a week later it came again as though it meant business. Mr. Ray had started a fire in the furnace. The rooms of the High Street house were comfortably warm as the rooms on Hill Street never had been. Betsy felt a pang when she remembered the glowing windows of the coal stove but she could not help enjoying a heated bedroom. And, of course, on Hill Street there had been no fireplace.

"The fireplace is going to be fun during the holidays," Mrs. Ray said.

"And Thanksgiving's almost here," answered Mr. Ray. "I've ordered a fifteen-pound turkey."

The Slades came for Thanksgiving dinner, bringing Tom who was home on vacation, which made the occasion eventful for Betsy. He was not only that highly desirable creature, a boy, but he was an old friend. He and Betsy and Tacy had started school together.

He was large and rugged with dark hair that always looked rough no matter how carefully he brushed it, greenish-brown eyes under glasses, and a dark skin. Not even his uniform could make him handsome but he was an original and interesting boy. He was musical; he played the violin; well, too, Julia said. His violin joined Julia's piano at all The Crowd parties.

Cox Military hadn't changed him, except that he now said "Hully Gee!" all the time. The Crowd had never even heard, "Hully Gee!" before. But everyone started to say it. Deep Valley rang with "Hully Gees!" after Tom went back to school.

December came in. The snow was still white and fresh but it was growing ominously deep. When the walks were shoveled, after a snowfall, the drifts were as high as a man's head. Betsy kept warm in a grey coat and a grey fur piece, and sometimes replaced her grey hat, which was topped by a red plaid bow, with a stocking cap or tam-o'-shanter, also red.

Clubs were in full swing; Mrs. Ray was frenziedly pre-

142

paring a paper for her Study Club. The lodges were giving dances. Julia and Fred went with Mr. and Mrs. Ray to the Knights of Pythias dances sometimes. Starting off in their party dresses, Mrs. Ray and Julia looked like sisters.

The Opera House began to have its visitations of plays. The best one was a musical comedy called "The District Leader," with a Joe Howard in it. Winona took the girls in The Crowd, and the following day she and Betsy and Tacy went up and down Front Street gathering up the advertising pictures of Joe Howard. They had cases on him, they said. Fred brought Julia the songs from the show, and The Crowd sang them around the piano.

"What's the Use of Dreaming?" Tony sang that one better than Joe Howard, everyone agreed.

The Crowd stood with locked arms to sing and often Tony's arm was locked in Betsy's. "My Wild Irish Rose," "Crocodile Isle," "The Moon Has His Eyes on You," "Dreaming." The songs they sang came to hold in their melodies the very essence of what Betsy felt for Tony, the magical sweetness.

For a few days after the Halloween party she had felt distressingly self conscious with him. His teasing eyes seemed to be searching her face to see if what Winona had said was true. But this had worn off; it was bound to; he was at the Ray house so much.

Yet there was a difference now. It was small; he was far too brotherly still; but Betsy was almost sure she saw a difference. He asked her to go with him to some of The Crowd parties; he didn't just go along. He paid for her when they went to the Majestic. He stayed later than the others did when The Crowd came to her house.

Going to and from classes in school he always hailed her. "Hi, Ray of Sunshine!" Sometimes he stopped to talk.

Sometimes he wrote her a note, but only when he had something to tell her. He didn't write notes just for fun as Herbert did. Betsy kept these careless scrawls in her handkerchief box under her handkerchiefs and the sachet bag.

Occasionally after school Betsy walked home with Tacy. She liked to visit the Kellys who all loved and petted her. She liked to call on the neighbors . . . the Riverses, Mrs. Benson, and the rest. It was satisfying to appear in the haunts of her childhood with the aura of high school about her. The hills were white now; she and Tacy couldn't go up to their bench. Betsy's old house was rented, and about the time she left Kellys, the lights would go on in the windows.

At this hour, often, the sky was the color of a dove's breast. The snow which all day long had sparkled in the sunshine looked pale. Walking homeward, looking up at the sky, and around her at the wan landscape, she felt an inexplicable yearning. It was mixed up with Tony, but it was more than Tony. It was growing up; it was leaving Hill Street and having someone else light a lamp in the beloved yellow cottage. She felt like crying, and yet there was nothing to cry about.

She made up poems as she tramped homeward, the snow squeaking under her feet. Sometimes when she reached home she wrote them down and put them with Tony's notes deep in the handkerchief box. But she did this secretly.

"What has become of your writing, Betsy?" her mother asked. "Are you sure you don't want Uncle Keith's trunk down in your bedroom?"

Betsy was sure; she didn't want it, although she still climbed to the third floor and visited it sometimes.

Writing didn't seem to fit in with the life she was living

now. Carney didn't write; Bonnie didn't write. Betsy felt almost ashamed of her ambition. The boys teased her about being a Little Poetess. She felt that she would die if anyone discovered those poems in the handkerchief box, and the bits of stories she still wrote sometimes when she was supposed to be doing algebra.

She told more stories than she wrote. She told them to Margaret. They were about Margaret herself and a girl named Ethel Brown who lived in Detroit and was gloriously beautiful and led Margaret off on enchanting adventures.

Anna liked to listen to them too.

"That Ethel Brown," she'd say. "She reminds me of the McCloskey girl. What was she wearing, Betsy?"

And Betsy would produce pale blue dresses and blue hats, or pale pink dresses and pink hats, or yellow dresses and yellow hats quite as she used to produce them for Tacy and Tib.

She told these stories mostly on evenings when her father, mother and Julia were out. Ethel Brown was a secret among Betsy, Margaret and Anna. When Betsy ran out of stories, Anna would tell some . . . not about Ethel Brown, of course. Hers concerned dragon flies who sewed up people's eyes, about horse hairs that turned into snakes.

One day after an evening of story telling in the kitchen, Margaret plotted to secure a hair from Old Mag's tail. She secured it, and put it in a bottle, and waited quiveringly to see it turn into a snake. It never turned but her faith in Anna was quite undiminished. Horse hairs had turned into snakes for Anna, as surely as Ethel Brown lived in Detroit.

At church now they were practising the Christmas

music. Some of it was familiar and caused to ring in Betsy's head the bells of childhood Christmases. Some of it was unfamiliar, for Episcopalian hymns were different from Baptist hymns. All of it was beautiful. It filled the empty chilly church with a glory like golden light.

Julia, who never cared what people thought, often went down into the nave and knelt and said a prayer. Sometimes Betsy went with her. She even went alone when Julia was practising a solo, and the nave was unlighted, and no one would see.

When she prayed alone like that, it seemed to her that she could hardly bear the painful sweetness of life. She prayed that she might grow prettier, that Tony might come to love her, that she might be a writer some day. It was amazing how light and free she felt, after she prayed.

Walking home on the rare occasions when they didn't have masculine company, she and Julia talked about the Episcopal Church. Betsy had definitely decided that she too wished to join it.

"There's a confirmation class beginning after Christmas," Julia said. "The Bishop comes to confirm people in the spring. Oh, Bettina, I wish we could go into that class together!"

"So do I," said Betsy. "Of course I'll have to be baptized. Papa asked me if I didn't want to be baptized this year but I put it off. I'd rather be baptized in the Episcopal Church if I'm going to be an Episcopalian." She pondered. "We have to talk it out with papa before that confirmation class begins."

"Shall we do it right now?"

"No, we want to be able to tell him we've thought it over thoroughly. Let's wait until after Christmas."

"You're so practical, Bettina! You have so much sense!" Julia cried.

She often said this, and Betsy did have sense. When Julia appealed to her for advice Betsy seemed to shuck off her romanticism as though it were an actor's dress and become in an instant a balanced capable person.

But Julia had more courage. She never, Betsy felt, would have put Uncle Keith's trunk in the attic and buried her poems in a handkerchief box.

Often Betsy strengthened herself with Julia's courage. And she valued her sister, too, for a gift she had of widening horizons. Betsy lived more intensely in the moment than Julia did. She loved some things more ardently. Her home, the Sunday night lunches, The Crowd, holidays, Hill Street, meant more to her than they did to Julia. The hills that shut in the town of Deep Valley shut Betsy into her own dearly loved world.

Julia loved the Great World. She longed to sing, to act, to study, out in the Great World. The Great World was more real and much more important to Julia than the Deep Valley High School.

Chapter Seventeen

THE BRASS BOWL

CHRISTMAS was definitely in the air now, not only in the churches. In school both literary societies were preparing Christmas programs, and teachers were growing indulgent under the influence of the approaching holidays. Anna was involved with Christmas cookies, plum pudding, mince meat, and two kinds of fruit cake. Mrs. Ray had thought one kind enough, but Anna had said firmly that the McCloskeys always had two. And when Anna quoted the McCloskeys, the Rays were silent. More and more they bowed to this legendary family.

Mrs. Ray was busy with Christmas shopping, and one night at supper she announced:

"I hope you haven't bought my Christmas present, Bob, for today I saw just what I want."

"I thought you were Christmas shopping for the rest of us, not yourself," jibed Mr. Ray, as he served Anna's excellent corned beef hash with poached eggs, a favorite winter supper.

"I've bought plenty for the rest of you," said Mrs. Ray, "and you'll think so after New Year's when the bills come in. But I can save you a great deal of shopping around by telling you exactly what I want!"

"What is it?" asked Margaret who had saved fifty cents.

Mrs. Ray was not ready to tell yet.

"It's expensive," she warned. "You can all go in together to get it. You don't need to buy me another thing. I'll be perfectly contented with just this."

"But what *is* it?" cried Julia and Betsy.

"It's in Dodd and Storer's window. Just what I want for the front parlor window. A big brass bowl!"

"A brass bowl!" said Mr. Ray disgustedly. "I will not give you a brass bowl!"

"It's perfectly stunning, Bob," Mrs. Ray said. "I just have to have it. It looks just like me."

"If a brass bowl looks just like you I'm sorry for your husband," Mr. Ray said. "I always thought you had a pretty shape."

"Don't be silly," said Mrs. Ray. "It looks just like our big front window, like our parlor, like our home."

"Well, you might as well forget it," Mr. Ray answered.

"I like to give you presents for yourself, not the house."

"I'd rather have that brass bowl than a mink fur piece."

"Bosh!" said Mr. Ray.

A few days later at supper Mrs. Ray mentioned the bowl again.

"I was shopping today," she said. "That brass bowl is still in Dodd and Storer's window. How does it happen you haven't bought it?"

"I have no intention of buying it," Mr. Ray answered. "I'm going to give you a personal present, not a house present."

"I love this new house so much that it's practically me."

"Bosh!" said Mr. Ray again.

Every day that Mrs. Ray went shopping she went to Dodd and Storer's to see whether the brass bowl was still in the window. It always was. And since she went Christmas shopping almost every day she mentioned the bowl at supper almost every night."

"Haven't you even seen it yet?" she demanded of Mr. Ray.

"I can't help seeing it," said Mr. Ray. "I pass Dodd and Storer's every day on my way to the store."

"I've seen it too," said Julia. "I went to look at it on my way to Mrs. Poppy's for a lesson. It's a beauty."

"Bob," said Mrs. Ray. "Do you hear what Julia says?"

"I hear," answered Mr. Ray, "but your present is all bought and paid for. It's in the safe at the store. And it *isn't* a brass bowl."

"Then you have to buy me two presents," Mrs. Ray said.

A night or two afterwards at the supper table, Anna, passing gingerbread, remarked: "Charley and I walked past Dodd and Storer's last night to see Mrs. Ray's brass bowl."

"Mrs. Ray's brass bowl!" repeated Mr. Ray. "What do you mean, Mrs. Ray's brass bowl?"

"The one you're going to buy for her," Anna replied.

"He certainly is," chimed in Mrs. Ray. "What did Charley think of it?"

"He thought it was lovely," said Anna. "And so did I. The McCloskeys used to have one just like it in their big bay window."

"Do you hear that, Bob?" Mrs. Ray asked. "We can't let the McCloskeys get ahead of us."

Betsy and Tacy went down town on their Christmas shopping expedition. This was a tradition with them. They went every year, visiting every store in town, and buying, at the end, one Christmas tree ornament. When Tib lived in Deep Valley she used to go with them, and sometimes Winona went. This year they went alone.

It was joyful, as always, to walk with locked arms along a snowy Front Street, gay with its decorations of evergreen and holly boughs, and the merry jingle of sleigh bells. Betsy drew Tacy to a stop before Dodd and Storer's window.

"Mamma has set her heart on that brass bowl," she said.

"It looks just like Mrs. Ray," said Tacy.

"That's what she says," answered Betsy. "I don't believe papa's going to buy it for her, though. He hasn't told us, but I believe he's bought the mink fur piece she was teasing for before she saw the bowl."

Even Margaret made a trip down to Dodd and Storer's to see the brass bowl, and Margaret brought up the matter of buying it. Mrs. Ray was in the kitchen with Anna, and Mr. Ray and the girls were in the parlor.

"Aren't we going to buy mamma her brass bowl?" Margaret asked. "I saw it today, and I thought it was very nice. I'll put in my fifty cents."

"We certainly won't buy it," Mr. Ray answered. "No sirree Bob. She's so sure I'm going to buy it that it wouldn't be any surprise. I've bought her something she's wanted a long time, and it's for herself, not the house." He lowered his voice to a whisper. "A mink fur piece."

"Then I'll buy her some violet perfume," said Margaret. "She always likes that."

"The fur piece will be wonderful, papa," Julia assured him. "She's been wanting one for ages."

"She'll be thrilled with it," Betsy said.

But Julia, Betsy and Margaret were secretly a little worried about the brass bowl as Christmas drew near. Mrs. Ray seemed so buoyantly satisfied that she was going to get it.

"Here's where I'm going to put the brass bowl I'm expecting for Christmas," she remarked to Tony when he came in and found her studying the front parlor window.

"What kind of a plant shall I put in my brass bowl?" she asked Tacy the very day before the day before Christmas. "A palm? Or one of those new poinsettias?"

The Ray house by this time was almost bursting with Christmas. Holly wreaths were up in all the windows. Mr. Ray had brought home candy canes; Washington had a red and green bow on his collar. And everyone had been warned by everyone else not to look in this or that drawer, or this or that closet.

"I don't dare to speak," Margaret said. "I'm so afraid I'll give something away."

"Don't worry, if you mention that I'm getting the brass bowl," said Mrs. Ray. "To be sure, it's still in Dodd and

Storer's window, but I think papa asked Miss Dodd to keep it there just to fool me. Didn't you, Bob?"

"Once and for all," said Mr. Ray, "you are not going to get that brass bowl."

But on the morning of the day before Christmas he weakened. Before he started off for the store he called the three girls into the kitchen.

"I'll be darned," he said, "if I'm not going to buy Jule her brass bowl. I believe she really wants it so much that she's going to be disappointed if she doesn't get it, in spite of the mink fur piece."

Julia, Betsy and Margaret heaved a triple sigh of relief. Then Julia had an anxious thought.

"But perhaps it's sold by now. This is so near Christmas."

"No, it's still in the window. I looked yesterday, and Miss Dodd wouldn't keep it there if it were sold."

Julia gave her father an ecstatic hug, and she and Betsy and Margaret hugged each other and jumped softly up and down.

"What is it? What's up?" Anna asked in a stage whisper.

"The brass bowl," Betsy whispered. "Papa's buying it for mamma. Won't it be fun when she sees it Christmas morning?"

Mr. Ray beamed all over his face.

When he came home that night, however, the beam was absent. He was smiling, but it was the fixed determined smile he wore when he was worried or unhappy about something. At the first opportunity he drew the girls aside.

"The bowl's gone," he said.

It was as though a door had opened, admitting a draft of wintry cold.

153

"Who bought it?" Margaret asked, her lips trembling a little.

"An out-of-town customer, Miss Dodd said. It's gone from the window."

"It doesn't matter at all, papa," Julia said. "Mamma is going to be so delighted with her fur piece."

"And she doesn't expect the bowl really," Betsy declared.

"I'm going to tell her," said Mr. Ray, "that I tried to get it and it was gone. I'll tell her tonight."

Anna's head with its knob of hair on top poked in at the door.

"Did you get that brass bowl, Mr. Ray?" she whispered. "Do you want to hide it up in my room? Where is it?"

"I couldn't get it, Anna," Mr. Ray answered. "It was sold."

"Oh, my poor lovey!" said Anna. "No brass bowl!" She slammed the door.

"Mr. McCloskey," Mr. Ray said ruefully, "would have bought it in time."

They all laughed because they felt like crying.

At Christmas Eve supper, which was oyster stew, Mr. Ray told Mrs. Ray that she wasn't getting the brass bowl. He told her it was sold to someone else. He made a joke of it, but something in his tone made it plain that he was telling the truth.

"Darn it all, Jule," he said, "I gave in and tried to get that silly bowl for you, but I was too late."

Mrs. Ray acted as though it didn't matter at all.

"I was only fooling about the whole thing," she said. "There are other brass bowls in the world."

"Not as puny as that one, lovey," said Anna lugubriously, clearing the soup plates to make way for chocolate cake.

"Just exactly as puny," Mrs. Ray insisted. "Maybe I'll get one for my birthday."

There was the usual Christmas Eve ritual. They decorated the tree. Betsy put on the golden harp from this year's shopping expedition with Tacy. She hung the red ball she had bought last year, the angel from the year before.

The tree stood in the dining room, and its candlelight mingled with the soft light from the fire in the grate as Julia went out to the piano and they all sang, "O Little Town of Bethlehem," "It Came Upon the Midnight Clear," "Hark, the Herald Angels Sing," and "Silent Night."

Then they gathered around the fire with Margaret in the circle of her father's arm, and Betsy read from Dickens' "Christmas Carol," the story of the Cratchits' Christmas Dinner. Margaret recited " 'Twas the Night Before Christmas," and Julia read the story of Jesus' birth out of the Book of Luke. Later they turned out the lights to fill one another's stockings which were hung around the fireplace. They all forgot about the brass bowl.

But next morning they remembered it. It was still dark and cold when Margaret clamored to see her presents. Mr. Ray went down to open the drafts in the furnace and rebuild the fire in the grate. Mrs. Ray went down to light the candles on the tree, and Anna started coffee to boiling and sausages to frying.

"I wish mamma was getting her bowl," Betsy whispered to Julia as they hurried into their clothes. Margaret didn't dress. She only put her bathrobe on over her outing flannel gown.

Mr. Ray came back upstairs to say that the dining room was warm now. Laughing and excited, they pelted down the stairs. Anna pushed through from the kitchen, intent upon her stocking. They all reached the fireplace at about the same time.

And almost all together they gave unbelieving exclamations. For on the floor in front of the fireplace, catching on its polished surface every gleam of every dancing flame, stood the brass bowl!

"Stars in the sky! Stars in the sky!" cried Anna.

"Santa Claus must have brought it," shouted Margaret, dancing about.

"Papa! You fooled us!" Julia and Betsy fell upon him.

Mr. Ray, however, looked completely mystified. He stared from the bowl around the circle, and his eyes came to rest at last upon his wife.

Then he began to laugh. He laughed until his face grew crimson. He laughed until he shook. He laughed so hard that all the rest laughed with him even before they knew what the joke was.

"You—you—" he said to Mrs. Ray, and went over to shake her. "She bought it herself," he announced to the rest. "*She's* the out-of-town customer!"

"That's right," said Mrs. Ray. "That brass bowl and I were meant for one another."

"She bought it herself!" cried Anna, rocking with laughter. "Stars in the sky, wait 'til Charley hears this!" She looked at Mrs. Ray, now snug in her husband's embrace. "It's just what Mrs. McCloskey would have done!" said Anna approvingly.

Chapter Eighteen

WHAT THE OUIJA BOARD SAID

THE rest of Christmas went like a glorified Sunday. It was Tuesday, actually. The family went to church in two different parties, and at the Episcopal Church Julia and Betsy in black vestments and four-cornered hats sang with all their hearts:

"O come, all ye faithful, joyful and triumphant . . ."

The church was rich with the fragrance of evergreen boughs brought into candlelit warmth from a snowy world.

There was plenty of snow, but it was old snow. The weather was mild; not Christmassy, everyone said. Dinner was Christmassy enough to make amends. The Rays ate to repletion, and afterwards Mr. and Mrs. Ray took naps while Julia, Betsy and Margaret on the hearth beside the tree read Christmas books, played with Margaret's toys and ran the Ouija Board which was one of Betsy's presents.

For a time the small three-legged table refused to budge. It sat stubbornly motionless upon its polished board with Julia's and Betsy's fingers poised on top, not stirring even after the five minutes of reverent silence recommended by the printed directions. At last, however, it began to move, at first hesitantly, then more and more briskly until it was sliding about the board with perfect confidence. It not only went to "Yes" and "No" but spelled out answers to all sorts of questions. This was later, after company had come in.

There was a great deal of company. Herbert and Larry came with their parents; Tom Slade . . . home for the Christmas holidays . . . came with his. Fred, Cab and Tony dropped in. Katie and Tacy made the long walk from Hill Street. Betsy and Tacy planned to exchange their gifts at The Crowds' Christmas tree at Bonnie's, the next night, but they had to see each other on Christmas Day, of course.

All the visitors had a fling at the Ouija Board and the little table on its padded legs flew about tirelessly spelling out messages for everyone.

"What lies ahead for me during the coming week?"

Betsy asked in theatrical tones, her fingers on the table. She and Tacy were running it at the moment with Fred, Cab, Tony and Herbert looking on.

Promptly the table moved. Betsy watched with delighted intensity. In a business-like fashion, as though it knew exactly what it was doing, it slid from letter to letter. The boys chanted the letters aloud:

"T-R-O-U-B-L-E."

"Trouble!" everyone shouted together.

Betsy was aghast. If she had been running the table with anyone but Tacy she would have thought her partner had pushed it for a joke. But if Tacy had pushed, she would have made it spell Happiness, or a Lot of Parties, or Fun. And certainly Betsy herself would not have pushed it to spell Trouble. Trouble was the last thing she had in her mind at the beginning of this party-spangled holiday week.

There was general laughter, but Tacy understood the look on Betsy's face.

"I don't believe in a silly old Ouija Board," she said.

"But what made the table spell that out, I wonder?" Betsy asked.

"Some thought in your mind," explained Julia over Fred's shoulder. "You pushed it unconsciously."

"But I wasn't thinking of trouble."

"Oh, probably you were. You're so dramatic, Bettina. Some impulse deep down inside you suggested that it would be dramatic to have the table spell out trouble."

Betsy pretended to be satisfied, but a tiny worry pricked her.

About twilight it started snowing. Soon there were rims of white on the dark branches of the trees, deep swathings of white on the bare young shrubs around the house. Everyone had gone except the Humphreys and the Slades, who had stayed for turkey sandwiches. By the time they left, lawns, roads and walks were one billowing drift.

"We should have had this last night," everyone said as Mr. Ray went out to sweep the soft snow off the steps before his guests descended. Parting cries of "Merry Christmas!" were muffled by the snow, still coming silently, steadily downwards.

It snowed during most of the following day, providing a shut-in time ideal for enjoying Christmas presents. But it cleared by evening. The stars were out, looking fresh and surprised, the moon was rising when Tony, Cab and Herbert stamped in to accompany Betsy to Bonnie's Christmas Tree party.

This was a real party, and although the weather was too cold for the blue silk mull, Betsy wore a festive dress of bright red velveteen. She had put a sprig of holly in her definitely curly hair, and she was well sprinkled with perfume . . . her own. Having announced far and wide her wish for perfume for Christmas, she had received several bottles. They were still under the tree and the boys doused her some more, for good measure. Julia was giving a party, and Herbert went to the kitchen to call on his friend Anna and sample the refreshments. At last Betsy tied on her party scarf, Tony held her coat, Herbert and Cab put on an overshoe apiece. She brought out the box in which she had packed her tissue-wrapped, ribbon-tied gifts for The Crowd. Tony took possession of it, and they started out gaily.

"I hope all the walks have been shoveled," said Mr. Ray following them to the porch.

"They have, Mr. Ray," Herbert assured him. "Of

course there are plenty of nice big drifts in case Betsy needs her face washed."

"Don't you dare!" cried Betsy, thinking of her fragile curls.

"The Ouija Board said she was in for trouble, you remember," Tony called.

"Now see here! This is a *party*. And I'm wearing my new dress."

Perhaps because of the new dress, the boys were very circumspect. They pushed one another freely into the drifts which rose fresh and soft on either side of the walk, but Betsy was spared. They took great scoops of snow in their hands and threatened to put it down her neck, but they didn't, and when they threw snowballs they managed to miss her.

Taking off her party scarf in Bonnie's bedroom, Betsy was delighted to find her hair still wavy. She ran happily down the stairs.

Entering the stately front parlor where a Christmas tree was shining, she received a surprise. It came in the form of two smacks, one on each cheek, one from Cab and one from Herbert who had bounced out from either side of the doorway.

"Why . . . why . . ." sputtered Betsy.

"There's mistletoe over the door," Herbert yelled.

Betsy looked up, forgetting to move away, and Tony dashed over and kissed her.

"Well, for Heaven's sake!" cried Betsy, blushing and rushing away through an uproar of laughter.

"Tacy's coming in next. Gosh, she'll be mad!" said Cab in a stage whisper as he and Herbert stationed themselves beside the door again.

Dr. and Mrs. Andrews enjoyed the fun as much as anyone, especially Mrs. Andrews. Betsy wondered sometimes whether it was the Paris influence that made them so different from other ministers and other ministers' wives.

When everyone had arrived except Larry, who would be late, Herbert said, and all the presents had been placed around the tree, Mrs. Andrews stood up, smiling. Earrings glittered in her ears beneath her crisp dark hair.

"We shan't wait for dear Larry," she said in her clipped speech. "He'll have to forgive us for going ahead. St. Nick's here." She clapped her hands, and a burly, red-jacketed, white-whiskered Santa came in from the hall. He crossed to the tree and it was three minutes, or anyway two, before anyone except Carney knew that he was Larry.

"I knew the second you came into the room. I knew from the way you walked with one shoulder higher than the other," Carney insisted later.

He began to distribute the presents, and through the noise and laughter Betsy kept thinking that Tony had kissed her.

She wished that he had kissed her before Cab and Herbert. Then his kiss would have been the first she had ever received from a boy, and that would have been fitting. She tried to forget that Cab and Herbert had kissed her first.

"My first kiss!" she thought romantically, referring of course to Tony's kiss and ignoring the others. She wished she could remember exactly what it was like, but unfortunately she couldn't. It had come so quickly and unexpectedly; it was as nondescript as the other smacks.

She glanced once or twice in Tony's direction. He was wearing his best dark suit, and a most becoming red tie. His black eyes shone with laughter but his lips wore the indulgent smile that was his usual reaction to Crowd parties. He always seemed a little aloof, more worldly than the rest.

Without intending to, she looked at him so hard and long that she drew his eyes to her. He winked.

It was a merry party. After the gift giving, they played charades. They were called to the dining room for a Christmas punch, and cakes, and little individual mince pies that Mrs. Andrews had made in November and had kept in crocks in the cellar ever since. English mince pies, she said.

When they left the house the weather was turning cold.

"I'll let Cab and Tony escort you home alone and unaided," Herbert said; and to Larry, he added, "I'll wait for you here. It won't take you long to say goodnight tonight."

"It never does. But that isn't my fault," Larry muttered, and Carney flashed her dimple.

So only Cab and Tony walked with Betsy up the Plum Street hill, and Cab dropped off at his own house as they passed it.

It happened that just as Cab left them Tony took Betsy's arm protectively. She felt her heart gyrate a little. Tony often accompanied her to and from parties but always with two or three other boys. They weren't often alone. And he was different, alone; he was more serious; he was never serious with the other boys around.

There were millions and millions of stars; big ones and little ones; and high above them glowed a great full moon. They walked slowly, the snow crunching under their feet, looking up at the moon. They tried to find the man in it, the lady in it. Betsy couldn't find the lady in it, and they stopped, Tony holding her arm while he pointed it out. They walked slowly on.

"This is beautiful," Betsy thought to herself. "I'll remember it always. Oh, I wish it was a mile to our house!"

But it was only half a block, and the music from Julia's party came out to meet them along with lights streaming from every window.

"Won't you come in?" Betsy asked. "We ought to be just about in time for refreshments."

"I certainly will," Tony replied.

The rugs had been rolled up in the music room and parlor. Mrs. Ray was at the piano, and four couples were dancing. Mrs. Ray knew how to play two dance tunes; a waltz and a two-step. She was playing the two-step now. Tony and Betsy took off their overshoes, and Tony swung Betsy into the dance.

Betsy had never been to a dance. But she had danced all her life. The rugs in the Ray house were often rolled up for an impromptu waltz or two-step to one of Mrs. Ray's two tunes.

"Gosh, Betsy! You can dance," said Tony.

"You've learned somewhere yourself," Betsy replied. And indeed he had. None of the other boys in The Crowd danced much, but Tony danced with the feeling for rhythm that made his ragtime singing so exceptional. He danced with subtlety, inventing steps as he went and Betsy followed him perfectly without missing a beat.

By mutual accord, when the music paused, they dropped their wraps on the nearest chair, and when the music resumed they started dancing again.

It was a waltz this time, but not Mrs. Ray's waltz. Looking around Betsy saw that her mother was dancing with Fred. Julia had sat down at the piano and she was playing, as only Julia could, the new hit waltz song, "Dreaming."

"Dreaming, dreaming,
Of you sweetheart I am dreaming,
Dreaming of days when you loved me best,
Dreaming of hours that have gone to rest . . ."

Tony hummed a few bars in his rich deep voice.

Julia's crowd, after calling out greetings, paid little attention to them. As for Tony and Betsy they forgot that the others were there. They did not speak to each other; they were too intent upon their dancing. Betsy danced on the tips of her toes. Standing so, she was just about Tony's height, and they moved like one person.

"I believe I like dancing better than anything else in the world," Betsy thought.

The music stopped, but to Betsy's amazement Tony's arms didn't fall away. Instead they tightened, and she felt a kiss on her cheek. She looked, confused, into Tony's laughing eyes.

"Wasn't it smart of me to stop under the mistletoe?" he asked.

They were in the doorway between music room and parlor, and there was indeed a mischievous white-berried spray hanging above them. Blushing, Betsy pulled herself away.

This was different from the kiss she had had at Bonnie's. No one had seen what had happened. No one was noticing them at all.

"It wasn't fair. I'm mad at you," said Betsy.

"Aw, come on! You're not really mad. Are you?" He still held her hand. It was delicious.

"I am too," said Betsy. "I'm not speaking to you."

The Crowd was moving into the dining room where

Anna had brought in the lighted chafing dish. Tony and Betsy followed; their hands parted.

After that, Betsy admitted reluctantly in thinking about it later, Tony acted exactly like himself. He joked with her mother, he joked with Julia, who tied on a ruffled apron and took charge of the chafing dish. And without ever quickening his gait, he managed to be extremely helpful which was always Tony's way. He brought in the coffee, toasted wafers, passed plates filled with shrimp a la Newburg.

After refreshments there was a little more dancing and Tony danced with Katie and Dorothy, and Leo and Fred danced with Betsy. When the party broke up, Tony waved at her over a number of intervening heads.

"Swell time, Betsy!"

He seemed to have forgotten all about the moment under the mistletoe, but she couldn't believe that. It must have been important to him since it was so world-shaking to her.

When she and Julia and her mother had at last finished discussing the party, and Betsy was ready for bed, she turned out the gas and went to the window. She looked out at the millions of stars; the smallest ones were only shining dust; she looked at the big calm moon that she and Tony had studied. She thought about Christmas night and the Ouija Board.

"Trouble!" she said. "Trouble!" Her tone was scornful. And yet the questioning joy that filled her, looking at the moon, was a little like trouble, at that.

Chapter Nineteen

THE WINTER PICNIC

THE next night there was another party. Parties came
thick and fast in Deep Valley during holiday week. This
one was a hen party. The boys not only were not invited,
they were warned that the woodshed would be locked.
There would be no stealing of refreshments tonight, Alice
said.

The party was at Alice's house, which was near

Tacy's but not on Hill Street. Her house nestled against a different fold of the hill. It was a long way from High Street, and Betsy was to stay all night with Bonnie in order to avoid the late walk home.

By request Betsy brought her Ouija Board, and after they had played games and admired Alice's tree the girls took turns asking the Ouija Board highly personal questions.

"What is the name of Carney's future husband?" laughed Bonnie, her soft plump fingers atop the magic table.

"Bonnie, stop!" cried Carney. But the table was already speeding about the board, spelling out "L-A-W-R-E-N-C-E."

"Why doesn't Tacy like boys?" asked Alice.

"But I do like them," protested Tacy. "I just don't think they are little tin gods."

"All right, table," said Alice. "What boy in the crowd does Tacy like best?"

The table did not move.

"See?" said Tacy, but they waited.

At last, laggardly, it spelled out, "T-O-M."

"Tom!" everyone shouted.

"Oh, well!" said Tacy unruffled. "It had to say something."

Betsy and Tacy were running the table now.

"What does this week have in store for me?"

"Don't ask that silly question, Betsy."

"But I want to see what the board will say tonight."

The table did not hesitate. Promptly it set about spelling out a word.

"T-R-O-U-B-L-E."

168

"Well of all things!" cried Bonnie, while Betsy and Tacy looked with real perplexity into each other's eyes. "Maybe you're going to freeze your nose at the picnic tomorrow."

"Or sprain your ankle when we go skating Saturday night," said Alice.

That was the more likely mishap. Betsy had weak ankles; she was a miserable skater; she hated skating although she didn't admit it any more. Since she had started going around with a Crowd, she always pretended radiantly to like whatever the others liked, and the others . . . Carney and Bonnie especially . . . adored skating.

Betsy barely listened to these clever conjectures. She thought about Tony and the kiss beneath the mistletoe, and her heart turned over. She hadn't told anyone about that kiss. Not even Tacy.

Before she and Bonnie went to sleep that night, Bonnie grew confidential. In spite of Alice's elaborate and delicious refreshments an hour earlier, Bonnie and Betsy had raided the Andrews' icebox and brought to the bedroom cheese, apples, olives, cookies, cold ham, and some of Mrs. Andrews' famous little mince pies. They sat on Bonnie's bed in dressing gowns, their feet tucked under them, munching.

"Don't you wish you could be crazy about someone, Betsy?" Bonnie asked. "Like Carney is about Larry, I mean? It must be wonderful."

"Yes, it might be interesting," said Betsy carelessly, thankful that Bonnie didn't suspect her feeling for Tony.

"You don't . . . do you, Betsy . . . have a crush on anyone?"

"Heavens, no!"

"Are you sure?" Bonnie's tone was pressing.

"Positive. I don't know why it is, but all the boys are alike to me."

"Me, too. Pin is swell but I just can't get thrilled about him."

Bonnie nibbled mince pie thoughtfully.

"I heard something about Tony," she said. Betsy waited, hardly breathing, and Bonnie went on. "I don't believe it, though. I heard that he smokes cigarettes."

"I don't believe it either," said Betsy. "Not for a minute."

"I *hope* he doesn't," said Bonnie, looking worried. "He really is just about our age, though he seems so much older. He does seem older; don't you think so, Betsy?"

Betsy agreed.

"It really worries me," Bonnie said. And then they talked about the picnic planned for the next day.

As soon as they woke up they looked out the window to take stock of the weather. It was pleasant. Sunshine glittered on the drifts covering Bonnie's lawn.

"It's a curious idea, a picnic in December," said Mrs. Andrews at breakfast. It was a very English breakfast, Betsy thought with satisfaction . . . ham, poached eggs, muffins, jam and tea.

"Don't walk too far," Dr. Andrews cautioned. "Remember the Christian Endeavor Christmas tree tonight."

"I won't forget, papa. How could I? I'm on the decorating committee."

After breakfast Bonnie remarked to Betsy, "I wish I could make Tony come to Christian Endeavor regularly. I think it would do him good."

"Why . . . I suppose it would," said Betsy.

"That smoking business!" A little line of worry

appeared again between Bonnie's wide calm brows. "Christian Endeavor would put a stop to that . . . if it's true. Christian Endeavor has such a good influence on the boys."

Betsy agreed that it had.

She hurried home to pack a picnic lunch and dress. She wore her heaviest dress, folded a red woollen muffler inside her coat and pulled on a red stocking cap, leaving a few curls outside to frame her face. She wore red mittens too.

Cab and Tony appeared with gunny sacks full of kindling over their shoulders. With Betsy they tramped to the Sibleys' to meet Carney, Bonnie, Tom and the Humphreys' boys. They joined the rest of the crowd at Alice's house.

The sun shone benevolently causing the snow to glisten as though strewn with diamond dust. They went down Pleasant Street and up a little hill leaving the last house of Deep Valley proper behind. On the other side of the hill, lying in the wide white valley was the cluster of small houses known as Little Syria. In childhood Betsy and Tacy had reached it by another route for by some trick of geography it was also over their own Big Hill. It had been a favorite haunt with them, and Tacy drew near to Betsy now, and took her arm and squeezed it.

"Remember Naifi?" she asked.

"I wonder what's become of her."

"They left Deep Valley a long time ago."

Betsy turned to Herbert who was swinging along beside them.

"Tacy and I once got to know the Syrians quite well."

"How did that happen?" he asked, and Betsy and Tacy, laughing, told him of a long ago contest between Julia and

Tib for the honor of being Queen of Summer, and of how it had ended with the coronation on Betsy's lawn of a little Syrian girl named Naifi who was actually a princess.

"You're fooling."

"No, really. She was a Syrian *emeera* . . . that means princess."

"Which house did she live in?" Herbert asked. They were now passing the settlement. The little houses were banked with snow; their roofs were laden with it. Woodsheds and chicken houses were almost submerged, and the only signs of life came from children building snow men on the lawns.

"She lived right here," said Tacy pausing before a small house.

She squeezed Betsy's arm again, and Betsy squeezed back as they walked on. It had been fun telling Herbert the story of that childhood adventure, such fun that she had not even thought of Tony. Usually she was conscious of his presence even when he was not near her, and as a matter of fact he was seldom far away. She looked about to see where he was.

Tramping through snow at the head of the party were Larry and Carney, hand in hand. Behind them Alice and Winona were accompanied by Pin, Cab and Tom. They had left Little Syria behind now but, turning around, Betsy saw Tony and Bonnie just passing Naifi's house. They were walking very slowly.

"She must be talking to him about Christian Endeavor," Betsy thought.

Larry and Carney paused and hailed The Crowd. Waving their arms to the east where a ridge of hill came down to meet the path and a frozen stream crossed it, they signified that they were turning off. Halfway up the glen a flat

172

rock was soon swept clean of snow. The kindling brought from home was sufficient to start flames among piled branches.

At first the fire was a thing of bright beauty, leaping like a dancer. But it was allowed to burn down to a more serviceable glow. Sticks were sharpened, and wienerwursts thrust upon them. The fragrant juices dripped into the embers.

"Gee, it smells good!" Winona said.

Alice put a pail of cocoa to heat. Carney and Bonnie were emptying the baskets, arranging buttered rolls, cookies, olives, and several cans of beans. Betsy and Tacy roasted their wienies with their arms about each other. It was good to be back picnicking beyond the Big Hill.

"After we eat," said Tacy, "let's follow this frozen brook up the glen. We'll find a waterfall, I think."

"Let's," said Betsy examining her wienie, cramming it into a roll and beginning to eat.

No one talked much and in fifteen minutes only a very small bird could have found a worthwhile tidbit. Then came snowballing and face washing and hilarious chases.

While Pin and Herbert washed Winona's face, those natural housewives Carney and Bonnie replaced cups and spoons and napkins in the baskets. Betsy and Tacy with Tom and Cab went off to find the waterfall.

Tony, Betsy observed, was helping Bonnie with the unexpected efficiency she had observed so many times. Bonnie was talking earnestly, but he wore his most superior expression.

"She certainly is having a time," Betsy thought, "getting him to promise to come to Christian Endeavor." She didn't exactly like these prolonged conferences. But she was happy to be exploring with Tacy. They found the frozen waterfall . . . icicles of every length made an iridescent drapery. They saw a cardinal flash against the snow. They found a bush with red berries and broke off a branch.

"You always take a bouquet home from a picnic," Tacy said.

Betsy was happy and yet there was a prick of unhappiness underneath. Walking back to the rock she wondered whether Tony and Bonnie were still talking.

"Probably by now he's fooling around with Winona," she thought. "And Herbert and Pin are with Bonnie."

But when they reached the picnic site neither Tony nor Bonnie were to be seen. Pin, Herbert and Winona were climbing trees; Larry and Carney were putting out the fire.

"Where are the rest of the kids?" Betsy asked casually, pretending that she wasn't sure who was missing.

"Tony and Bonnie went on ahead," Carney answered.

They had gone on ahead! Well, why shouldn't they? Bonnie, Betsy remembered, had to help decorate the Christian Endeavor tree. It was early for that, though. Probably Bonnie had gotten cold? But Bonnie never got cold.

Betsy suddenly felt very cold indeed. The sun had disappeared. The world was pearl-colored from hill to hill upward and from hill to hill downward. Two saucers of pearl met around the horizon.

Betsy wound her red muffler more tightly and pulled down her stocking cap. She didn't care how far she pulled it down now; she was willing to poke all her curls out of sight if Tony was not there to see.

"That cross country tramp *did* tire you," her mother said at supper.

"No, it didn't, mamma."

"You seem awfully tired."

"I'm not tired, really."

"I don't think you ought to go to the Christian Endeavor party tonight."

"Now you're talking sense," Mr. Ray put in. "She's been to parties two nights running and she's going to one or two more this week, if my ears haven't deceived me."

"Oh, no, papa," said Betsy. "Tomorrow night we're going skating, that's all. And coming up here for Welsh rarebit afterwards."

"And you don't call that a party? Well, it's too much. Why do you want to go to a Presbyterian Christian Endeavor party, anyway? You're a Baptist."

"And an Episcopalian. She seems almost more Episcopalian than Baptist to me," Margaret said innocently.

Betsy and Julia both squirmed.

"Oh, please let me go!" said Betsy. To her annoyance tears rushed into her eyes. "Maybe I am a little tired," she added, wiping them quickly. "But I do want especially to go."

"Well," said her mother, weakening. "If you go upstairs and rest until time to dress it might be all right. Don't you think so, Bob?"

"I suppose so," said Mr. Ray. "And tomorrow night's the skating, but the night after that you stay home. Do you hear?"

"Yes, papa," said Betsy readily. That night was the one night of the week for which there was no party planned.

Up in her own room she didn't light the gas; she went to the window and looked out. The snow had the brilliant almost unearthly glow it often had at twilight.

"I must be tired," she thought, taking off her dress and

shoes and getting into her bathrobe. "Otherwise I wouldn't feel so blue. There's nothing to feel blue about."

But she couldn't get out of her mind the memory of Tony and Bonnie, lagging behind on the walk to the glen, and deep in conversation on the picnic rock. What had they done when they reached home, she wondered? Had Bonnie made him tea, as she did for the girls sometimes? Real English tea. It would have tasted good after their cold walk. Cold was becoming to Bonnie, too. It made her cheeks like roses.

"It makes my nose red," Betsy thought, and tears came into her eyes.

She crawled into bed and buried her face in the pillow. The pillow was quite damp presently.

Julia came into the room.

"Do you feel all right, Bettina?"

"Just tired. Don't light the gas."

"I won't. But when you're ready to dress, I'll do your hair. I want to try it in a pompadour."

"Do you?" Betsy asked. Furtively she dried her cheeks on the blankets. She turned face up as Julia sat down beside her, smelling of her sweet cologne.

"What are you going to wear?" Julia asked.

"My white waist over pink, I guess. With a pink hair ribbon. And my pleated skirt."

"Wear it over blue, and a blue hair ribbon. Blue is so becoming to you, Bettina. You look divine in it."

Julia leaned over and kissed her sister lightly.

"You rest now," she said. "I'll be back in half an hour."

"I wonder if Julia suspects," Betsy thought, as the door closed.

The possibility that Julia suspected was comforting

somehow. Betsy stopped crying and rested hard. Afterwards Julia did her hair in a lofty pompadour, and the blue underwaist peeping through eyelet embroidery, the blue hair ribbon, were becoming indeed.

Cab called for her before she was dressed, and as she was coming down stairs the bell rang again. As usual Anna rushed to answer it.

"What did you have for dessert tonight, Anna?" Betsy heard in a familiar teasing tone. Then, "For gosh sake, look at Betsy in a pompadour!"

Cab took up the cry.

"A poetess in a pompadour!"

"Come, Ray of Sunshine," Tony said, "and give us a look. It's stunning. It's altogether too stunning for Christian Endeavor."

"Are you going to Christian Endeavor?" Betsy asked. She asked it quite naturally for already she felt all right. Tony was just the same.

"Might as well," he answered lazily. "Bonnie asked me to. She thinks I'm going to the dogs." He stretched his arms and added in a gratified tone. "Yes sir, Bonnie thinks I'm going to the dogs."

Julia, who had seated herself at the piano, whirled around sharply.

"*Bonnie* thinks so?" she asked. "Bonnie's trying to reform you or convert you or something?"

"I guess so," Tony answered. "Why?"

"Nothing," answered Julia. "I just wondered."

"Now she knows," Betsy thought.

Julia's glance was shrewd but her tone, as she turned back to the piano, was light.

"Well, go get religion if you must," she said. "But come

back here afterwards. I got all the songs from 'The Time, the Place and the Girl' for Christmas. I thought we could try them out tonight."

"That sounds like fun," said Tony. "I'll be back all right."

With this expert sisterly backing, Betsy felt her last qualm vanish. As Tony helped her into her coat, she even forgot that the Ouija Board had spelled out T-R-O-U-B-L-E.

Chapter Twenty

T-R-O-U-B-L-E?

SHE remembered at the Christian Endeavor party. There was no religious service tonight, just Christmas carols, the tree, games, and refreshments. But Bonnie, as hostess, was as poised and gracious as when she presided over a meeting.

Tony sauntered over to her at once. Betsy, watching out

of a corner of her eye, saw Bonnie's welcoming smile. They did not spend much time together, but it wasn't Tony's fault. She made it clear that as President of the Christian Endeavor she must scatter her attention over the entire group. This she did with tactful kindness, drawing awkward and bashful members into the circle, making sure there was a candy cane on the tree for everyone, serving cider and doughnuts.

Tony gave up after the second try. He did not relish rebuffs. He joined Cab, Herbert and Betsy and they sat together, played together, ate together. He was in high spirits, and Betsy had fun, but the pricking was back.

As the party was breaking up, Bonnie came over to Tony.

"I'm sorry I couldn't pay much attention to you, Tony. You know, it's a big responsibility, being President of Christian Endeavor."

"Sure, sure!" said Tony. "I had a good time. I don't aim to associate with Presidents anyway. Or with Vice Presidents, or Secretaries, or Treasurers, or even Sergeants at Arms."

Bonnie looked troubled.

"You're angry," she said. "I'm so sorry. I'm sure I could make you understand if I had more time. You know I want you to come to Christian Endeavor regularly, not just for parties."

"Not a chance!" said Tony scornfully. "How do you like Betsy's pompadour?"

"I love it." Bonnie smiled at Betsy. "*You* think he ought to come. Don't you, Betsy?" she asked.

"I certainly do," Betsy replied.

"If I could just talk with you!" Bonnie repeated. But Tony answered cryptically:

"Sorry. I have a date with 'The Time, the Place and the Girl.' "

Betsy inwardly blessed Julia.

"Well, *I* have a date to walk home with Pin," said Bonnie, sounding annoyed. "I was going to suggest your stopping off at my house before we go skating tomorrow night, but I withdraw the suggestion."

"You can't withdraw it," said Tony triumphantly. "You never made it."

"Well, don't come!" said Bonnie sharply, forgetting she was President of Christian Endeavor, "because I'll be busy."

"Certainly I won't come," replied Tony. "I'm busy myself. But I'll bet a nickel that if I did come you'd open the door with a bright and smiling face."

"I would not!"

"You would too!"

"I would not!"

"Children, children!" said Cab. "Remember this is Christian Endeavor. Remember this is the Christmas season of peace and good will." He began to laugh and Betsy joined in. She laughed almost too hard.

"Come on," said Tony, taking Betsy's arm. "Let's go."

Betsy didn't enjoy the walk home as she had enjoyed another walk just two days before, although the same moon was shining and Cab again dropped off at his own home.

"My family's fit to be tied," he said. "They don't see why I go to Christian Endeavor anyway when I'm Welsh Reformed. But I wouldn't have missed that brawl you and Bonnie had tonight for a farm, Tony."

"Bonnie," said Tony, "gives me a pain."

"Are you going to call for her tomorrow night?"

"I am not! What's more, I'm going to smoke a cigarette as soon as we get to the pond."

"Tony! You wouldn't!" cried Betsy.

Tony laughed. "Wait and see," he said.

After that he and Betsy went to the Ray house, and with Julia and Fred they sang all the songs from "The Time, the Place and the Girl." They popped corn and made fudge. They had a marvelous time.

"How did Bonnie's reforming Tony come out?" Julia asked casually as she and Betsy were preparing for bed.

"Ran into a snag," said Betsy. "I think he likes her though."

"That reforming," said Julia, "is one of the oldest lines in the world, and one of the best."

"But she's really and truly interested in getting Tony to join," Betsy said soberly.

"And she really and truly likes him," Julia answered tartly.

"Yes, I think she does," said Betsy. She remembered the midnight confab she and Bonnie had had after Alice's party. Bonnie had been trying to find out then whether Betsy liked Tony. Perhaps she should have confided?

"They had a quarrel tonight," Betsy said slowly. "And Tony says he's going to smoke a cigarette at the pond tomorrow night just to make her mad."

"Hmm!" said Julia. She looked worried. "But you don't really care for Tony, do you, Bettina?" she asked. "Not seriously, I mean."

"No," answered Betsy, glad to salvage her pride. "All the boys are alike to me. I think I like Cab the best. But in a *very* unromantic way."

"That's good," said Julia, and kissed her, and went off to bed.

Betsy wound her hair on the Magic Wavers so tightly that it hurt. She had a terrible feeling inside. She felt as though her mother were sick, or as though she had been flunked out of school, or as though the end of the world were drawing near. She wound her hair on the Wavers so tightly that tears came into her eyes.

The weather turned cold that night. The thermometer dropped like a bucket into a deep well.

"I think it's too cold for skating," Mrs. Ray said the next afternoon, and Betsy's hopes rose. "Maybe the boys and girls would just as soon come here for the rarebit and forget about skating."

"Oh, I don't think so, mamma," Betsy answered vivaciously, for if there was going to be a skating party she wanted to be allowed to go. "But I'll telephone Carney and Bonnie and see what they think."

How wonderful, she thought on the way to the phone, how marvelous it would be if the skating party were called off! It seemed to her that the threat implicit in Tony's cigarette would melt into nothingness if The Crowd were assembled around her own fire.

"I'll try to make them call it off," she said over her shoulder.

But Carney scoffed at the idea.

"Why, this is grand skating weather," she replied. "The pond is swept and the boys are out there now laying a bonfire. I just love a cold night for skating, don't you?"

"The colder the better for me," Betsy answered. "It was mamma's idea to call it off. I was going to telephone Bonnie and ask her opinion but I won't bother now."

"She's right here," Carney answered. "We're sitting by the fire doing shadow embroidery on our new waists. Come on down and I'll make some fudge."

183

"No, thanks. My family thinks I'm going out too much."

"Where have I heard that before?" laughed Carney. "Wait, then! I'll call Bonnie."

"Hello, Betsy?" came Bonnie's soft voice.

"Hello," said Betsy. "My mother had some insane idea that it was too cold for the skating. But Carney and I have decided to forget it."

"Oh, yes!" said Bonnie. "It isn't a bit too cold. Unless your mother is really worried, Betsy?" It was like Bonnie to add that.

"No. It was just a suggestion."

"What did you think of the fracas Tony and I got into last night?"

"I think he's smitten with you," said Betsy, laughing heartily.

"Oh, Betsy!" said Bonnie. "You're the one Tony's always hanging around."

"He's just part of my long voluminous train," answered Betsy. "It's so long I have to measure it every night."

"Do you use a yardstick?" giggled Bonnie.

"I use algebra," said Betsy. "X plus X plus Y plus Z. Wouldn't O'Rourke be pleased if she could hear me spouting algebra?"

"Betsy, you're killing!" Bonnie dissolved in mirth. "Carney wants to know what the joke is. She says, why don't you change your mind and come on down."

"No," said Betsy. "Tell her I'm sitting by my own fire doing algebra problems about how many boys are smitten with me. Goodbye, Bonnie. Don't forget what I said. Tony has a case on you."

"You're killing. Goodbye," Bonnie replied.

Betsy felt better when she came away from the phone.

She felt rather shaky; there was something upsetting in the air. But she no longer felt like crying.

"Tony has a case on Bonnie," she said gaily to her mother.

"I don't wonder," Mrs. Ray replied. "Bonnie's a very attractive girl. And she'd be good for Tony; don't you think so?"

"Oh, yes," said Betsy. "And the skating party is definitely on, just as I thought it would be."

Chapter Twenty-One

T-R-O-U-B-L-E!

CAB, Herbert and Tony arrived together that evening to walk to the pond with Betsy.

"I thought you were stopping by for Bonnie," Betsy said jokingly to Tony.

"Like fun!" he answered. "Too much Christian Endeavor around that house for me!"

"Bonnie's going with Larry and Carney," Herbert remarked. "When I heard of that set-up I telephoned and volunteered my invaluable services. But she turned me down."

"You see?" said Betsy. "She's expecting you, Tony."

"What about Pin?" Tony inquired.

"He's taking Winona."

"How does that happen?" Julia asked.

"Bonnie turned him down too," said Herbert. "What ails the girl?"

Betsy glanced at Tony.

"Pin sort of likes Winona," he said. "They're both tall, and they're both thin, and they're both crazy."

Betsy felt dazed.

She put on the red stocking cap, determinedly pulling out her curls, tucked the red muffler at its most becoming angle, picked up her skates and swung them.

"Who wants the great and supreme honor?"

"Humphreys," said Herbert, and grabbed them. But when he had them in his hands he regarded them disapprovingly.

"They look dull," he said.

They did look dull. Betsy had not skated that season. She hated skating so much that even the sight of skates was abhorrent to her, and she had dug these out of the basement cupboard only that afternoon.

She had dressed warmly, but as soon as she went out of doors she realized that she hadn't dressed warmly enough. The air went down her throat like an icy drink. Inside her coat and dress and the extra warm underwear she shivered.

"You'll warm up when we get to skating," said Tony, who was holding her elbow.

"I'm not a very good skater," Betsy said.

"If you skate half as well as you dance I'll be satisfied."

"Maybe I *have* improved since last year," Betsy thought, meaning that she hoped she had. But her spirits were low.

Even the sight of the pond did not lift them although the bonfire was beautiful. Branches had been piled higher then her head and their wild glow reddened the snow.

"Gosh, we're going to have fun!" said Herbert. "Sit down, Betsy, and let me get your skates on."

"I'll do it," Tony said. That should have made her feel better but it didn't. Her qualms mounted as she sat down on the bench while Tony expertly buckled on her skates.

Carney and Bonnie hailed her. They had shed their coats but they didn't look cold. They wore heavy turtle neck sweaters and stocking caps, pulled efficiently down.

"You'd better pull that cap down around your ears," said Tony, and even helped to stuff her curls back underneath it. Betsy felt that she looked hideous with no hair showing and her big clumsy coat. She struggled to her feet.

Tony was kind about her poor skating. He said her ankles must be weak, and gave a long dissertation about how to strengthen weak ankles. After a turn or two around they came back to the bench beside the fire. About that time Tacy, Alice and Tom arrived. Cab asked Betsy to skate, and Tony skated off to take Carney away from Larry.

Cab, too, was kind about Betsy's deficiencies. Herbert, however, who skated with her next, was brutally frank.

"Gosh darn it, Betsy!" he said, "Skating's so easy. Why haven't you learned?"

"I just don't like to skate," said Betsy crossly.

"Well anybody born in Minnesota ought to like to skate," said Herbert. "And ought to know how."

Betsy's ankles wobbled. She lurched and leaned on Herbert heavily. Larry and Carney flashed past her, together. Cab and Bonnie came behind. Pin and Winona were skating separately. Both were skilful. Tall and thin, Pin looked like a dragon fly as one long leg after another swung easily through the air.

"I think I'll go back to the bonfire," Betsy said.

"Heck!" answered Herbert. "If you want to skate I'll drag you around."

"I don't want to skate," said Betsy. "You have enough to do, dragging yourself."

"Well for Pete's sake!" said Herbert, breaking off the spat with an exclamation so sincerely startled that Betsy said, "Who? What? Where?"

"There," said Herbert. "Tony! What do you think of that?"

Tony was standing beside the fire, one foot on the bench in a nonchalant attitude. Between two fingers he held a cigarette at which he took an occasional careless puff.

"Some of the fellows smoke of course," said Herbert hastily. "But just behind the barn, as it were. Not at a party with girls around. What's got into Tony?"

Betsy did not answer.

Carney had seen him. Betsy saw Carney tug at Larry's arm. Larry turned to look and then Larry and Carney skated rapidly toward Bonnie, and tugged at Bonnie's arm.

Tony blew smoke thoughtfully upward, threw the cigarette down and mashed it out, took a pack from his pocket and selected another.

"For Pete's sake!" Herbert said again.

Betsy saw Bonnie speak to Cab, then leave him alone on the ice. Skating expertly, looking round and cute in her big sweater, she went rapidly toward Tony.

"Hello," said Tony, when Bonnie reached him, and with ostentatious politeness threw his cigarette into the fire.

"Tony," said Bonnie, "will you skate with me?"

"Isn't it customary," asked Tony, "for the boy to ask the girl?"

"Maybe," said Bonnie. "But I'm asking you. Please, Tony."

"Do you want to skate or preach?" he asked.

Bonnie smiled. After all, she was not at Christian Endeavor now. She smiled and put out a mittened hand.

"Skate," she said.

Pin and Winona started clowning on the ice. Winona sat down with a bang and laughed. Cab was trying to skate backward with Tacy. Tom was with Alice. Betsy told Herbert that she had twisted her ankle, and insisted that she liked to sit by the fire alone. He skated off, and she sat by the fire alone.

Tony and Bonnie skated slowly, in perfect harmony, their arms crossed in front, their hands clasped. Betsy tried not to look at them. She looked at the fire. She looked up at the cold disinterested moon and off at the pale unfriendly landscape.

She watched the other skaters, and laughed at their mishaps, and waved when they waved to her. Now and again one or another skated over to sit with her and talk. But Tony didn't come, nor Bonnie.

By and by Tacy noticed that Tony and Bonnie had skated together for a long, long time. She and Cab skated over to Betsy.

"I'm cold," said Tacy. "Can I keep company with you?"

"I'm hungry," said Cab. "When do we start back to the Ray house?"

"Any time," said Betsy. "But people still seem to be having an awfully good time."

"Tony and Bonnie especially," said Cab. "He's smitten and smitten hard. She'll make a Presbyterian out of him yet. Bet a nickel."

"I'll bet you haven't got a nickel," said Tacy.

"And I wouldn't bet even if you had," added Betsy, refusing Tacy's offer to change the subject. "It looks to me like a perfectly awful case."

"Maybe the big bum will stop hanging around your place, getting under my feet," said Cab.

"I'm going to round the others up," said Tacy quickly, "and tell them that we're starting on."

It was very cold, going home. Betsy's hands ached, and her feet ached, and she knew that her nose was as red as a beet. But she laughed at Cab's jokes even harder than usual, and at Tacy's jokes too, for Tacy was full of jokes. Tacy kept her arm twined through Betsy's, and thought of very silly things to say about Betsy's crippled condition.

Betsy's ankle felt all right now; as a matter of fact, it had felt all right all along. But she was glad that Julia, after they reached home, offered to make the rarebit.

"Keep off your ankle, Betsy. You know my rarebit is perfect."

Betsy took off the stocking cap and resurrected her curls. She sat by the fire and her nose was its normal color by the time the rest came in. But it didn't matter, for Tony paid no attention to her. He was teasing Bonnie.

"She pulled me out of the gutter practically," he said to Julia who received his joke coldly. She sent him to the kitchen to make toast, but it only made things worse.

"Come along and help me, Bonnie. I'll go to the dogs out here in the kitchen all alone."

Bonnie went along and helped him. They were a long time making toast, and they burned it.

Betsy laughed continuously, even at Herbert's jokes about her terrible skating. Now that they were at home, Herbert relented about her sad showing on the ice. He offered to take her out the next day and teach her to skate.

"And get my head snapped off?" asked Betsy. "I'm afraid of you when you get near ice, Herbie. I wouldn't even let you go to the ice box with me."

"Aw, I wasn't that bad!" Herbert said.

For the first time he looked at Betsy with a faintly romantic eye. His adoration of Bonnie had died for lack of nourishment, and he hadn't even noticed now that she was burning toast in the kitchen in Tony's company.

"Gosh, you have red cheeks tonight, Betsy," he said. "Do you paint?"

He took out his handkerchief and rubbed her face to find out. Cab helped him until Betsy cried for mercy. Tony and Bonnie were back from the kitchen then, but Tony didn't join in the fun.

He joined, of course, in the singing that followed the rarebit. Arms locked, The Crowd circled about the piano, and sang until the room quivered.

> "Dreaming, Dreaming,
>   Of you sweetheart, I am dreaming,
>   Dreaming of hours when you loved me best,
>   Dreaming of days that have gone to rest . . ."

Tony's arm was locked in Bonnie's, and now and then she looked up at him to smile. Betsy didn't sing much. She was laughing with Herbert.

192

She was still full of laughter when she and Julia went up to bed.

"That reforming line worked all right," she said. "Bonnie didn't know it was a line, though."

"I notice that Herbert looks at you with new eyes. And he's so handsome! Much handsomer than Tony."

"Tony, the dear departed," Betsy said.

It was all very well until the lights were out, the slit in the storm window opened, and Betsy beneath the blankets. Then the tears she had been holding back gushed out in a relieving flood. She cried and cried, holding the pillow tight in her arms for comfort.

T-R-O-U-B-L-E, her Ouija Board had spelled.

This was trouble, all right.

Chapter Twenty-Two

NEW YEAR'S EVE

BETSY sunk that night into a well of grief, and in the morning she did not propose to climb out. Her father knocked on her door as usual but she did not budge. Margaret, on her way downstairs, put her head in.

"Time to get up, Betsy."

Still Betsy did not budge.

When Mr. Ray called Julia from the foot of the stairs, he called Betsy too. Betsy did not even answer.

Julia came in, tying the violet ribbons of a most becoming dressing sacque.

"What's the matter, darling?"

"I just don't want to get up," said Betsy.

"It must be your ankle," Julia said quickly. Of course! Her ankle! Julia was wonderful. She closed the window, adjusted the shades, and plumped up Betsy's pillows. She went to the bathroom and returned with a wet washcloth and a towel. She handed Betsy a comb.

"I'll explain to papa about your ankle," she said, departing, "and bring you some breakfast."

Betsy didn't even say "Thanks." She just burrowed deeper into the pillow. With her eyes shut and her face half smothered she could keep out the picture of Tony smiling down at Bonnie, but she could not keep out an ominous feeling of something bad and sad waiting for her if she stirred.

Her father brought her tray himself.

"Sit up and wash your face," he said cheerily. "I'll have a look at that ankle."

Betsy sat up reluctantly. She scrubbed her face with the cold washcloth, poked her foot out of bed beyond the hem of her outing flannel nightgown.

"No swelling," Mr. Ray observed.

Drawing up a chair he poked the ankle. "Hurt?"

"No," said Betsy.

He poked it again. "Hurt?"

"No."

When he poked it a third time, Betsy said, "Ouch!"

"It hurts *there?*" asked Mr. Ray, sounding surprised. He poked it again.

"Ouch!" said Betsy, pulling the foot away.

Mr. Ray looked perplexed.

"Must be a strained ligament. You can get up after breakfast, but no skating or rampaging today," he announced.

"I'd just as soon stay in bed," said Betsy. "I don't feel very good. Not *too* bad," she added hastily, remembering Tacy's party the following night. Mrs. Ray had come into the room.

"A day in bed wouldn't do Betsy any harm," she remarked.

"If the ankle isn't better tonight I'll put a strap on it," Mr. Ray said and patted her head, and departed, his wife following.

Betsy took the tray on her knees.

"I'm not a bit hungry," she thought, looking morosely at the sausages and fried potatoes, the hot buttered toast, the jam, the steaming cocoa. But when Anna came up to get the tray, it was empty.

"I'm glad your ankle didn't go to your stomach, lovey," she said. "As long as a person can eat, he can put up with anything. That's what Mrs. McCloskey used to say."

"Did the McCloskey girl ever sprain her ankle?" Betsy asked listlessly.

"Both of them," answered Anna. "I made her apple dumplings for dinner that day. How'd you like some apple dumplings, lovey?"

"Oh, Anna, I'd love them! That is," Betsy added, "if I don't get to feeling worse. If I move my ankle I feel terrible. But if I stay in bed I think I could eat some apple dumplings."

"Sure you could," Anna replied.

When the tray was gone Betsy had the feeling that the

time had come to face her sorrow, but somehow she couldn't get around to it. Margaret came in with one of her Christmas books and suggested hopefully that Betsy might feel better if she read aloud for a while.

"It's a very appropriate book," Margaret said. "It's about a little lame prince, and you're lame, Julia says."

Betsy read out loud and grew so interested that she almost forgot to say, "Ouch! That hurts!" when her mother helped her into a chair in order to freshen the bed. While her mother dusted the room, they gossiped cheerfully. Julia came in next.

"I'm going to beautify you," said Julia. "There's no reason why you shouldn't look like an interesting invalid."

"I don't care how I look," said Betsy, feeling suddenly completely wretched.

"You know how I love to fix people up," Julia answered. "Where do you keep your best dressing sacque?"

"In the bottom drawer," said Betsy.

It was made of pale blue silk and embroidered with little pink rosebuds. It tied with pink ribbons and was very becoming. Before Betsy put it on Julia brushed her hair and dressed it in a pompadour with two pink ribbons. She went into her mother's room and came back with a chamois skin dipped in powder and ran this over Betsy's face.

"Now lick your lips and wet your eyebrows," Julia commanded. "And you'll look pale and interesting enough for anybody."

Betsy licked with rising interest.

Julia helped her into the dressing sacque, tied the ribbons, and put a small beribboned pillow back of her head. Betsy enjoyed having Julia work about her. She liked the touch of her small white hands, and the smell of that cologne she used.

"Now," said Julia, "I'm going to manicure your nails."

They often manicured each other's nails. Betsy was clumsy at it but Julia was skilful. She filed and clipped and buffed until Betsy's nails looked like pink pearls.

"You have beautiful nails. I never saw such half moons," Julia said.

In the midst of all this Cab and Herbert arrived.

"Come on up," Julia called.

"Betsy's sick, but it isn't contagious," Margaret explained gravely at the top step.

The boys tiptoed in clumsy solicitude into the blue and white freshness of Betsy's room.

"You don't look sick," said Cab.

"Gosh, you look pretty!" exclaimed Herbert. The admiration which had dawned in his eyes the night before was brighter now. He looked at Betsy much as he had been wont to look at Bonnie.

Betsy languished on the pillow.

"It's my ankle. Any time I go skating again!" she said, looking at Herbert reproachfully.

"Gosh, I'm sorry," said Herbert. The boys sat down to watch the manicure. The doorbell rang again, for Tom and Pin.

"Hully gee!" exclaimed Tom looking at Betsy.

"What's the matter?" asked Pin.

"Ankle. I twisted it last night. I was skating with a big brute who doesn't know what it's like to have weak ankles."

"Help! Betsy! Go easy," begged Herbert.

"Yes, you're the brute," said Betsy.

Flirting while my heart is breaking, she thought to herself. She was doing a good job of it too. Herbert straddled a frail chair, grasped the top of it with strong brown fingers, and stared in enchantment.

"You're Anna's favorite," said Betsy. "But you're not mine. I'm going to put a stop to that piece of pie business."

"I would too," said Julia, buffing.

"Make Anna give it to me," said Cab.

"Or me," said Tom.

"I never even tasted Anna's pie," said Pin.

"You ought to come to see me oftener," said Betsy, giving him a radiant smile. Dog that I am, she thought. Pin had veered to Winona. He didn't belong to Bonnie any longer. He wasn't Betsy's rightful prey. But she was too reckless to care.

"There's an idea," said Pin. "Just what nights do you have pie?"

"Betsy's beaux," said Julia, "are eating us out of house and home."

Everything was going beautifully when the doorbell rang again. Betsy heard Tony's voice speaking to Anna. She heard his lazy steps on the stairs. He lounged in the doorway.

"What do I see before me?" he asked. "Betsy or Madame DuBarry?"

"We all know you're taking sophomore history." But it was Julia who said it, not Betsy. At the sight of his curly thatch, his laughing black eyes, Betsy's high spirits vanished. She leaned back and didn't say a word.

Someone explained about the ankle. Someone else explained that Herbert was in bad. And anyone could see what Herbert's condition was. He was staring at Betsy, rapt and tongue-tied. Anyone could see who looked, that is, or cared. Tony did neither. He seemed sorry about Betsy's ankle, but having expressed himself in his usual offhand way, he lapsed into an abstracted silence. The banter went on but Tony didn't join in, any more than Herbert did, or Betsy, who felt misery invading her again. He was so charming, so casual, so incomparably superior to all the other boys. How could she give him up? But she had given him up. She didn't feel old enough or wise enough even to try to take him back from Bonnie.

"I'm tired," said Betsy suddenly.

"And the manicure is finished," Julia said, getting up. "I think Betsy had better rest now."

"Clear out, all you kids," said Herbert.

There was a scraping of chairs and pushing toward the doorway. Herbert was the last to go out.

"Going to be able to go to Tacy's tomorrow night?" he asked.

"I hope so," said Betsy, closing her eyes. Wretched as she was, she gave thought to the picture she must make, lying pale and exhausted on the lacy pillow.

"I wish my eyelashes were thick and curly like Margaret's," she thought. "I'm thankful that they're dark at least."

She hoped they looked startlingly dark, and that her fingers, helplessly curled, looked startlingly white against the blue counterpane.

Julia glanced at her approvingly, tiptoed out, and closed the door.

The boys stayed downstairs to sing a while. Tears slipped through Betsy's fortunately dark lashes as she listened to the dear familiar tunes. She heard the boys departing one by one. Then Anna brought up her dinner.

The afternoon was punctuated with callers, female callers now. Tacy sat on the bed beside Betsy, holding her hand. Carney and Bonnie came, laughing, bringing the winter in on pink cheeks and snowy furs.

Betsy bestirred herself out of listlessness for them.

"Didn't I tell you, Bonnie," she asked, "that Tony was smitten? He's simply crazy about you. He was in here this morning and just mooned around."

"He phoned her three times this morning," Carney chuckled.

Three times! Three dull blows at Betsy's heart. He must have phoned her twice before he came over to Rays, and probably once after he left. She couldn't remember that Tony had ever phoned her. He wasn't a telephone addict as some of the boys and most of the girls were.

"Did he call up just to talk?" Betsy asked.

"Oh, he called up the first time to ask me to go to your party with him, Tacy," Bonnie said. She sounded amused. "And the second time he asked me not to forget that I had promised. And the third time he asked me not to let anybody else come along. But nobody would be apt to come anyway. Pin has gone over to Winona."

"And Herbert," said Tacy, "as you all may have noticed last night, has transferred his affections with a bang to Betsy."

"Good!" said Bonnie. Her sincerity knocked Betsy's triumph over like a house of cards.

During supper and the early evening Betsy was alone in her room. Sad as she was, she enjoyed lying in bed, warm, petted, while familiar household sounds floated up from below. This was only an interlude. Tomorrow she would be up on her two feet, facing the world and her trouble.

"No visitors for Betsy tonight," Betsy heard her mother say after a ring of the bell. Then Margaret came upstairs.

"Herbert sent you this," she said, holding out a small box of candy. "He says he's sorry about your ankle. He wants to know, will you let him take you to Tacy's party tomorrow night?"

"I'll go with him if I'm able to go," said Betsy. "You can have the candy, Margaret. Oh, I might take just a piece or two," she added, thinking better of this gesture.

Julia went out that evening on a sleigh ride. Mr. and Mrs. Ray went out too. Betsy and Margaret and Anna ate Herbert's candy to the last stale chocolate drop, and Betsy told them Ethel Brown stories. It wasn't an unhappy evening. But when the gas was turned out and the snowy world was quiet, her grief came back, seeking a little attention. Betsy gave it the tenderest attention. She thought of Tony, his charms and falseness, until she fell asleep.

The Crowd saw the old year out at Tacy's. Betsy's father, fearing for her ankle, drove her up in the sleigh but Cab and Herbert went along. Tony and Bonnie arrived late.

The rambling white house at the end of Hill Street was full of greens and Christmas cheer. The Crowd played games, and the refreshments—as always at the Kelly house—were superabundant. These were served about half past eleven, and the company was still eating when the bells and whistles of downtown Deep Valley sounded faintly. Everyone jumped up and began to cry "Happy New Year!" Betsy and Tacy kissed each other.

Breaking away from the rest they ran out of doors. The winter stars were icily bright. Snow gleamed on the hills where for so many years, winter and summer, they had played together.

In the little yellow cottage which had once been the Ray house, lights were shining. It could almost have been home still. Betsy and Tacy could almost have been children again.

"I wish I still lived there," said Betsy, hugging Tacy, partly from love and partly from cold. "It's such trouble to grow up."

"I hope you have a very happy new year," Tacy said.

Chapter Twenty-Three

THE TALK WITH MR. RAY

IT WAS arranged that Betsy . . . the ankle had to be
treated tenderly . . . was to stay all night with Tacy. The
Kellys would drop her at home on their way to church
New Year's morning. She enjoyed sleeping in the slant-
roofed bedroom with Tacy and Katie and eating breakfast
with the large merry Kelly family. The Kellys were full of

204

anecdotes about her childhood and Tacy's, and it was comforting somehow.

Later Betsy and Tacy had a serious hour alone. They made their New Year's resolutions, and when she got home Betsy wrote them down. Never had she made such serious, such sobering resolutions. She resolved to work harder at school, to read improving literature, to brush her hair a hundred strokes every night, not to think about boys . . . especially not about Tony . . . and to have the talk with her father about joining the Episcopal Church. After the holiday dinner when Mr. and Mrs. Ray went to take naps and Margaret departed with her Christmas sled for a little sedate coasting, Betsy broached the matter to Julia.

"It's almost time to talk to papa about this church business."

"I know it," said Julia looking troubled.

"The confirmation class begins in February; along about Lent."

"And that's another thing, Betsy. We'll want to keep Lent this year."

Julia was incredibly bold at times. Betsy had thought, of course, about keeping Lent after she became an Episcopalian. She had dreamed about giving up something for Lent, as Tacy did. It had seemed delightfully romantic. But she had played with these ideas only in reveries. Julia was actually proposing to carry them out.

"Do Episcopalians eat fish on Friday?" Betsy asked weakly.

"I'm not sure," said Julia. "There's High Church and Low Church. I think we're Low Church here in Deep Valley. But Anna wouldn't mind cooking fish for us."

"Julia!" cried Betsy, shuddering. "Can you imagine papa?"

"It's pretty awful," Julia agreed. "What shall we do, Bettina?"

After some thought Betsy asked, "Do you suppose papa would think we knew our minds by now?"

"We've been singing in the choir all winter."

"We go back to school a week from tomorrow. Let's talk to him a week from today."

"That's a good plan," Julia said.

The second week of vacation was outwardly much like the first. Boys and girls dropped in, and there were parties. But Betsy ploughed through the parties as though they were ordeals comparable to the examinations looming ahead in school. Tony and Bonnie came to everything together, late usually, looking moon-struck. Tony dropped in at the Ray house, but in the flesh only; his thoughts were plainly on Broad Street.

It helped, Betsy found, to adhere to her resolutions as though they were laws laid down. No matter how tired she was at night she brushed her hair a hundred strokes before rolling it up on Magic Wavers. She banished Robert W. Chambers from her room and brought in Longfellow, Whittier and Poe. She ruled Tony sternly from her thoughts. And the Sunday before school resumed, in the robing room at church, she said to Julia: "Today is the day we talk to papa."

Julia looked grave and beautiful in her black robe and the black four-cornered hat.

"How do you feel?" she asked.

"Queer in my stomach. And why do we always say, 'talk to papa'? We have to talk to mamma, too."

"We know mamma will understand," said Julia. "She's

a very Episcopalian type. But papa is such a Baptist!"

"And you remember all he told us about his mother. It's going to be hard," Betsy said gloomily.

"Bettina," said Julia. "When you pray in church this morning, pray about it, and so will I. Maybe we can find a chance to pray alone after everyone is gone."

That was the sort of thing that Betsy thought of doing, and Julia boldly did.

Organ music sounded, and the girls formed into a line, two abreast, for the processional. They marched and sang:

> *Clear before us through the darkness,*
> *Gleams and burns the guiding light,*
> *Brother clasps the hand of brother,*
> *Stepping fearless through the night.*

When she came to "Brother clasps the hand of brother," Betsy glanced at Julia. Julia wasn't looking at her, of course. Nothing ever disturbed Julia's rapt expression when she was singing. Betsy doubted that it would alter if the church burned down. But surely, Betsy thought, she must see the significance of the hymn. Change that "Brother clasps the hand of brother," to "Sister clasps the hand of sister," and how perfectly it fitted!

"Let us pray," the Reverend Mr. Lewis said.

The Reverend Mr. Lewis as usual prayed for a number of things, for remission of sins, for peace, for grace, for the President of the United States, for the Clergy and People, and for all conditions of men. But whenever the ritual permitted a personal supplication, Betsy made only one prayer.

"Please help us to tell papa," she prayed, digging her

forehead into her curved arm, forgetting even to try to look pretty.

After the service Julia with calm authority told Fred and Herbert not to wait for them. She and Betsy went down into the body of the church and said their special prayer.

Walking home through the bleak cold, Betsy said, "Now after dinner today, we'll do it."

"After his nap," Julia added.

After dinner and his nap their father, as usual on Sundays, settled down in the parlor with the Sunday paper. He liked best to sit in a curved leather chair that his Lodge had given him after he was Grand Master and to cross his feet on an ottoman in front. With a cigar in his mouth and the paper folded neatly, he read with absorption.

Today Mrs. Ray was reading, too. And Margaret and Washington were looking at the funnies. Julia and Betsy came down the stairs together, as though still marching two abreast in a procession.

"Papa," said Julia, "Betsy and I want to have a talk with you."

Mr. Ray looked up, and he must have seen from their faces that they had a serious matter on their minds, for he put the paper down, and placed his cigar carefully across an ash try.

"Do mamma and Margaret get in on this?" he asked them.

"Yes," said Julia. "They might as well."

"Sit down, then," said Mr. Ray, and they sat down gingerly on the edges of their chairs. Mr. Ray took his feet off the ottoman, crossed his legs and leaned back calmly, tucking a thumb into his striped Sunday vest.

"Go ahead," he said, looking from Julia whose pointed

face was pale under her pompadour to Betsy whose cheeks were red as fire.

"Papa," said Julia, "Betsy and I want to join the Episcopal Church."

Mr. Ray continued to lean back, but no longer calmly. Julia's announcement had really startled him.

"You do, eh?" he said. He kept his tone offhand, but he sounded as startled as he looked. "What do you think of this, Jule?" he asked, playing for time.

"I've seen it coming," Mrs. Ray answered.

"Do you mean," he said to Julia and Betsy, "that you like all that kneeling down and getting up, kneeling down and getting up?"

He was talking fast, half jokingly. He was . . . Betsy knew . . . trying to adjust himself to their bewildering idea.

"Papa," said Betsy, "don't joke. Julia and I know that you'll feel terrible. In the first place it will be so embarrassing to you; you're a prominent Baptist. People will think it strange of you to let us join the Episcopal Church. They'll criticize you, and we can't stand the thought of that. And yet we both want to be Episcopalians. That's why we thought we'd ask you to . . . sort of . . . talk it over."

Mr. Ray grew serious then. Still with a thumb in his vest he looked at them out of wise, kindly eyes.

"Let me set you right on one thing first of all," he said. "We aren't going to decide this on the basis of what people will say. You might as well learn right now, you two, that the poorest guide you can have in life is what people will say. What the Baptists in Deep Valley will think of mother and me if our girls go off and join the Episcopal Church has nothing to do with the matter."

Margaret got to her feet, standing straight like her father. Crossing the room she rubbed against his knee and he made a place for her in his chair. He kept his arm around her while he talked, and Margaret stared at her sisters with black-lashed disapproving eyes.

"Don't you agree with me, Jule?" Mr. Ray asked.

"Yes, I do," said Mrs. Ray. "I've done lots in my life the Baptists didn't approve of. Papa has too. We belong to a dancing club; we play whist; we go on picnics sometimes on Sundays. But we don't do anything we think is wrong, and the Baptists respect us. They even asked papa to be a deacon."

"But there's another thing," said Betsy. "We know how much the Baptist Church means to papa. We know about Grandma Ray starting the church down in Iowa. It makes Julia and me feel bad to stop being Baptists." Her eyes filled with tears. "It makes us feel terrible," she said.

Julia's eyes filled with tears too, although she didn't cry as easily as Betsy did. She winked violently, and then took out a handkerchief. But since Betsy was groping vainly for a handkerchief and needed one even more, Julia passed hers along and kept on winking. Betsy wiped her eyes and blew her nose.

"See here," said Mr. Ray. "Anybody would think from the way you talk that *I* was the one who had a problem about what church to join. You are the two who have the problem. What makes you think you want to be Episcopalians, anyway?"

But now Betsy was tongue-tied. Not because she was afraid she would cry, although that entered in, but because she was shy of putting into words deeply-felt emotions. She didn't mind putting them into written words. She could

have written her father an essay on her feeling for the
Episcopal Church, but she couldn't tell it to him.

Julia spoke eloquently. "It's the beauty of the service,
papa," she said. "Betsy and I both respond to it. The
music lifts us up, and the ritual is like a poem. We were
just made to be Episcopalians."

"You've thought this over? It isn't just a whim?"

"We've thought it over for weeks and months," said
Julia, glad to be able to say so. "We're sure of everything
except whether or not we ought to hurt you and . . ."

"Julia," said Mr. Ray. "You'd never make a lawyer. I
repeat that mother and I don't enter into this. You're
seventeen years old, and Betsy's past fourteen. Both of you
are almost women, and personally I'm glad to discover that
you've given some thought to religion. It's a right thing to
do when you begin to grow up. It's what I did, and what
your mother did, and what . . . I am sure . . . your
Grandmother Ray would approve if she were here. The
important thing isn't what church you want to join but
whether you want to join a church at all.

"Certainly you can be Episcopalians. I'm sure mother
agrees. Don't you, Jule?"

Mrs. Ray nodded and reached for the handkerchief
Julia had given Betsy.

"And I hope," Mr. Ray continued, "I hope very much
that if you're going to be Episcopalians, you'll be good
Episcopalians."

"We'll try to be," Julia said quickly.

"But that isn't what I hope most," Mr. Ray added. He
knotted thoughtful fingers around his chin.

"Yes, I hope you'll be good Episcopalians," he repeated.
"I hope you'll go to church as regularly as mother and I

do. We miss a Sunday now and then, when it's fine picnicking weather. We know that God made the out-of-doors, too. But year in, year out, we go to church pretty regularly.

"And we support the church. You have to think of that. Churches need an income just as a family does; and it is your duty to support your church if you join one. With more than money, too. A church needs members who take an active part in the church work. Mother and I don't do as much as some, and some folks overdo it, in my opinion, but we try to carry our load. My point is that if you're going to join a church, you want to be prepared to support it, both with money and time."

"Yes, papa," Julia and Betsy said.

"But that's just the beginning," Mr. Ray went on, and sat straight in his chair. "It isn't enough to go to church, and to support the church. The most important part of religion isn't in any church. It's down in your own heart. Religion is in your thoughts, and in the way you act from day to day, in the way you treat other people. It's honesty, and unselfishness, and kindness. Especially kindness."

He paused.

"Well, that's that," he ended, his face breaking into a smile. "You two go and be Episcopalians, if you can stand that everlasting kneeling down and getting up. I never could. Everything's settled now, until Margaret here comes and tells us that she wants to be a Mormon."

"I won't," said Margaret, sitting very straight. "I don't know what a Mormon is, but I want to be a Baptist. I'm always going to be a Baptist." And she turned and buried her face in her father's striped Sunday vest.

Mr. Ray hugged her. He got up. And everyone got up,

Mrs. Ray, and Julia, and Betsy, and Margaret. They all embraced in a big family hug, tighter and tighter.

"Now," said Mr. Ray. "I'd better go put the coffee pot on." For that was what the family always did in moments of stress. Margaret didn't drink coffee of course, and Betsy's Sunday cup was mostly cream and sugar. Yet they understood what their father meant when he moved with a competent tread toward the kitchen.

Chapter Twenty-Four

AN ADVENTURE ON PUGET SOUND

THE next day they went back to school, and it was an excellent time for being religious, for being serious-minded, for being heart-broken. The thermometer was far below zero and examinations were looming ahead. Stiffly wrapped, Betsy and Tacy hurried along High Street muttering Latin conjugations. When boys and girls dropped into the Ray house after school, they all studied. Tacy,

Alice and Winona came to stay all night and study.

"Why do you have to study *together?*" Mr. Ray asked. "When I was a boy we didn't study in droves. And what help is all the fudge?"

"Nourishment, papa, nourishment," Betsy explained. "We need strength. Composition is a cinch, of course; and history won't be bad, Clarke is such a darling. But Latin and algebra! Wow!"

Julia too was ferociously intent upon study. She was going to no dances; she quarreled with Fred and refused to make up.

"I'm tired of him anyway," she confided to Betsy. "And it's a very convenient time to be between beaux . . . examination week."

When Fred telephoned Julia was out. When he came Julia was busy. She wouldn't make up. Fred grew haggard. His eyes showed sleepless nights.

"This is pretty hard on Fred," said Betsy indignantly. "He's going to flunk everything, because he's worrying about you."

"Very foolish of him," said Julia, settling down to her Cicero.

The last examination came on Friday, and after school The Crowd surged into the Ray house not only to make fudge but to sing and to ask the Ouija Board who had passed and who had not. Saturday night The Crowd went sleighing. Bells jingling on the frosty air tried to compete with harmonizing from the boys and girls tucked under robes in the big sleigh. Tony and Bonnie sat side by side, his arm draped along the back of the seat. It was a horrible party for Betsy who remarked at frequent intervals that she never had had so much fun in her life.

Monday, the new term began and Betsy found that she

had passed in everything. She squeezed through algebra by a breath, through Latin by a hair. Her history mark was fair, but gentle Miss Clarke was disappointed that students who were so brilliant in class made such a poor showing on examination papers.

"You must have been nervous," she said consolingly to Betsy.

Mr. Gaston, although he had seemed so unappreciative of Betsy all term, gave her a high mark . . . ninety-six. It was topped in the class only by Joe Willard's ninety-seven. And shortly Betsy was given another proof of her composition teacher's good opinion.

Miss Clarke approached her after school.

"I've been talking with Mr. Gaston," she said, "and he and I both think that, although you are only a freshman, you can write an essay good enough to be read at Rhetoricals."

"Really?" cried Betsy. Her modest surprise was assumed, but her pleasure was genuine.

"Aren't you proud?" Miss Clarke asked, patting her shoulder. "We are planning an All-American program, and we want you to write a paper on Puget Sound."

"Puget Sound?" Betsy echoed vaguely.

"Just go to the library," Miss Clarke said, "and read all you can find on Puget Sound. Then write an interesting essay about it."

"Yes, ma'am," said Betsy.

She was delighted with the assignment. It not only provided a highly creditable excuse for absenting herself from the gatherings of The Crowd and the presence of Tony and Bonnie, but it poulticed her sore heart. An essay for Rhetoricals on Puget Sound!

She told the family about it at supper, and they were pleased and impressed.

"Your Aunt Flora lives on Puget Sound," Mr. Ray observed. "You might write her for some material."

"Where is Puget Sound?" asked Margaret, and Betsy, who had not yet looked it up, was relieved when her father answered for her.

"It's an arm of the Pacific extending into Washington state. Seattle where your Aunt Flora lives is built on Puget Sound."

"Papa and I once took a trip on the Sound," Mrs. Ray added. "We went from Seattle to Olympia on the Steamer Princess Victoria."

They talked about the trip throughout supper.

After supper Betsy collected all the pencils she could find. She took them to the kitchen and sharpened them while Anna looked on admiringly. She hunted up a notebook and wrote on the first page, "Puget Sound." The next day after school she ignored the social advances of her friends and turned toward the library.

There was a driving north wind. The cold air stung her cheeks above the grey fur piece and numbed her hands. Her feet were numb too, inside her overshoes, as she crunched along the snowy walk. But she was happier than she had been for days. She felt a fierce proud satisfaction. It was an adventure to be going to the library to learn about a strange new place called Puget Sound.

"I think I'll name my essay that," she planned. " 'An Adventure on Puget Sound.' I don't believe Clarke would mind if I worked a little story in."

Miss Sparrow, the small twinkling-eyed librarian, was glad to see Betsy. They were old friends.

"You haven't been down for a long time," she said. She unearthed endless fat and fascinating volumes on the state of Washington and the Pacific Northwest and Puget Sound.

Betsy walked home through a cold even sharper than she had faced coming down, but she didn't mind. She was thinking of pines standing ruggedly above green water, of Mt. Rainier rising white and fair, or colored like candle flame by sunset. She didn't think once of Tony and Bonnie.

At the supper table, she was bursting with the glories of Puget Sound, but she had to divide talking time with Julia.

Julia had had a singing lesson that day, and *she* was bursting with news of some new records Mrs. Poppy had played on the gramophone.

"They're Caruso records. Enrico Caruso. When you hear him sing that 'Laugh, Pagliaccio,' you absolutely have to cry."

"Who is Enrico Caruso?" Margaret wanted to know.

"Just a fat little fellow who likes his spaghetti," Mr. Ray joked.

"Just the greatest singer in the world," Julia said, giving her father a crushing look.

"Not so great as Chauncey Olcott, I'll bet," said Betsy.

"Chauncey Olcott! You can't mention him in the same breath. You'd better stick to Puget Sound, Bettina."

Steamers on Puget Sound, Mt. Ranier, spaghetti and Caruso surged through Betsy's dreams that night. The next day after history class she spoke to Miss Clarke.

"Miss Clarke, you wouldn't mind, would you, if I put some characters into my essay? Took them on a trip through Puget Sound, maybe?"

"I think it would be a nice idea," Miss Clarke answered, beaming. "It would put a little color, a little life, into the paper."

"That's what I thought," Betsy said.

She went to the library every day after school and at home, in front of the fire, wrote industriously in her notebook. Cab was disgusted and Herbert's budding romantic interest died. Betsy didn't mind. She had given herself heart and soul to Puget Sound.

Her father was much interested in the essay. He talked about Puget Sound every night at supper, and when he paused for breath Julia chimed in about Enrico Caruso. She went often to Mrs. Poppy's to listen to his records.

"I'd give ten years of my life to hear him utter one note," she cried dramatically.

Betsy grew almost as absorbed in Enrico Caruso as she was in Puget Sound. She asked questions about him. He was an Italian she discovered, stout and dark, with a tenor voice so divine that his stoutness and darkness didn't matter at all.

The essay was finished at last and the day for Rhetoricals arrived. At noon Betsy changed from her school waist and skirt into the red velveteen. Mrs. Ray dressed up too. She was going to hear the program as parents often did when their children performed.

"I wish I could go," Mr. Ray said. "I'll have to wait until supper to hear all about it. Will you let me read the essay tonight, Betsy?"

"Of course," said Betsy. Up to now no one in the family had read it; and this worried Mr. Ray a little.

"Has one of the teachers read it?" he asked now. "Somebody ought to check your facts. I suppose you covered the salmon fisheries?"

"Miss Clarke read it," Betsy answered evasively, "last night after school."

"Did she like it?" Mr. Ray inquired.

"She liked it all right," Betsy said.

As a matter of fact Miss Clarke had seemed surprised by the essay. She had changed color two or three times while she was reading. She had coughed and gone out for a glass of water. She had taken off her eyeglasses and polished them and put them on again.

"It's not exactly what I expected, Betsy," she had said. "But perhaps it will do our Rhetoricals good."

This was such a queer compliment that Betsy did not repeat it to her father, and she thought about it with some trepidation when, sitting on the platform with the others taking part in the program, she watched Miss Bangeter, tall, dark and majestic, walk to the front of the platform. After a few words Miss Bangeter turned the meeting over to Miss Clarke.

Miss Clarke explained that the program was to cover all parts of the United States. She announced the opening number, a contribution from the chorus. Since Betsy sang in the chorus she had a chance to stand on her shaky legs and get accustomed to the audience. It was vast and frightening.

The chorus sang "Dixie," and that covered the South. A girl read one of Brett Harte's stories, and that covered California. A boy recited from Whittier's "Snow Bound" and that covered New England. Betsy sat on the platform with her hands clutching her essay, copied out on foolscap paper in her best handwriting. Her legs were still shaky, her hands were like ice, and her mouth felt as dry as a piece of carpet.

Miss Clarke announced that the next contribution

would cover the Pacific Northwest. It was an essay on Puget Sound, written and read by Betsy Ray.

Betsy rose and walked to the front of the platform.

There was a burst of the hearty applause that high school students love to give as a welcome change from being quiet. She saw Herbert's wide grin, Cab's twinkling eyes, Tacy's pale face. Julia too looked anxious but her mother was calm and confident, a little stern, as she was when Julia sang.

"An Adventure on Puget Sound," Betsy said.

She started to read to the accompaniment of the fidgeting, whispering and paper rustling that usually keep pace with the reading of an essay to a high school audience. But after a moment you could have heard a pin drop. For Betsy's essay wasn't an essay, exactly. It was an account of a trip which half a dozen girls in stiffly starched sailor suits and breezy sailor hats were taking on the Steamer Princess Victoria on Puget Sound. The girls were named Betsy, Tacy, Julia, Katie, Carney and Bonnie.

Betsy—in the story—was afraid the sea air would straighten out her home made curls. This brought a gust of laughter from the audience. Bonnie quoted the guide book, trying to make the trip educational. Carney flashed a lone dimple and cried, *"O di immortales!"* Katie talked with an Irish brogue, and Tacy was seasick.

The gust of laughter became a wind. Miss Bangeter rapped for order.

Betsy's essay had a plot. Julia burst into the luxurious salon, richly upholstered in brown leather, where the ship's orchestra was playing and a gay throng was assembled, to tell her companions that Enrico Caruso was on board. She was determined to have a look at him, and the girls searched the faces of their shipmates but saw no one who looked godlike enough to be Enrico Caruso. They saw, however, a short fat swarthy Italian; he seemed, indeed, to be eyeing them.

In the dining room, hung in palest green, full of women in ball gowns, flowers and candlelight, with the orchestra now playing behind potted palms, they continued to search for Caruso. Failing to find him, they watched the stout Italian who consumed five spring chickens and vast quantities of spaghetti. It was at this point that Tacy grew seasick.

They went out on deck and noted the panorama of wooded hill and fertile plain. Bonnie told them that Puget Sound was the Mediterranean of America. When not searching for Enrico Caruso they watched the sun set on Mt. Rainier, the color of candle flame.

"How Caruso must be enjoying this!" sighed Julia. The Italian who was in the next deck chair, seemed interested in her remark. "I'd give ten years of my life to hear him utter one note," Julia remarked dramatically.

The moon rose, and someone suggested singing.

"Girls!" rebuked Julia. "We couldn't sing with Enrico Caruso on board!" But they talked her down, the moonlight called for singing so strongly. They began to sing.

They sang "Shy Ann, Shy Ann, Hop on My Pony," and "What's the Use of Dreaming" and "Crocodile Isle" and "Cause I'm Lonesome." Then Katie suggested "My Wild Irish Rose."

"We need a tenor. Fake one, Katie," Julia said.

But Katie didn't need to fake one, for at that point the Italian joined in their song in a tenor voice so golden that the stars above Puget Sound swam in glory as they listened. At the end the little man rose and bowed to Julia.

"The lady might like to know me. I am Enrico Caruso," he said.

"And he ate five spring chickens!" breathed Julia.

That was the final line.

The auditorium of the Deep Valley High School rocked and roared applause. Miss Clarke looked timidly toward Miss Bangeter. Miss Bangeter was laughing and clapping her hands. She wiped her eyes too before she rose and rapped for order and walked to the front of the platform.

"Betsy certainly surprised us," she said. "She left out a few important facts about the Sound, I must admit. And I think she should turn in a report on the Salmon Fisheries, just to show that she knows about them, as I have no doubt she does. But she certainly made us all want to take that trip. Didn't she?"

Uproarious applause was the answer.

Betsy's knees that stopped shaking now. Her mouth felt natural again. She was happy. She was proud. Let Bonnie have Tony if she wanted him!

"The pen is mightier than the sword," she thought. Sword wasn't the word, exactly. But it was the best she could find with the Deep Valley High School whistling and stamping its feet.

Chapter Twenty-Five

CHANGE IN THE AIR

"When the days begin to lengthen,
Then the cold begins to strengthen."

MR. RAY quoted the old saw every February and every February it was true. The weather was mercilessly cold. Good black coal rattled steadily into the furnace. Bluejays took refuge under the eaves of the house, ruffling their feathers.

"You can put molasses on the end of a stick and catch one," Anna said. Margaret tried. She didn't succeed, but it helped to defeat February.

Mrs. Ray defeated it with a thimble bee; Betsy and Tacy wore their best dresses and served. Julia defeated it by writing to the music store in Minneapolis and ordering another opera score; Aïda this time. She also acquired a new beau named Hugh. The examination papers were barely dry when she started throwing bright glances at this slender studious youth who soon was completely at home in the Ray house. Only Washington now served as a reminder of the hapless Fred.

Julia and Betsy were busy too with confirmation classes. They observed Lent rigorously for a time. Julia gave up dancing, a sacrifice Betsy could not very well make since The Crowd had not started going to dances. She equaled it, however; she gave up candy; she gave up fudge.

"What shall we do with the money we save on the grocery bill?" Mr. Ray asked. "Would you like a trip to California, Jule? How about an auto?"

In the after school gatherings at the Ray house there was a great emptiness, most imperfectly satisfied with cookies. When The Crowd gathered elsewhere and fudge was offered, Betsy accepted her portion, took it home and put it in a box.

"I'm going to eat it Easter Sunday," she explained.

Before Easter she and Julia would be confirmed, and even sooner Betsy would be baptized. She had asked Mr. and Mrs. Humphreys to be her godparents.

"Doesn't that make us practically related?" Herbert asked, walking home from confirmation class.

"I'd be glad if it would," Betsy answered. "I never had a brother."

"You don't seem like a sister exactly," Herbert said. "I'll tell you what you are; you're my Confidential Friend."

After that Herbert and Betsy, writing notes to each other in school, put C.F. after their names.

But Betsy did not confide in Herbert. She was not much of a confider, except to Tacy. Herbert, however, poured into Betsy's ear his infatuation for a round-cheeked girl named Irma. This was not very flattering but it was good experience for a writer, Betsy thought. Since her triumph with Puget Sound she was very much the writer.

"That affair with Tony helped my writing," she told Tacy. "I mean, it will when I get around to write. It's good for writers to suffer."

Tony dropped in often, teasing and affectionate as ever, and quite unaware of having improved her art.

The girls in The Crowd were making friendship pillows. Carney and Bonnie had started the fad. They asked friends to write their names, nicknames and pet jokes on pillows, and then they embroidered over the penciled scrawls. Betsy was as poor at embroidery as she was at algebra but she started a friendship pillow. After school she often went down to the Sibleys' to work on it with Carney and Bonnie.

Usually there was a fire in the library grate, and beyond the windows stretched the snowy side lawn. Betsy's thread tangled and knotted, the work bored her unspeakably. So shortly she took to reading aloud while the others sewed. Curled in Mr. Sibley's chair she read "Helen's Babies," and they laughed until they cried into their friendship pillows. Carney finished Betsy's pillow for her.

When they fell to talking she was always surprised anew by how different Carney and Bonnie were from herself.

They actually enjoyed embroidering and sewing; they were interested in learning to cook and keep house. They expected to marry and settle down, right here in Deep Valley, perhaps.

A contrast to these domestic chats was provided by her bedtime talks with Julia.

"When we're out in the Great World" . . . Julia would begin. She spoke freely of New York, London, Berlin and Paris and expected to know them all intimately some day.

March and St. Patrick's Day brought the annual supper in the basement of the Catholic Church. Katie and Tacy with shamrocks on their shirtwaists, green bows in their hair, waited on the Rays.

"Who do you think I just waited on?" Tacy asked Betsy. She went on without waiting for an answer. "O'Rourke and Clarke. I was scared to death. I couldn't get over the idea that O'Rourke was going to ask me to work an algebra problem."

"I suppose you chatted with Clarke about the Ancient Romans," said Betsy.

"No, we talked about you. That is, they asked me whether this supper was as good as the one we ate on Puget Sound. And Clarke said you were a very talented girl."

"Did she, really?"

"Yes. And then she said something funny. She said you were going to have a chance to prove it. What do you suppose she meant by that?"

Betsy found out the next day after school. Miss Clarke called her into the empty classroom, and it was plain that something important was in the wind. Miss Clarke was smiling tremulously; her soft cheeks were flushed. She

227

took off her eyeglasses, polished them, and put them back.

"I'm sure you know," she began at last, "about the Essay Contest. The Philomathians and Zetamathians compete every year for the essay cup. Each society chooses one senior, one junior, one sophomore and one freshman to make up a team. A subject is assigned, and the two teams are excused from all homework in English in order to have time for library study.

"Then on a Saturday morning in May, they are locked into a classroom with Miss O'Rourke and myself. They are not allowed to bring any notes, and they are given three hours in which to write. The essays are graded on the point system, and the society whose team piles up the most points, wins. The awarding of the cup, as Julia may have told you, is an event of Commencement Week.

"Since the Philomathians have won the cup for debating," Miss Clarke went on, "and we hold the athletics cup, the contest this year is extremely important. Naturally we are very anxious to win. I have selected with great care the students for the Zetamathian team. You will be interested to hear who our freshman representative will be." She smiled at Betsy, and her eyes gleamed through her glasses. "After a conference with the English teachers," she continued, "I have selected Betsy Ray."

Betsy blushed vividly. Her heart pounded with joy.

"I am sure," Miss Clarke said, "that the freshman points, at least, will go to the Zetamathians."

Betsy tried to look modest but she was sure of it too. She could almost hear her name read out when the winning contestants were announced. All eight contestants sat on the platform. The four who had won the higher ratings rose when the cup was presented.

"What is the subject?" she asked.

228

" 'The Philippines: their Present and Future Value.' And Betsy, there's one thing Miss Bangeter advised me to mention. You mustn't mind. I thought your story about Puget Sound was delightful. In fact, it led to your being chosen now. But on the Essay Contest you have to be serious. Your paper has to be a sound piece of work, well fortified by facts. Do you think you can write that sort of thing?"

"Oh, yes," said Betsy. In her thoughts she added airily, "Just give me a pencil." There was nothing she would have hesitated to write from an epic poem to an advertisement. "And I love to work at the library," she added.

"I know." Miss Clarke smiled. "I always talk with Miss Sparrow before selecting students for the Essay Contest. She knows who is capable of study, and who is not. You haven't asked," Miss Clarke added mischievously, "who your Philomathian freshman rival is."

"Who is it?" asked Betsy politely.

"Joe Willard," Miss Clarke replied, "and he is an excellent English student. You'll have to work to keep up with him."

"I certainly will," laughed Betsy, but she was only saying what she thought was expected of her. True, Joe Willard wrote well, and he topped her grade in Composition. But had Joe Willard, or anyone else in high school, been writing poems, stories and novels all his life? Had Joe Willard written a paper on Puget Sound that was the sensation of the year? Betsy considered the freshman points as good as won.

"The Zetamathians are relying on you, Betsy," Miss Clarke said.

Betsy was very, very pleased, and Tacy, waiting for her outside, was overjoyed.

"Of course you'll win," she said. "Oh, Betsy, I'm so proud of you!"

"Shucks!" said Betsy, but she was proud of herself.

They burst into the house and told Mrs. Ray. She was busy with Miss Mix who was making her disturbing spring visit, but for a moment Mrs. Ray forgot about her checked brown and white suit, and Julia's pink silk, and Betsy's canary-colored silk, and Margaret's plaid. She ran downstairs to tell Anna and to telephone Mr. Ray.

Miss Mix gave Betsy one of her rare smiles.

"I hope you'll win," she said.

"Oh, she's sure to win, Miss Mix," said Tacy.

"I have to do a lot of work between now and the middle of May," Betsy said, feeling important.

After Tacy left she hunted up a notebook and some pencils. She went to the kitchen to sharpen the pencils and enjoy Anna's admiration.

"I think I'll go down to the library and start studying now," she announced.

But when she had put on her grey coat and fur piece and the hat with the plaid ribbon, it seemed too bad not to go down to the Sibleys' and share her exciting news with Carney and Bonnie.

"I'll start work at the library tomorrow," she decided.

She burst into the Broad Street house breathless, but before she had taken off her overshoes, she saw that Carney had news of her own.

"What's the matter?" she asked.

"Matter enough," said Carney darkly. "Come on in. Bonnie will tell you herself."

In the library Bonnie looked up from her friendship pillow, but she didn't smile.

"Has Carney told you?" she asked.

230

"Told me what? Whose funeral is this, anyway?"

Bonnie's big blue eyes filled with tears.

"It's mine, I guess," she said. "I'm going back to Paris."

"To Paris!" cried Betsy. "Aren't you glad?"

"Glad!" echoed Bonnie. "Why should I be glad? If you think Paris is half as nice as Deep Valley, Minnesota, you're mistaken, that's all."

She threw her arms around Carney, and they buried tearful faces in each other's shoulders.

Betsy felt ashamed. "I know just how you feel," she said. "It was like that with Tacy and Tib and me when Tib went to Milwaukee. And of course Milwaukee isn't half as far away as Paris. But we have lots of fun writing letters. We'll write you dozens of letters, Bonnie."

"That will be g-r-r-and," wept Bonnie. "But when I hear about all your parties it will only make me feel bad."

"They won't be half so much fun without you," Carney said, sniffing.

"We'll miss you terribly," Betsy said. She began to feel a little weepy herself.

Bonnie straightened up and wiped her eyes.

"This is very silly of me," she said. "But oh, I've enjoyed this winter! We've had such wonderful times!"

"When are you going?" Betsy asked.

"Right away. That's what's so awful about it. Papa's been called back to that American church in Paris, and we're sailing from New York the last of the month."

Sailing from New York! Bonnie said it as carelessly as though she were saying, "Going to the Majestic."

"I'm going to give a big party for her," Carney said. "And Mrs. Humphreys is going to give one too, Larry says."

"And I'll give one too," said Betsy. "And I'm sure that

231

Tacy will, and probably Alice and Winona. There will be party after party, Bonnie."

"That will be grand," said Bonnie, cheering up.

Not until she was out in the twilight did it occur to Betsy that this round of parties might interfere with her study for the Essay Contest.

"But it doesn't matter," she thought. "I'll have plenty of time to study after Bonnie goes. Anyway I can win that contest with one arm tied behind me. I'm almost sorry for Joe."

In her mind's eye she had a sudden picture of him. Blond, bright-eyed, with that determined smile.

"I wish I knew him better," she thought unexpectedly. "But I don't think he likes me. And then, he's so busy, working every day after school. He won't be able to go to the library much. So it's really more fair if I don't."

This reasoning led her back to parties and thence to Bonnie's departure. Not until that moment, which caught her at the corner of High Street and Plum, did it occur to her that Bonnie's going left Tony free again. She was glad to note that she felt no pleasure in this disloyal thought, although the quick memory of Tony and Bonnie made the winter twilight deepen, made her feel homesick on the very steps of home.

Chapter Twenty-Six

OF CHURCH AND LIBRARY

As Carney and Bonnie had prophesied, Bonnie's impending departure brought a most unlentenlike round of parties. Except for the fact that she was saving candy in a box instead of eating it, Betsy would have forgotten that it was Lent. Parents were indulgent because they too regretted Bonnie's going. To The Crowd it was a real sorrow which must be drowned in endless high jinks.

The girls went down to the Photographic Gallery and had their pictures taken with Bonnie. Boys and girls together went to the jewelry store and bought her a locket and chain. And on an afternoon toward the end of March she left on the four-forty-five which went to the Twin Cities where she would change for Chicago and New York.

The Crowd saw her off, and she wept when they gave her the locket.

Dr. and Mrs. Andrews, after saying their goodbyes, retired to the parlor car but Bonnie stayed out on the observation platform until the train pulled away. She wore a green suit and hat and a big corsage of flowers . . . from Tony, who looked far too nonchalant. Her blue eyes kept brimming, and she dabbed at them with a very clean white handkerchief. Carney looked grimly determined not to cry, and Larry kept a protective hand on her arm.

The train moved away, and Bonnie waved the white handkerchief. Everyone waved back as the little green figure grew smaller and smaller, and blurred, and disappeared.

Tony took Betsy's arm.

"Come on," he said. "Let's go raise the roof." But Betsy felt no triumph in this return. She knew that his heart was on the four-forty-five speeding toward St. Paul.

Cards came from Chicago and New York, and at last a letter from Paris. Still Bonnie's soft laugh was missed at The Crowd gatherings, and interest in Christian Endeavor . . . especially among the boys . . . dwindled regrettably.

Yet the spring held important matters for them all despite Bonnie's going. It was important to watch the giant snowdrifts melt, to hear joyful rivers rushing in the gutters and to see brown patches of last year's grass. And early in April Betsy was baptized. It had been planned that this event would take place just before her confirmation, but Mr. Humphreys had to go to California on sudden mysterious business, so they hurried it up.

It occurred during Evening prayer just after the Second Lesson. Betsy was impressed when she noticed that the Reverend Mr. Lewis used the rites prescribed for Baptism to Such as Are of Riper Years. "Riper Years" had a solemn sound. And it was a solemn occasion. Mr. Humphreys looked grave, and so did pretty, fluttery Mrs. Humphreys. But there was a mischievous gleam in the blue eyes of the irrepressible Herbert as Betsy passed him on her way to the font.

She was wearing her vestments, for she came down from the choir for the ceremony. Candles were glowing, and to Betsy the simple church looked like a cathedral. A chill ran down her spine when the Reverend Mr. Lewis asked "Dost thou renounce the devil and all his works, the vain pomp and glory of the world . . . ?" She renounced them according to the prayer book but the "vain pomp and glory of the world" rang accusingly in her ears. She was not entirely sure that she renounced them; she hadn't even seen them yet.

In a moment Mr. and Mrs. Humphreys had spoken her name, "Elizabeth Warrington Ray," and she was being sprinkled.

She was a little disappointed when it was over to find that she felt exactly as she had felt before. She wondered how she had looked during the ceremony. She had forgotten to look the way she planned to look, which was just the way Julia had looked when she was baptized. It served her right for thinking of the "vain pomp and glory of the world!"

The Humphreys came for Sunday night lunch and gave her a gold cross on a chain. Betsy felt self-conscious. It didn't seem right to exchange quips with Larry and Herbert when she had just been baptized.

The following Sunday was even more momentous. With Julia and Herbert and Herbert's new love, Irma, and many more boys and girls, she was confirmed.

While she waited for her turn to kneel before the white-haired Bishop, Betsy watched Julia kneel, her face exalted. She heard the Bishop say:

"Defend, O Lord, this Thy child with Thy heavenly grace; that she may continue Thine forever; and daily increase in Thy Holy Spirit more and more until she comes unto Thy everlasting kingdom."

Presently the Bishop said the same thing to Betsy. His words sank into her heart as gently as the kind old hands touched her head.

Out in the robing room Julia, still with an exalted face, took Betsy's hand and pressed it.

"We're Episcopalians now."

Mrs. Ray and the three girls bought new Easter hats. And Betsy and Tacy helped Margaret dye eggs. They put on a patronizing manner but they enjoyed it as much as Margaret did. They told her how they used to color eggs, and save the dyes and later color sand and have sand stores. Margaret loved to hear about when Betsy and Tacy were little girls.

"I can even *remember* when you were little girls," she boasted.

On Easter morning, Julia and Betsy went to early communion. No doubt about it, they were Episcopalians now! At eleven o'clock they started off again, and Mr. and Mrs. Ray and Margaret started off for the Baptist Church, and Anna, in a huge hat laden with flowers, stiff bows of ribbon and a bluebird, started off for the Lutheran Church.

"It's too bad there isn't a Mormon in the family," Mr. Ray said.

That afternoon Betsy opened the candy box she had filled during Lent.

"You're going to pass it around, aren't you?" asked Hugh. "It's only Christian to do that."

"It looks awfully stale," said Tony, "especially that peanut fudge."

"It tastes delicious," said Betsy, but since it was, decidedly, stale she passed it generously.

Tony had come to the Rays every day since Bonnie left. One day during Easter vacation he came seven times. Betsy had planned to devote vacation to study for the Essay Contest. But it was difficult with Tony dropping in and out.

One day when she knew he was going to the Majestic, she went to the library but she told him what time she planned to leave. Oddly this coincided with the time he would be leaving the Majestic.

"I may come around and pick you up," he said.

Betsy made sure that her hair was in curl. She put on a crisp hair ribbon and a white ruffled shirtwaist, fresh from Anna's iron. Then she hunted up the still empty notebook, her still unblunted pencils and went to the library.

"I've been looking for you," Miss Sparrow said. "Miss

Clarke told me you had been chosen for the Essay Contest team. Congratulations, Betsy!"

"I'm awfully pleased about it," Betsy said, smiling.

"You'll have to work hard," Miss Sparrow warned. "The others have a head start. They have been coming almost every day for a couple of weeks now."

"I can catch up," Betsy said.

"You can't take any books on the Philippines out of the library," Miss Sparrow explained. "They are all assembled on a special shelf and there is a table where the contestants may read and take notes. Come, I'll show you." She led Betsy through the stalls to a table at the back of the library where a senior girl and Joe Willard were reading. They looked up briefly and smiled as she approached. Miss Sparrow nodded toward the table, toward a shelf, and withdrew.

Betsy loved the library; especially she loved the open stalls where she had often wandered happily. But there was to be no wandering now. The volumes dealing with the Philippines confronted her, looking ponderous and more than a little dull. Filled with zest for her new enterprise, she chose three of the heaviest and sat down at the table.

"The Philippines: their Present and Future Value," she wrote in her notebook, and opened a book importantly. She started to read it and she liked the descriptions of the scenery, the natives. But she knew this could be no Adventure on Puget Sound. She must grapple with facts, with figures, with statistics. She began the long hard pull.

After a while the senior girl got up, replaced her volume on the shelf, nodded and departed. Joe and Betsy read with absorbed concentration until they discovered themselves in the dusk. Elsewhere in the library, lights had come on and Joe snapped on the green-shaded light over their table.

Betsy smiled at him.

"I'm surprised," she said, "that they allow Philomathians and Zetamathians to study at the same table."

Joe returned her smile.

"The Zetamathians don't come very often," he said. "I'm worried about them. I don't want to take an unfair advantage."

"They can look out for themselves. They're good," Betsy said. She said it with a blush that ran down to the collar of her fresh white shirtwaist.

"Yes, but look what they're up against. Terrific competition," Joe returned.

He was, Betsy thought, as she had often thought before, very good looking. His yellow hair gleamed in the light of the overhanging lamp. He had thick eyebrows of a somewhat darker shade, with eyelashes to match. His eyes were as blue as Herbert's but their expression was different.

He almost always wore the same red tie and the same blue serge suit, carefully brushed and pressed, but in spite of this obvious shortage of clothing and the well-known fact that he worked after school and Saturdays, there was nothing humble about him. He held his head at a cocky angle, and there was a swing in his walk. He was touchy; Betsy knew that; but people liked him just the same although no one knew him very well. He had no time for the athletics which drew the boys together, and he ignored the girls . . . perhaps because of a lack of pocket money.

"I have an idea," he announced now. His eyes shone as though he were pleased with himself. The defiant lower lip was outthrust. "Want to hear it?"

"Yes. Of course I do."

"The Philomathians have a head start on the Zetama-thians," he said, "and they don't like it at all. They are men of honor, the Philomathians are. The Philomathians have been coming down here every Sunday and every day during vacation. They can't come in the evening for they work in the evening, they toil for their daily bread. But they are unusually bright, and they've learned practically all there is to know about The Philippines: their Present and Future Value. They are darned worried about the Zetamathians. Especially," he added, "since the Zetama-thians are just a poor weak girl."

Betsy blushed again.

"Now, here's the idea," said Joe Willard. "The Philo-mathians might walk home with the Zetamathians, and on the way they could tell them the whole sad story of the Philippines. What do you say?"

Betsy didn't know what to say. She wished to Heaven that she had not thrown out that suggestion to Tony. Tony was wonderful, of course. And he had broken her heart. And she couldn't hear the song, "Dreaming," without wanting to cry. And it was all very romantic. But there was something about Joe Willard . . . any girl in high school would like to have him walk home with her.

"It's a grand plan," said Betsy. "But . . ." She was groping for the casual significant words which would in-dicate that although she had an engagement tonight, she would not have one on another night. "I'm sorry . . ." she began, and faltered, for at just that moment Tony came swaggering through the stalls. He barely glanced at Joe Willard.

"Ready?" he asked possessively.

"Not quite," Betsy said. "Won't you wait for me outside? I'll be with you in a minute."

"That's a bum idea," said Tony. "Where's your coat?" He found it and held it up. "I'll tell you all you want to know about the Philippines walking home," he said.

It was a most unfortunate remark. Betsy turned to Joe Willard but his blonde head was bent over his book. His ears were red and when he said goodnight his manner was icy.

Betsy was exasperated, all the more so when she reached the library steps. Tony wasn't even alone; Herbert and Cab were waiting. This was no romantic saunter through the melting spring twilight, but just the usual impersonal bantering and pushing about.

Joe Willard didn't ask Betsy again to let him walk home from the library with her. He didn't pay any attention to her beyond civil hellos and goodbyes. Once, most unethically, in an attempt to draw him into conversation again, she asked him where to find a certain piece of information. He told her, but bent over his books before she could manage more than "thank you."

And Betsy's visits to the library were few and far apart. For April was bringing true spring. Buds were swelling, bold bright robins were back. The Crowd had no trouble beguiling Betsy out on expeditions behind Old Mag or Dandy. She went on picnics with Tacy, too, building fires, drinking smoky cocoa, searching in matted leaves for violets and Dutchmen's breeches.

In the ecstasy of the season she almost stopped suffering, she took no interest in school, and telling herself that May eleventh was a very long way off, she quite forgot about the Essay Contest.

Chapter Twenty-Seven

THE ESSAY CONTEST

HER father reminded her of it on the morning after her birthday. She had become fifteen with all due ceremony of claps on the back, birthday cake and gifts, and at breakfast Mr. Ray remarked pointedly:

" 'The Philippines: their Present and Future Value' " is a mighty big subject. A *mighty* big subject."

"I know, papa," said Betsy penitently, and during the next few days she really did study for the Essay Contest. She went to the library and delved into the fat dull books. They depressed her by revealing the magnitude of her task.

"Dear me!" she said to Tacy. "In May I must buckle right down."

But early in May a blow descended. The heavens, so to speak, fell.

The trees along High Street wore pale green chiffon now. Plum trees were in heady bloom. Birds were flying about with bits of straw in their bills, or sitting on eggs, or at least singing madly. Human beings were almost as busy, uncovering flower beds and raking last autumn's leaves.

Carney passed Betsy a note. "Bonfire at our house tonight. Can you come? Herbert will call for you."

"Assisted by the amiable Herbert," wrote Betsy, "I will wend my way to your residence as requested."

Carney received this sparkling reply without a smile, which was odd, and the note that Betsy presently received from Herbert was also strangely sober.

"I'll call for you early tonight. Something to tell you. H. Humphreys."

"I wonder what's up?" Betsy thought.

When Herbert arrived, Mr. Ray was out rolling his newly seeded lawn. And Betsy coming down the steps, hatless, her hands thrust into the pockets of her light spring coat, was deeply startled by what she heard.

"Yes, I saw your father," Mr. Ray was saying. "He told me about the move to California."

"California!" Betsy ran down the walk.

"It's true," Herbert said. "We're clearing out, just as

soon as school is over. We're going out to San Diego to live."

Betsy was aghast. First Bonnie, now Larry and Herbert! The Crowd could not survive this second blow.

"How perfectly awful!" she cried.

"Isn't it?" asked Herbert. Yet there was discernible in his bright blue eyes the stirrings of adventurous interest. "Dad says California's fine, though. No winter, which is tough, but there's swimming in the Pacific Ocean."

"Betsy's grandparents live in San Diego," Mr. Ray said.

"Gee, Betsy, come out to visit them and I'll show you around."

They developed this idea as they walked through the spring twilight to Carney's. Betsy was quite intoxicated with the notion of seeing orange trees, poinsettias, the mountains and the Pacific in Herbert's company.

"It won't be for a couple of years, probably. We'll be so grown up we'll hardly know each other."

"I'll bet you'll still blush when I call you Little Poetess," Herbert said. "Do you know, Betsy, I was in love with you in fifth grade?"

"You were?" Betsy was amazed. "Why all the girls were crazy about you."

"Well, you certainly had me going. You wore a locket and you used to swing it when you studied."

Betsy started to say, "I guess I'll buy myself another locket." But her sidelong glance showed his eyes brimming with mischief. She remembered how much more fun he was when he wasn't in love, and changed her mind.

"Now you're my C.F.," she said. "And I want lots of letters. All about the California girls."

They were having such a good time that their "hellos" at the Sibleys' side lawn were completely cheerful. Herbert went to the giant pile of leaves already burning in the driveway and Carney came to meet Betsy.

"I see that Herbert hasn't told you," she said looking at Betsy's smiling face. Betsy felt a disloyal pang.

"Yes, he has," she said sobering. "Isn't it awful?"

"Awful," repeated Carney, not a trace of dimple showing. "Awful doesn't describe it. I think it's cruel of Mr. Humphreys, absolutely cruel. What does he have to go to California for? Isn't Minnesota all right?"

Larry joined them, his face a thunder cloud. Here was no glimmer of the adventurous zest Herbert had shown. He took Carney's hand, which startled Betsy for a moment. Larry and Carney "went together" and had since seventh grade but they weren't spoony. Carney detested spoony girls.

Now, however, her hand closed around Larry's. Without speaking they went back to the fire.

If it were Tony going away, I'd feel like that too, thought Betsy, and glanced toward his lounging figure.

Carney's small brothers were bringing wheelbarrows full of leaves to feed the flames. The fire crackled briskly and threw out a brazen heat. The smell of the smoke brought back to Betsy bygone Hill Street springs.

"I must be getting very old," she thought, "the way things remind me of things."

When the fire had burned low the boys piled on branches from trees Mr. Sibley had been trimming, and when these in turn were reduced to embers they toasted marshmallows on pointed sticks. Spreading coats and blankets, they sat down around the fire and now it was the time for singing. They came at last to "Dreaming."

"Dreaming, dreaming,
Of you sweetheart I am dreaming,
Dreaming of days when you loved me best . . ."

Tony was sitting near Betsy singing in his deep rich voice. She expected the melody to flood her heart as usual with melancholy memories, but it didn't somehow. She glanced toward Larry and Carney.

Boldly Larry held Carney's hand in his, and they didn't even try to sing. Carney sat stiff and straight, like a hurt child.

The imminent departure of the Humphreys for California was very, very sad. But at least it meant another rash of parties. One day it was suddenly, alarmingly, the tenth of May and the following day would bring the Essay Contest.

"Are you well prepared, Betsy?" asked Miss Clarke after school, looking a little anxious.

"Oh, yes," said Betsy. "I'm going down to the library though to check on a few facts."

Miss Sparrow looked anxious too.

"You haven't done much reading, Betsy. Do you have some books on the Philippines at home?"

"No," said Betsy. "But I've talked with my father. And I'm going to work a while right now."

She went through the stalls to the table reserved for the contestants. Seniors, juniors and sophomores were there, reading with frenzied concentration. But not Joe Willard.

"He knows all there is to know about the Philippines," thought Betsy with a sinking heart. She skimmed through the big books aimlessly. "Oh, well," she thought. "I'll get by on my writing." But Joe Willard, she remembered, wrote very well indeed.

Tacy who called for her cheered her as they walked homeward.

"You can write circles around Joe Willard," she said.

"Oh, sure, sure," said Betsy. "I ought to know a few more facts though."

"Just skim lightly over the facts," Tacy advised. "Your essay will be so interesting that the judges can't put it down."

Julia at the supper table took the same attitude. Mr. Ray had asked Betsy some questions about the Philippines, receiving evasive answers.

"Betsy writes so well, papa. She doesn't need to know those dull old dates."

"Betsy," said Mrs. Ray, "has been writing since she could hold a pencil. I remember her when she was five years old asking me how to spell 'going down the street.'"

"Ja, Betsy will win all right," remarked Anna, clearing the plates. "Maybe you'd better take coffee with your breakfast, lovey, like on Sunday mornings?"

"I believe some coffee *would* be a good idea," said Betsy importantly, "but I don't have a qualm about the contest. Not a qualm." She spent the evening going over her notes. There were gaps, alarming gaps in her information.

Cab came over, but she did not see him. Herbert telephoned but she did not talk. Tony arrived but she did not even go downstairs.

Tony . . . she could hear from upstairs . . . wanted to sing.

"I'm afraid we'd disturb Betsy," she heard Julia say. "She's concentrating on the Philippines. It can't really be necessary, though. She's sure to win."

Tony laughed. "I told Joe Willard today he might as well be buying some black crepe for his hat band."

247

"What did he say?" asked Julia.

"He only grinned."

Betsy didn't like the sound of that. She slapped her notebook shut, wound her hair on Magic Wavers, and went to bed.

"Sleep is what I need," she thought. "With a good night's sleep I can write better than anyone in Deep Valley High School."

And she had a fair night's sleep although, she told the family at breakfast, she dreamed about Aguinaldo. Her father said he was glad to hear that she knew there was such a person but the rest of the family was impressed. When Margaret asked Betsy to help with her hair ribbon, Mrs. Ray told her not to bother Betsy; Betsy had something important on her mind. Anna brought her coffee, and although Betsy always combined it with so much sugar and cream that its stimulus was diluted, it did her good to drink it.

"Here I go," said Betsy. "Joe Willard, watch out!"

She snatched up a hat and a pen, and ran outdoors.

It seemed strange to be going to school on Saturday morning. Children were playing on all the lilac-scented lawns. It had rained last night, but today the sun was out, and the air was filled with moist sweetness.

The high school, of course, was deserted. But Miss Clarke and Miss O'Rourke were waiting in the upper hall, behind a small table.

"All notes and books must be left here," Miss Clarke said.

"I haven't any with me," Betsy answered smiling.

"That's right," Miss Clarke beamed. "Go into the algebra classroom. You will find paper on the desk, but don't start to write until the bell rings."

Betsy found two seniors, two juniors and two sopho-mores in the classroom.

"I wonder where Joe Willard is," she said to herself. "I should think he'd like to get here in time to collect his thoughts a little."

But it was exactly one minute to nine when Joe Willard sauntered in. He walked up to the desk and helped him-self liberally to foolscap, then walked back to a desk in the corner and ran his fingers over his yellow hair.

Miss Clarke and Miss O'Rourke came in and closed the door.

"When the bell rings," said Miss O'Rourke, "you may start to write. And you must stop at twelve o'clock. If you finish sooner, put your essay on the desk and go out quietly. The subject, as you all know, is 'The Philippines: their Present and Future Value.'"

As she spoke the last word, a gong sounded. Eight boys and girls dipped their pens in ink.

First Betsy wrote the title, "The Philippines: their Pres-ent and Future Value." She puzzled a moment about what to write next. Miss Clarke had advised that she think out her opening paragraph in advance but she had not done this, being a great believer in the inspiration of the moment.

And inspiration did not betray her. As always when she took a pen or pencil in her hand, inspiration cast a golden light. A flowery opening paragraph soon found its way to paper, the final sentence leading, just as it should, into a second paragraph.

But unfortunately today she could not write entirely by the light of inspiration. Her essay was supposed to have a solid core of knowledge based on six weeks' study. Instead of going happily where her fancy led, she was obliged in every paragraph to conceal the absence of facts. History was padded with legends that happened to stick in her mind. For exports and imports she substituted descriptions of orchids and volcanoes and sunsets on Manila Bay. It took ingenuity. It took thought. It took time.

At eleven o'clock Joe Willard rose, strolled to the front of the room and laid his paper on Miss O'Rourke's desk. There was a slight swagger in his walk. Closing the door he looked back over his still struggling colleagues. Betsy felt sure that he had not intended it so, but his gaze met hers.

"He is positive, sure, he's going to win," she thought. "Well, so am I." And in desperation she put in some snappy conversation between Aguinaldo and Commodore Dewey. It livened up the essay a good bit.

Except for Joe Willard, everyone wrote until twelve o'clock. The gong rang then and somewhat soberly the contestants took their papers up to the desk and filed out. Two weeks would pass before it was known which society had won. The cup would be awarded and the winners of the class points announced at the term's last assembly.

"Satisfied, Betsy?" Miss Clarke asked.

Betsy nodded brightly.

"We certainly are lucky that you are a Zetamathian," Miss Clarke said. But Betsy's homeward walk was slower than usual and considerably more subdued.

Chapter Twenty-Eight

RESULTS

But she ran up the steps of home smiling.

"Fine! Fine!" she replied to all family queries about how the Essay Contest had gone. At dinner she described the events of the morning dramatically.

"So this Willard boy ran out of things to write about at eleven o'clock, did he?" her mother asked.

"It really wasn't fair," said Julia, "to put anyone up against Betsy."

"Hail the conquering heroine!" said Tony when he dropped in that afternoon.

In a little while Betsy forgot the misgivings which had filled her at Joe Willard's departing gaze. Everyone from Miss Clarke to Margaret was convinced that she had safely won the freshman points; she began to believe it herself.

There was little time to think of the matter, however, for again examinations were upon her. Betsy and Cab took up the greeting she and Tacy had originally evolved.

"*Hic, haec, hoc,*" he would cry from the front door every morning.

"*Hujus, hujus, hujus,*" Betsy would respond from within.

"*Huic, huic, huic,*" they chorused together. "Who says Latin isn't spoken familiarly now?"

"I'd like to get hold of the fiend who invented algebra," Betsy groaned to Tacy as, well fortified with fudge, they studied after school.

Composition did not worry her, but she read the Ancient History from cover to cover.

"It's extremely interesting," she remarked in surprise. Studying, as she had done all year, only the paragraph she expected to be called on to discuss, she had missed the immense, moving sweep of the narrative.

Julia was even more desperate then Betsy. She was not only faced with examinations. She was singing a solo for Commencement. "An Open Secret," it was called, and she practiced it from morning until night.

"*Pussy willow has a secret,*" Julia warbled, and in Betsy's mind Pussy Willow's secret was mixed up with

Latin conjugations, algebraic equations and the Punic Wars. It added to her confusion on all these topics.

The chorus, in which Betsy and Tacy sang, was also preparing a number for Commencement:

> "My heart's in the highlands,
> My heart is not here.
> My heart's in the highlands,
> Achasing the deer."

Betsy and Tacy had their private version.

> "My heart's in the high school,
> My heart is not here.
> My heart's in the high school,
> Achasing my dear."

This was supposed to refer to Betsy's infatuation for Tony, and Betsy and Tacy considered it gloriously funny. When they had studied until they were groggy, and Betsy was walking halfway home with Tacy through the late afternoon, they sang it:

> "My heart's in the hi-i-i-i-gh school
> My heart is not he-e-e-re . . ."

The light green world of May echoed to delirious laughter.

Examinations began. These were followed by daily indignation meetings at the Ray house.

"How could Morse be so beastly?"

"How can O'Rourke look so pretty and give such hideous exams?"

Larry and Carney alone were not concerned about

exams. They did not even seem to care whether they passed.

"The Time, the Place and the Girl" came to Deep Valley. Carney was allowed to go with Larry . . . in the evening . . . alone. Sympathetic parents hoped this would afford a measure of consolation. The Humphreys were leaving for California on the day after the day after Commencement.

The first event of Commencement week was the joint evening meeting of Philomathians and Zetamathians at which the essay cup would be awarded.

Which society had won the cup was still unknown to all except the judges. There was no doubt, however, in the minds of those around Betsy about the freshman points, and by this time there was no doubt in Betsy's mind either. That feeling she had had was crazy. Of course she would win.

The eight contestants were to sit on the platform along with Miss Bangeter, Miss Clarke, Miss O'Rourke and the presidents of the two societies. The four who had received the most points would rise when the cup was awarded.

"I'm glad you have your canary-colored silk to wear to-night, Betsy," Mrs. Ray said. "Since you have to stand up and bow."

"Let me do your hair," said Julia. They hurried upstairs after supper, and Margaret looked on while Julia worked.

Katie, Tacy and Alice called for them.

"See these new gloves? I wore them just so I could split them clapping for you," Tacy said. "Gee, you look nice!"

Betsy's cheeks were burning. The canary-colored dress fitted to perfection, and her pompadour stood up like a fan.

The assembly room was divided between Philomathians and Zetamathians, and the Zetamathians this year had the alcove side. This was most desirable, for on these evening meetings boys and girls were allowed to perch on the bookcases.

The Crowd, parting from Betsy, rushed for them. Betsy hurried to the platform. Four Philomathians, their president and Miss O'Rourke, four Zetamathians, their president and Miss Clarke, flanked Miss Bangeter's tall table. Betsy sat opposite Joe Willard. They smiled at each other.

The crowded assembly room looked gayer than usual, for the Zetamathians wore streamers of turquoise blue; the Philomathians were decked with orange. Defiant chants were hurled first from one side of the room and then the other.

"Zet! Zet! Zetamathian!"

"Philo! Philo! Philomathian!"

Tony sat with Winona, Pin and the Humphreys on the Philomathian side. Tacy sat on a bookcase with the crowd of Zetamathians; all of them were eating peanuts. First one and then another waved to Betsy, or threw kisses, or clapped hands softly high in the air. Betsy did not respond except by smiling. She sat with her hands folded, her ankles crossed.

Tall and benign, Miss Bangeter called the meeting to order. The high school song was sung, and the opening ceremonies, minutes of previous meeting, announcements and reports ran their usual course.

"And now," said Miss Bangeter, "we come to the main event of the evening, the awarding of the Essay Cup." She indicated a table on which three silver cups were prominently displayed. One was tied with an orange bow, one with turquoise blue. The Essay cup stood in the center, unmarked.

"As you know," she continued, "eight students have competed, two from each high school year. Freshmen are judged together, sophomores are judged together, and juniors, and seniors. That is our attempt to make the Contest perfectly fair. We *think* you increase in knowledge and ability as you go on through high school." (Laughter.)

"I will announce the class awards in turn, and at the end the total number of points piled up for each society. First, the freshmen." She paused, and Betsy blushed. She glanced swiftly at Joe Willard's cocky blond head, his handsome determined-looking profile.

"The freshmen contestants, as you all know, are Joe Willard and Betsy Ray. Both are excellent English students. The one who gained the freshman points is . . ." She paused and smiled while a wave of subdued laughter and exclamations of anxiety swept across the hall. A whispered chant came from the alcove:

"Betsy, Betsy, Betsy."

A similar chant rolled from the opposite wall:

"Joe, Joe, Joe."

"The winner of the freshman points," Miss Bangeter repeated, "is Joe Willard."

Betsy was stunned. So for a moment were the Zetamathians. Automatically she found herself smiling. She found herself applauding frenziedly as Joe Willard, looking both poised and abashed, rose and sat down again. The Philomathians cheered and applauded so enthusiastically that he had to stand up a second time. Betsy applauded too and even turned her radiant smile toward the alcove.

Tacy was not applauding. She was shaking her fist at Joe Willard. She was joking, of course; and yet she meant it too. Cab and Tony had taken out big white handkerchiefs and were pretending to be weeping.

Betsy felt as though she were in a dream. Her ears were ringing, and the events that went forward on the stage seemed unreal. The other winners were named in turn. The final scores were announced. The Philomathians won the cup. It was presented to the Philomathian president.

Before joining her surprised indignant Crowd, Betsy sought out Joe Willard.

"Congratulations," she said, putting out her hand. "I'm sure your essay was wonderful."

For once Joe's blue eyes were friendly.

"Got just what you deserved," he said. "You should have let me walk home with you that night."

Of course, as usual, Betsy blushed.

Betsy did not sleep very well that night. The next morning she woke up so early that even Anna was not about. She dressed and went softly out of the house. If she had still lived on Hill Street, she would have gone up on the hill. As it was, she sat on the porch steps, but it was nice there. The dawn colors were still in the sky above the German Catholic College. The lawn was brushed with silver, and the birds were so bold, so abundant . . . it seemed as though they knew that for this hour they owned the world.

Betsy was ashamed of herself. She was deeply and thoroughly ashamed. This feeling had nothing to do with her hurt pride. And its deepest cause was not the disappointment of her family, her friends, Miss Clarke. That had been loyally masked with assertions that "it doesn't matter anyway," "you'll show them next year," "the judges were crazy." Her mother especially was sure that the judges had taken leave of their senses. But in her father's eyes Betsy

257

had seen the opinion that the judges had shown excellent judgment. It was this view, shared by Betsy herself, which troubled her now.

"Maybe, of course," she thought, "Joe Willard writes better than I do. And if he does, that's all right. The world is probably full of people who write better than I do." (She doubted it.) "What makes me feel bad is that I didn't give myself a chance."

When Julia had a part in a home talent play, her social life went by the board. If she had a solo to sing, she practised it, even though she neglected everything else.

"That's the way my writing ought to be treated," Betsy thought.

She looked back over the crowded winter. She did not regret it. But she should not have let its fun, its troubles, its excitements squeeze her writing out.

"If I treat my writing like that," she told herself, "it may go away entirely."

The thought appalled her. What would life be like without her writing? Writing filled her life with beauty and mystery, gave it purpose . . . and promise.

"Everyone has something, probably. With Julia it's singing, with Anna, it's cooking, with Carney and Bonnie, it's keeping house and having families . . . something that's most important of all because it's theirs to do."

She jumped up and went down the steps and started walking.

She walked down High Street, past the high school, and on and on, trying to beat out on the sidewalk her angry self reproach.

"Help me to straighten this thing out!" she said to God. "Please, please, help me to straighten this thing out!"

Presently she found herself tired, hungry, happy and knowing exactly what to do. She turned and hurried toward home.

The house smelled of coffee now. Anna was in the kitchen. Betsy burst in smiling.

"You're out early, lovey. Hungry?"

"Starved! What's for breakfast?"

"Bacon and eggs."

"Bacon and eggs! They're just what I want," Betsy cried. "Anna," she said, "will you do something for me after breakfast?"

"Sure, lovey! What is it?"

"That old trunk in the attic, that big square trunk of my Uncle Keith's. I want you to help me bring it down."

"Where you going to put it?"

"In my bedroom," Betsy said.

"In your pretty blue bedroom?" Anna demanded. "It won't look nice there, lovey. There's plenty in that room already."

"That trunk's going in," said Betsy, "if everything else goes out." She walked around the kitchen smiling. "Gee, I'm hungry! I could eat nails."

"Strike the gong," said Anna. "And as soon as the dishes are done, we'll move that trunk."

No one in the Ray family made any comment when Uncle Keith's trunk came back to Betsy's room. Her mother found a shawl with which to cover it when it wasn't being used as a desk . . . the very same shawl that had covered it on Hill Street. Margaret came in to sit on it, looking pleased. Betsy brought her Bible and prayer book, a dictionary and the volume of Poe, a pile of freshly sharpened pencils and what notebooks she could lay her hands on.

"Stand up, Margaret," she said. "I'm going to arrange the tray. And I'm going to buy a whole pile of new notebooks as soon as Commencement is over."

Chapter Twenty-Nine

THE HILL

AND now Commencement week was in full swing, along
with a burst of Minnesota heat. Betsy had trouble keeping
her hair in curl for the class play, Class Day and all the
other festivities.

The chorus was rehearsing daily in the Opera House
where Commencement exercises would be held. Betsy and
Tacy wandered behind the scenes, reminding each other

of the time they had played in Rip Van Winkle and discovered Uncle Keith.

Commencement night came, and Julia in the pink silk dress sang, "An Open Secret."

"Pussy willow has a secret," she sang, leaning toward her audience, almost acting the words out.

Betsy in the canary-colored silk, Tacy in pale green mull sang that their hearts were in the highlands.

"I almost sang 'My heart's in the high school' " Tacy giggled, walking home.

"So did I. I started to, even. Let's sing it now."

They sang it, arms entwined, walking home along the dark streets. *"My heart's in the hi-i-igh school . . ."*

"There's no one I can be so silly with as I can with you," said Tacy.

Report cards were issued next day, and they both passed. Betsy Ray: algebra, 75; Latin 78; ancient history, 91; composition, 92.

Mr. Gaston infuriated the class by telling them that they must read *Ivanhoe* over the summer. Betsy had read it, but she didn't say so. She acted as cross as everyone else.

That night, the night before the Humphreys left, The Crowd was invited to the Ray house.

"I want to make it like all the other parties we've had this year," Betsy planned.

But she couldn't. It was far too warm for a fire in the grate. Doors and windows were open, and the porch was hung with baskets full of daisies and geraniums and long trailing vines. A hammock swung there too.

They sang the old songs, though. Julia played the piano as usual and The Crowd, with arms locked, stood behind her. They sang "My Wild Irish Rose," and "Crocodile Isle," and "Cause I'm Lonesome," and "Dreaming." Julia made Welsh rarebit in the chafing dish.

Herbert and Cab disappeared from the party, and soon Margaret came running into the dining room to say that everyone should come to the music room to see a show.

"I'm to say that it's for Larry and Carney," she announced.

Herbert in Mrs. Ray's best silk dress and Anna's big feathered hat leaned over the stairs pretending to be Juliet, while Cab, wearing Julia's new cape and strumming on a pot cover was Romeo, serenading. They were very funny, and it did everyone good, especially Larry and Carney.

"Anna wouldn't have loaned that hat to anyone but you," Betsy told Herbert. "Her heart is broken because you're going away."

"Maybe I'll get a little of her cooking now," said Cab.

"No," interposed Tony, "I'm stepping into Humphreys' shoes."

When The Crowd left Tony stayed behind. Mr. and Mrs. Ray had already retired.

"Betsy and I are going to do the dishes," Tony said. "My first step toward getting in with Anna."

"I can take a hint. Goodnight," said Julia. She blew them a kiss and went upstairs.

Tony washed and Betsy wiped. Tony was good at washing. He scraped and rinsed and stacked the dishes before he began, and kept a kettle of hot water boiling.

"You're the most efficient lazy person I ever knew," said Betsy.

They talked about the Humphreys' going, and about

how sad it was to see The Crowd break up, and about what they would do next year with Bonnie and Larry and Herbert all gone.

"So long as the Ray family doesn't move away, I'll do all right," Tony said.

The dishes finished, they went into the dining room, the parlor, the music room. They put them all in order. It was strange to be alone with Tony in the deserted downstairs with the family asleep above. Not asleep, exactly. Her mother would come into her room to talk the party over. But there wasn't a sound anywhere in the house.

Betsy and Tony went out on the porch and sat down in the hammock.

The night was very warm and soft; stars spangled the sky behind the German Catholic College. The air was sweet with the smell of syringa bushes from the house next door. Tony's rough sleeve touched Betsy's arm. She was wearing the short-sleeved canary-colored silk. They pushed the swing and rocked slowly back and forth.

And suddenly it came to Betsy with electric force that she wasn't in love with Tony any more. She liked him, she liked him enormously, but if Cab, or Herbert, or Pin had been sitting in the swing beside her, she would have felt no differently.

Thinking back she realized that this had been true for some time. Not for weeks had there been any magic in the sight of that curly thatch, those bold black eyes, that lazy sauntering walk. The feeling she had had was gone; it had vanished; it just wasn't, any more.

"Tony," said Betsy. "I'm so happy."

"So am I," said Tony. His tone was caressing and he moved his arm slightly as though with a little encouragement he might become sentimental. Betsy jumped up.

"Will you come over in the morning to help me make fudge? I promised Herbie a box for the train."

"Sure," said Tony. "It will give me a chance to see my new inamorata, Anna."

Betsy laughed.

"I'm glad you have an inamorata, Tony. But as far as I'm concerned, I'm fancy free."

The Humphreys left for California the next day, and half of Deep Valley was at the station. Mr. and Mrs. Ray and all the High Fly Whist Club were there to say goodbye to Mr. and Mrs. Humphreys. Larry's and Herbert's crowd was there, and the football crowd, and some of the teachers, and a delegation of business men.

"Everything but the band," Tony remarked.

"And a band wouldn't do. We're too sad," Betsy said.

"Remember to write to me, all you kids," said Herbert.

Larry held Carney by the arm. They didn't talk or joke. And when the four-forty-five moved out of the station with the Humphreys on the observation platform, Betsy slipped her arm through one of Carney's arms, and Tacy took the other.

This, thought Betsy impressively, closes a chapter in our lives.

She didn't say it, for it sounded sad, and she wanted to comfort Carney.

For several days she devoted herself to comforting Carney. Bonnie, she knew, could have done it better. But Betsy did her best. She went to the Sibleys' every afternoon and Carney played the piano, classical pieces, while Betsy listened. Curled in Mr. Sibley's chair, Betsy read out loud while Carney sewed.

Letters from Larry came from St. Paul, from Omaha, from Santa Fe. There were picture postals from Herbert, too, for Betsy. Indians, the Grand Canyon, and at last the orange trees and poinsettias of California.

"I really must go out to visit Grandma," Betsy thought, sticking these alluring post cards into her mirror.

One afternoon Tacy telephoned.

"Mamma's baking cake for supper. That kind you like, without any frosting on it."

"I get your point," said Betsy. "I'll be there. Walk down to meet me; will you?"

"I'll meet you at Lincoln Park."

It was mid-June now, and very hot. Betsy wore her pink lawn jumper, the one she had worn, she remembered, when she went to the Majestic and saw Cab chopping wood, the day Anna came, almost a year ago. She carried the same pink parasol and walked slowly through the heat.

Tacy met her, and they locked their damp arms.

"Gee, I'm glad to see you," Tacy said. "I've missed you since school ended."

"I've missed you too," said Betsy. "I'm going to come up to Hill Street lots this summer."

"Are you going out to that farm again?"

"The Taggarts? I don't know." She had a sudden smothering memory of her homesickness. "I wonder whether I'd be homesick if I went again? Probably not. I'm so much older."

She did feel unbelievably older.

And Hill Street emphasized the change. They stopped at almost every house, to talk with the old neighbors, pat familiar dogs, exclaim over children who had put on inches and acquired big front teeth. All the neighbors exclaimed that Betsy was a real young lady.

Mr. and Mrs. Kelly said they couldn't get over how she had changed.

"I haven't changed inside," said Betsy. "I'd like to eat supper up on our bench."

"Oh, let's!" cried Tacy. "May we, mamma?"

"Papa," Mrs. Kelly said. "Fix a plate for each of them."

So Mr. Kelly filled Tacy's plate, and Betsy's. And they each took a glass of milk and a piece of Mrs. Kelly's cake, still warm from the oven. Laughed at by the family and laughing at each other, they walked carefully out of the house and up the road to the bench at the top of Hill Street.

Hill Street looked very green and fresh with sprinklers running and roses in bloom. The sun was setting behind Tacy's house.

"Just where it ought to set," said Betsy. "It hasn't set in the right place since I left Hill Street. Oh, Tacy, it's wonderful to be back!"

And yet, even as she spoke, she knew that she did not wish to come back, not to stay, not to live. She loved the little yellow cottage more than she loved any place on earth, but she was through with it except in her memories.

She thought of the High Street house which had looked so bare at first on its windy corner. It was still a little bare, although now the vines Mr. Ray had transplanted from Hill Street covered it with their familiar pattern, and baskets full of flowers hung around the porch and shrubs were set out. It was bare, but it was full of the things that make a house, a home.

How many songs the music room had echoed to! How many onion sandwiches had been eaten on Sunday nights around the fireplace! The brass bowl in the big front window looked like High Street, not Hill Street. Uncle Keith's trunk still seemed out of place in her bedroom, but it was a challenge there.

In the High Street house she had fallen in love and out of it again. She would never forget Tony kissing her under the mistletoe even though now, to her continued amazement, he was just like anyone else . . . all the magic gone.

On the steps of the High Street house she had met her disappointment after the Essay Contest. She thought suddenly about Joe Willard. He had never been inside her house . . . yet.

She and Tacy sat looking down Hill Street while the clouds in the sky behind Tacy's house turned pink. Their hands met and as always, unfailingly, joined in a loyal clasp.